YESTERDAY'S TROUBLE

ALSO BY DALLAS GORHAM

The Carlos McCrary PI Mystery Thriller Series

Six Murders Too Many

Double Fake, Double Murder

Quarterback Trap

Dangerous Friends

Day of the Tiger

McCrary's Justice

Yesterday's Trouble

Four Years Gone

Debt of Honor

Sometimes You Lose

YESTERDAY'S TROUBLE

CARLOS MCCRARY PI
BOOK 7

DALLAS GORHAM

Book and cover design by eBook Prep
www.ebookprep.com

August 2022
ISBN: 978-1-64457-265-8

ePublishing Works!
644 Shrewsbury Commons Ave
Ste 249
Shrewsbury PA 17361
United States of America

www.epublishingworks.com
Phone: 866-846-5123

PROLOGUE

Lester

L ester watched the YouTube video again. The lead singer's blonde hair waved and danced in time to the music. The rhinestones on the cuffs and collar of her western jacket flashed and sparkled in the spotlight each time she strummed her guitar. Despite the poor quality of the cellphone video, it had garnered over a million views and ignited demand for the new country singer.

He muted the sound. *Without music, she looks like a silly disjointed puppet. That's what she'll be if this tour gets off the ground—a puppet with me jerking her strings.*

She wiggled her left thumb as she fingered the frets. Lester had studied the move hundreds of times in the three weeks since he had found the girl of his destiny. Found her after years of searching. He knew the video frame by frame. He poised his finger over the sound button. The chorus was coming... *now.* Unmuting the sound, Lester cranked the volume and sang the haunting chorus with her.

> *Heart, don't fail me now.*
> *Now that he's come my way.*

Give me power in this joyful hour.
To rise at dawn to a brighter day.

Lester screamed, "Bitch, bitch, bitch," and logged off. He stared at the wall as if he had x-ray vision to see her miles away. *The man you sing about who's come your way is the wrong man for you. Your joyful hour will never come. You don't realize it, but your brighter day will never dawn, bitch. Not until you're with me.*

He opened an email website. *Let's see... What would be an appropriate email address for this one? Let's try* purewhiteblood.

He tapped the keyboard on his laptop, then frowned. "Name in use." *Maybe if I add a number to it, say,* purewhiteblood21. *No, that's imitative. Let's try* whiterulemillenium. *Excellent. whiterulemillenium it shall be.*

He composed an email and edited it until it conveyed his disapproval, his rage, and his message with the emotional overtones he wanted.

Send.

ONE

Carlos McCrary

T he young woman—little more than a teenager—rose to her feet when I walked into the reception area.

Most people who visit my office near downtown Port City are not keen to meet me. I'm a private investigator, and most of my visitors are in trouble. Some are suspicious, leery—even hostile. The rest often come with a problem they expect McCrary Investigations—that's me, Carlos McCrary—to solve.

This one was different. She flashed me a dazzling smile with straight white teeth that belonged in a toothpaste commercial. A smile that lit up the room as if the sun had emerged on an overcast day. Ah, the excitement of youth.

"Tank Tyler sent me. He made an appointment for me."

Tank Tyler was my CPA and financial advisor. Tank had telephoned the previous week to make the appointment. "Cleo Hennessey is a budding country music star. She's preparing to start her first concert tour. Her boyfriend LeMarvis Jones is a client. You know him?"

"Sure. Marvelous LeMarvis averaged 28 points per game last season

7

for the Port City Peregrines. Makes $30 million a year and worth more. Over seven feet tall."

"That's the guy. FYI, he's way over seven feet. Somebody's been sending Cleo Hennessey threatening emails, and LeMarvis thinks she needs security on her concert tour."

"You have an opinion?"

"Security is your job, sport; my job is to manage LeMarvis's money. He's been a client since the Peregrines drafted him eight years ago. I met Cleo a couple of times. Nice girl. Pretty too. LeMarvis is worried about her safety. I suggested he hire you to provide security. LeMarvis will foot the bill."

"Is he aware that security for a concert tour will cost him enough cash to choke a trash compactor?"

"He's underwritten the concert to the tune of over ten million dollars. A few hundred thousand more won't matter."

"Is this a millionaire sugar-daddy deal?"

"Nothing like that, chief. LeMarvis is not a woman-chaser who cavorts with girl-of-the-month types. He's good, solid people. He and Cleo are in love, not lust. Between us, they plan to announce their engagement after the concert tour."

"Thanks for the heads-up. Anything else I should know?"

"Cleo is a country girl at heart. She doesn't believe she needs extra security. She's afraid it will cramp her style—keep her away from the fans. Also, she grew up poor and she's tight as a guitar string with money, especially with LeMarvis's money. He tells me she'll be a tough sale."

"I'll turn on my celebrated charm and dazzle her with my fancy footwork."

"*Humph.* I've seen you dance, white boy. You try fancy footwork, you'll trip on your celebrated size 12 feet and fall on your celebrated ass."

From the looks of Cleo's smile, perhaps she looked forward to meeting me despite what Tank Tyler said.

Cleo gazed down at me with pale blue eyes set in an unlined face that could have belonged to a twelve-year-old. She wore gold sandals with flat heels. She was six-foot-four at least. I stand six-foot-two, and she made me feel short. It was disconcerting.

She grabbed my hand. "Cleopatra Jane Hennessey. My friends call me Cleo."

Her sky-blue slacks and shirt matched her eyes. She didn't look like a country singer, even if her accent carried the sound of weathered Appalachian Mountains and tall trees. Perhaps she was out of uniform today. No rhinestone shirt or fancy boots.

"Carlos Andres McCrary. Everybody calls me Chuck." We shook hands. "Is LeMarvis joining us?"

She peeked at her phone. "He's stuck on I-95. An eighteen-wheeler jackknifed in the rain. He'll be here soon. Can we start without him?"

"Sure. Can I offer you something to drink?"

"Bourbon and branch would be good." It was ten o'clock in the morning, but she wasn't kidding. Was her southeast Kentucky birthplace speaking? Her website said she was born in the Appalachian Mountains. Too bad I couldn't offer moonshine.

"I'm fresh out of both. Sorry. How about coffee?"

She shook her head and her blonde curls swayed around her ears. "I try not to drink caffeine."

We settled on a ginger ale for Cleo and a coffee for me.

I punched the intercom. "Betty, a ginger ale for my guest and a coffee for me, please. And when LeMarvis Jones arrives, call me, then send him back. Otherwise, hold my calls."

Whenever I meet with a client, I always tell Betty to hold my calls. It makes clients feel special, but Betty knows whose calls to put through regardless.

Cleo followed as I led her to my so-called conference room. With three people, it's crowded. On rare occasions, I squeeze in five and it's a circus clown car.

Like most people who see my conference room the first time, Cleo's eyes wandered to the right-hand wall.

Matching picture frames displayed my PI license, my degree in criminology from the University of Florida, and a picture of my graduating class from the Port City Police Academy. To the right hung my Bronze Star, the medal citation, a photo of my Special Forces unit in Afghanistan, and my honorable discharge.

Cutting my eyes to the wall for an instant, my thoughts escaped to Ghar Mesar in the Afghanistan mountains. An old battle scar on my left bicep throbbed.

"I never seen a Bronze Star medal before."

For the thousandth time, I wished I had never been there to earn it. That battle cost the life of a brother-in-arms. He was awarded his Bronze Star posthumously. For the thousand-and-first time, I pushed that image aside.

"A former girlfriend who was a marketing guru insisted I display all that. She framed them as my birthday present the day I opened my PI office. She calls it an *ego wall*."

"What did you do to earn the medal?"

"I was in the wrong place at the right time. My whole squad was. The general had to give someone a medal; he chose me." I didn't mention the other Bronze Star recipient; that would depress us both.

"I'm impressed."

"That's what my girlfriend intended. If I ever see her again, I'll tell her she was right. Please, have a seat." I gestured at a chair where she wouldn't see my ego wall. I didn't want the wall to distract her during our interview.

She sat. "Why not?"

Betty tapped on the door and walked in with our drinks. "Here you are." She set the tray down and left.

"Why ain't you and her together?"

I swallowed once and changed the subject. "Let's talk about you. Tank said you received email threats."

"Don't change the subject. I'm nosy; everybody always says that. Momma says everybody needs to love somebody. When me and LeMarvis met, it was almost love at first sight."

I wasn't there to discuss my life, so I followed her lead. "How did you and LeMarvis meet?"

"I was singing at the Tarnished Spur in Humbolt Springs last year. LeMarvis and some of his Peregrine players, they come in to listen to the music. I noticed right off on account of they were real tall. Do you know the Tarnished Spur?"

"I've heard of it, but I go to the Pick 'n Fiddle on South Beach to hear country music."

"I ain't played the Pick 'n Fiddle. I heard it's a nice place."

"Go on. LeMarvis and friends came into the Tarnished Spur…"

"The manager sat them down front at a reserved table because they were celebrities. Some drunk cowboys behind them, they complained they couldn't see because LeMarvis and his friends were so tall. LeMarvis, he offered to buy them a round of drinks, but they wouldn't have none of it."

She lifted her ginger ale. "They were looking for a fight no matter what LeMarvis and his friends did. You know how some people are mean drunks?"

"Yeah. Some drunks get happy, some get sleepy, and some get mean."

"Right. Before I knew it, chairs and bottles started flying. I seen bar fights before, and this was a bad one. LeMarvis, he seen how scared I was, and he left the fight and run to the stage. Stood like a shield between me and the fight until the cops got there. He apologized real nice. Said he felt responsible. He invited me out for a late supper and saw I got home safe. The next day, he called to ask me on a proper date."

"That's a great story. Now, about those emails—"

"You changed the subject again. Why ain't you together with your girlfriend? What happened?"

Drinking my coffee, I gained control of my emotions—Lord knows I'd had enough practice doing that the last few months. "My girlfriend got angry because I put my clients first. She said I canceled one date too many for a client emergency, and she gave up on me." That was true-*ish*. Maybe Cleo would buy it and get off the subject.

"Now, tell me about the threats."

She set down her soda. "It's some redneck country boys living in the past and talking whiskey talk. I wouldn't pay it no mind, but LeMarvis…" She sighed. "He takes everything serious."

"Does anyone you know want to harm you?"

"No. I don't have no enemies."

"Could it be someone you have a nagging suspicion about? Somebody who gives you a bad vibe?"

"Not really. I get along with everybody."

"Is there anything in your past that might jump up to embarrass you or harm you?"

Cleo gazed out my window at the boulevard traffic. "Nope. I've led a pretty normal life."

"What's your background?"

She chuckled. "You being a private detective and all, I woulda figured you already read about me on my website."

"I did, but marketing gurus write those things, so they're usually full of BS. Besides, it said nothing about your family."

"I ain't seen my family in years." She sipped her ginger ale.

The silence stretched as I waited to see if she would say more. She didn't.

The wireless handset beeped and I picked it up.

"LeMarvis Jones is here," Betty said. "I sent him your way."

I stood as the door opened. The tallest man I had ever met ducked his head, bent his knees, and almost duckwalked into the room. My door is a standard six-feet-six-inches. When Tank Tyler comes over, he leans his head to one side. LeMarvis Jones folded his giant body. The Peregrines website listed LeMarvis as seven-foot-three.

I stuck out my hand. "Chuck McCrary."

"LeMarvis Jones. Pleased to meet you." His giant hand encircled mine.

"Take a seat. Is Betty getting you something to drink?"

"She offered, but I told her I was good." He smiled at Cleo. "Hey, babe, sorry I'm late." He bent low to kiss her on top of her head.

She beamed at him and the room lit up again. "That's okay, honey. It's raining hard enough to float a stump. I'm glad you made it safe."

"Did you show Chuck the emails?" He took the chair between Cleo and me.

"There was more than one?" I asked.

"Three." Cleo handed me three sheets of paper. "I printed them out. You can keep these. I keep the originals on my computer, or maybe they're in the Cloud. Tech stuff confuses me."

"Okay if I read these first?"

The emails were racist diatribes that white people and black people shouldn't mix, let alone date. They predicted dire consequences to the human race and civilization if "mongrelization of the Caucazian race" continued. It read like an historical drama from before the Civil Rights Act passed—and that was before I was born. It was almost before my parents were born. In my head, I realized people such as the sender existed, but I had never met one. If I had, they had kept their opinions to themselves. When I finished reading, I smoothed out the printed sheets on the table and gazed at LeMarvis. "I presume Cleo showed these to you?"

He nodded. "Is this guy dangerous? Or am I acting like a frightened old woman?"

"If Cleo were my girlfriend, I would worry too. The guy who sent these emails is a few cards short of a full deck."

"You think it's one person?"

"It doesn't matter whether it's three people or one, the potential danger is there."

"Each message came from a different email address," Cleo said.

"True, but each email address contained the word *white*, and the sender misspelled *Caucasian* the same way in all three emails. My job is easier if the suspect is one person, because I have to guard against one enemy instead of three, but it might be three separate people working together. But let's hope not."

"I hate to see LeMarvis waste money on security I don't need. He already risked millions to underwrite my tour."

"Your tour is the best investment I ever made, babe. As for the extra security... we're talking about your *life*. What's another million or two since I already invested twelve?" He grinned.

"Besides," I said, "even though nine times out of ten it's a good bet nothing bad will happen, this guy might be the tenth case. Most emails in this vein are what you said—an anonymous idiot blowing off steam, counting on the anonymity of the internet to ensure that you can't identify him. But if there is an actual threat hidden behind these emails, then this is a risk to your life. We can't play the odds. If you hire me, I will prepare for what *could* happen, not for what will *probably* happen."

"This is the twenty-first century," LeMarvis said, "but we realize there are people opposed to interracial marriages."

Cleo grinned at LeMarvis. "Me and LeMarvis have a philosophy about those people." She patted his hand.

"Screw 'em," they said together and laughed.

She released LeMarvis's hand. "I don't see why you need to spend so much money on security for my tour. When I opened for Cody Wayne last month, he used his roadies and the local police. We never had no trouble. Other singers don't use outside security. It's unnecessary and expensive."

LeMarvis raised a hand as big as a tennis racket. "You don't know what other singers do for security, babe. You're new at this business. You've never done your own tour. You opened for Cody Wayne Davis, but he hadn't received any threatening emails."

"They're not threats, honey. Not exactly. Whoever he is, he's spouting off. He hasn't threatened to harm me; he just don't want me to be with you."

"Cleo, you saved the emails on your computer?"

"Yes, or in the Cloud somewhere."

"I want to take your computer and your Cloud passwords to my computer guru and see if he can back trace the IP address they came from. It may help find this nut."

"You want my computer?"

"For a day."

She frowned. "You never realize how you depend on them things until someone takes it away for a while." She sighed. "Okay. I'll bring it tomorrow."

"If you prefer, my guy can visit your place and do his magic in your apartment."

"That would be great, but I'm not in my apartment. LeMarvis insisted I move in with him after this email stuff started."

"I live on Magnolia Island." LeMarvis gave me the address.

"I know the place," I responded. "Good security." I noted the address. "Tell me about this tour."

Cleo sat straighter. "We open the Summer Fun Concert Tour at the Falcon's Nest arena next week on Saturday and Sunday. Then we skip a weekend and evaluate the first two concerts. We allowed an extra week to tweak the music, sets, and costumes. The weekend after that, we play Tampa on Saturday and Sunday. The next week we play Orlando on a Friday and Saturday night. After that, it's Jacksonville on Friday and Saturday with a Sunday matinee. We finish the following weekend in

Atlanta with four performances, Friday and Saturday nights, and two shows on Sunday."

She handed me another piece of paper. "These are names and addresses for each concert hall and the contact information for the local hall management."

"You had this list already prepared?"

She grinned. "LeMarvis told me he wanted this protection gig real bad. LeMarvis and I haven't told nobody, but we intend to get married before next basketball season. Most times, LeMarvis does anything I ask, and I know I'll do anything *he* asks." She smiled at him. "That's what a husband and wife are supposed to do. I'm giving him a chance to back out. It's a pot full of money, honey."

"Babe, I'm worth over a hundred million. None of it's worth a week-old pizza if anything happens to you. You're worth every penny I own." He patted her knee. "Let's use the extra security, babe."

Cleo put her hand on his and squeezed. "If you both say so…"

"We do," he replied.

LeMarvis patted her hand and faced me. "You need a retainer?"

"Yes." I told him my rates and the amount of the retainer.

His eyes widened, but he pulled out his checkbook, signed a blank check, and pushed it across the table. "You fill it out."

After I did, I showed him the filled-in check. He nodded, and I stuck it in my pocket.

If something bad happened to Cleo on this tour, I hated to imagine LeMarvis feeling as bad as I felt after it happened to me. I wouldn't wish that on anyone.

TWO

Lester

L ester frowned. What the hell was she doing there? She had never been to this building before, at least not in the weeks he had been following her.

He waited while Cleo's Hyundai and LeMarvis's BMW left the lot. He could find them later; he knew where they lived. After the BMW disappeared in the distance, he parked his car and entered the building. He wrote down the tenant names from the directory in the lobby.

The first tenant was an insurance agency. Lester opened the door and stuck his head inside. "Was that Marvelous LeMarvis Jones the basketball player I saw walk out of here?" he asked the woman at the desk.

Her eyes grew as big as silver dollars. "LeMarvis Jones? He was in the building?"

"I saw him in the parking lot. Did he come in here?"

"Nope. He must have visited another office."

Lester thanked the woman and left. In the hall, he drew a line through the agency's name. The next tenant was an engineering and survey firm where he did the same routine with the same results.

Twenty minutes later, he finished the ground floor and started on the second floor. He stepped into the lobby of the executive suite where Chuck McCrary officed. "Did I see LeMarvis Jones come out this door a while ago?"

"Yes. Isn't it exciting to have him in the building?"

"I'm a big fan," Lester said. "Did you get his autograph? Or a selfie with him?"

The receptionist shook her head. "No, Chuck wouldn't approve of me bothering a client."

"Chuck?"

"Carlos McCrary, the private eye. He's kinda famous too. Anyway, we respect our clients' privacy."

Stupid bitch, you violated your client's privacy and you don't even recognize it.

"That's a good idea," Lester agreed.

Lester searched *Carlos McCrary* and found more than four hundred thousand internet entries ranging from an Argentine socialite to soccer players in three countries to criminals in four states. Halfway down the first page of results he found the right Carlos McCrary: owner of McCrary Investigations, U.S. Army Special Forces veteran, Bronze Star medal recipient, University of Florida graduate with a degree in criminology, and former Port City police detective. Cleo must have hired this McCrary fellow as her bodyguard.

That would make his project more difficult, but difficult didn't mean impossible. He would just have to be even more careful.

THREE

Carlos McCrary

C leo had given me two concert tickets which I held in the air. "I have a present for you, bro."

Clint Watson flipped his book face down on the glass-topped side table. "It's not my birthday and I graduated last month. What's the occasion?"

Over the last two years, Clint had become close like a younger brother or nephew. He burst into my life, a runaway bus careening down a mountain road with no guardrail. My client had been framed for murder and my investigation led me to Clint Watson. When I found him, Clint was a sixteen-year-old kid who survived hand-to-mouth on the streets of an iffy neighborhood where the murder happened. His drug-addict mother had no desire to parent him, and his father was never in the picture. The foster-care system failed him for a variety of reasons. Since he had no one else, I took him in and enrolled him in Port City Preparatory School as a boarding student. He had graduated the previous month and would begin his freshman year at the University of Florida in a few weeks.

"My new client is Cleo Hennessey. She gave me two third-row tickets for you and a friend to her concert Saturday night." I handed him the tickets.

"Can I take a date?"

I had never seen Clint with a girl and he had never brought one home to our condo. I had begun to wonder if he was a late bloomer or perhaps there was something else he hadn't told me.

"I didn't realize you had a girlfriend."

"I don't. At least, not yet. There's this girl I met at Port City Prep… We ate lunch together in the cafeteria, but we never dated. Unless you count sitting together at school football games."

"That counts as a date in my book. How come you never mentioned her during football season?"

"It was no big deal. I was a boarding student and she commuted from Port City Beach. You didn't give me the car until I graduated, so I couldn't pick her up for the games. She drove her own car to the stadium and I walked. We sat together."

"If I had known, I would have loaned you my car. Why didn't you ask?"

Clint spread his hands. "I just didn't. She lives on the beach. Madison Wycliffe is her name. She finished her junior year at Prep."

"Congratulations. Have a great time." I handed him a hundred dollars. "Take her to dinner beforehand; she'll love that."

"Thanks." He stuffed the bills in his pocket. "There's one thing I didn't tell you…"

I waited.

"Madison is white."

"Lots of people are. Don't hold it against her."

"She said that her parents didn't want her to date a black boy."

"Black *boy*? They called you *boy*?"

Clint grinned. "No, it's not bad as that. Remember, Madison is seventeen. Her contemporaries are boys. Her parents said that last year. They didn't intend any racism in the comment. At least, I choose to believe they didn't. She mentioned it last football season when I asked her to a game. She met me there instead of me picking her up."

"Forbidden love. Some people say it tastes sweeter, although I have no personal knowledge."

Clint smiled. "Maybe I'll find out."

19

"You carrying?" On his sixteenth birthday, I gave Clint a box of condoms and advised him to carry one with him twenty-four/seven.

"Bro, it will be our first date."

"Stranger things have happened. Don't get some girl pregnant until you intend to, preferably *after* you're married."

"I haven't asked her out yet."

"When she says yes, you'll have to meet her parents. What happens when you appear at her house? You suppose they'll notice you're black?"

Clint grinned. "I have no idea what they'll do. I'm kinda new at dating."

"You should discuss this with her. Call her and plan how to handle the introduction."

"What would you do, big bro?"

"Bro, you have faced situations like this your whole life. Skin color is the first thing people notice when they meet a stranger, even if they're not racist. For most people, race is no more significant than eye color or height. But for some..." I shrugged. "I wish I could help, but I don't have a clue. I seldom face any friction from being a Latino."

FOUR

The Port City concert venue was the Falcon's Nest, the arena where the University of Atlantic County Falcons play their home basketball games. Snoop and I had an appointment with Elise Spector, the arena manager.

As I parked near the entrance, Snoop asked, "Any chance Cleo would wear a Kevlar vest?"

I laughed. "I'm pretty sure she won't wear a bulletproof vest."

"What if we sewed sequins on it?"

When I opened the glass door, we heard the soft susurrus of a nearly-empty building. Distant clangs and bangs emanated from the double doors which opened from the lobby to the arena floor.

We found a door marked *Administration* and went in. A middle-aged woman with gray streaks in her hair sat behind a standard-issue institutional desk.

"Hi, I'm Chuck McCrary. This is my associate, Raymond Snopolski."

"Call me Snoop."

The three of us did the pleased-to-meet-you routine.

Spector handed each of us a set of passkeys. "You will be handling concert security tonight?"

"Yes, ma'am, McCrary Investigations at your service." I handed her a business card. Perhaps I should change the name to *Security R Us*.

She laid the card on her desk without looking at it. "We normally wouldn't rent the Nest to a music concert. We avoid events that might bring drugs to campus."

"Why did you make an exception for Cleo Hennessey's concert?"

She wrinkled her nose as if she smelled a bad odor. "It wasn't up to me; the Board of Trustees overruled me. LeMarvis Jones is a big donor to UAC. He paid the usual rent for the Nest, plus he funded two academic four-year scholarships for next semester." She frowned. "You know there will be drugs."

"At least, with your no-smoking policy, there won't be any marijuana smoked in the Nest."

"Yeah, right. I suppose you both need to inspect the arena."

"Yes ma'am."

"Come with me." She locked her office door behind us and led Snoop and me to the cavernous arena. We stood in the aisle between two grandstand sections. Harsh light shone through skylights spaced between the roof girders to light the floor and leave the grandstands in darkness.

A crew was setting a wood floor in place for the concert. Eerie echoes from the work crew bounced around the cavernous space, sounding like a flock of birds arguing with a machine shop.

Snoop held up the passkeys. "If you'll excuse me, Ms. Spector. I'll go poke around." Raymond "Snoop" Snopolski had been a police detective for over thirty years. After his partner was killed on the job, he took early retirement and became a private investigator. He worked mostly for law firms and insurance companies. I hired him frequently as backup, for surveillance, and legwork.

I revolved a slow 360. "Did Cleo's agent tell you about the email threats she received?"

Spector made a noise with her mouth, somewhere between a sigh and a scoff. "Another reason I didn't want to host her concert. Some weirdo might bomb the Nest, but the Trustees said UAC wouldn't bow to fear."

"I see a dozen places a sniper might hide and another handful of places to hide a bomb. Snoop and I will check them out."

"I figured as much. Those keys open every lock in the place. Climb around the rafters if you want. Bring the keys back after tomorrow night's concert. I won't be working that late, but you can leave them on my desk and lock the door when you leave."

By my definition, the first concert was a success. Nobody was shot, bombed, stabbed, overdosed, or otherwise killed.

I sent Cleo and LeMarvis home with two agents. The rest of my team assembled in a conference room on the upper level for an after-action debrief.

Snoop, Pedro "Pete" Martinez, Gunner Knudson, and I poured from a pot of coffee we had bought at a concession stand before it closed.

"Any more suggestions for improvements to tonight's security plan?" I asked.

Pete swallowed his coffee. "What did the clients say?" Pete was a Miami-Dade private eye I used for extra manpower.

"We met briefly in Cleo's dressing room before they went home. They seemed delighted. Cleo was over the moon after her first concert. She wouldn't know *sic 'em* from *come here*. LeMarvis grinned a lot, and he pays the bills."

"And nobody got killed," Gunner added. Erik Gunnar Knutson was my teammate in the Triple Seven Special Forces squad in Iraq and Afghanistan. Naturally, we nicknamed him *Gunner*. With a good rifle, he could hit a poker chip at 1,000 yards as easily as I could at fifty, but I was better looking.

"Let's stick with a winner. What's the attendance tomorrow night?" he asked.

"Cleo's agent, Avery Harper, told me before he left that tonight's performance has already lit up social media like a fireworks show. YouTube videos posted during the concert have already tallied tens of thousands of hits. Avery expects the lower bowl to sell out all 5,000 seats. He told the Nest to open the upper bowl for an extra 3,000 tickets he expects to sell online before tomorrow night's performance."

"That's what we need. Four thousand more suspects to watch."

"Then watch them we will, Snoop," I responded. "I'm adding two more agents for the upper bowl."

We tweaked the roving patrols and ticket-taking procedure and everybody went home. At least, I did.

FIVE

I mixed a *Cuba Libre* and kicked off my shoes.

Clint had texted he would be late, but it was after midnight. The concert had let out over two hours before. Perhaps he had learned if forbidden love did taste sweeter.

A key rattled in the lock and I walked to the foyer as Clint opened the door. I felt like an eager father, wanting to hear about his son's first date.

Clint stood in the open front door, one hand on the knob. He wore a blue raw silk blazer with a Florida Gator patch on the pocket, a Gator-orange silk shirt, and khaki pants. I had left for the arena before Clint dressed for his date. I felt proud of how grown up he seemed, but I resisted the temptation to take a picture of him in his fancy clothes.

"How was the concert?"

"There's been a complication." Clint peered over his shoulder and spoke to someone in the hall. "It's okay, Madison. Chuck loves company."

Clint led a girl through our front door. My Grandpa Magnus McCrary would say she was so white that chalk would make a black mark on her. Pale blue eyes, long blonde hair that curled past her shoulders. She was a knockout, even with her eyes red and puffy and her expertly-applied mascara trailing black streaks down her cheeks. Her designer jeans had been professionally frayed for that fashionable homeless-person look. She wore a scoop-neck gold shell with a layered vest over it. She wore two earrings in each ear, one pair of gold hoops, and one pair of some colored stone. Her multi-colored sandals laced halfway up her calves.

My knowledge regarding women's fashion is sketchy to non-existent, but to my unskilled eye, her outfit could have come straight out of a fashion magazine. Port City Prep wasn't cheap, and she did live on the beach. Her folks had real money. Of course, I was pretty well fixed too.

She extended her hand. "Madison Wycliffe, Mr. McCrary. Pleased to meet you. Clint told me all about you." She had a firm grip, even though her voice quavered a bit.

Seeing her in better light, it didn't take a detective to know she'd been crying. "Welcome, Madison. Everybody calls me Chuck, as I'm sure Clint told you. Would you care for something to drink?"

She sniffed. "Seven and Seven, or ginger ale if you don't have Seven-Up."

"We have Seven-Up," Clint said, "but Chuck won't serve whiskey to a minor." He winked at me. "I'll have the same."

"Great. Clint, why don't you show Madison around while I fetch your drinks. I'll meet y'all on the big balcony."

I poured two Seven-Ups and set them and my drink on a tray. Carrying the tray to the big glass-topped table, I sat and waited for them to finish her tour of the condo. The evening had cooled off and I left the sliders open for fresh air. It didn't hurt that I could eavesdrop on the conversation inside. Madison seemed as if she was struggling to hold herself together.

Murmuring voices grew louder as the young couple approached through the living room.

An unfamiliar cellphone rang behind me.

Madison's voice said, "It's Daddy."

Madison and Clint stepped onto the balcony. Her phone kept ringing.

Madison took a deep breath and moved to the railing. She glared at her cellphone. It rang again.

She stood with her back to me, looking at the bay. She lifted the phone to her ear. "Hello... Yes, Daddy. I'm fine. We're at Clint's brother's apartment... No, he's white—not that it's your business... No, he's not his biological brother. Clint calls him his 'brother from another mother' because they're like family…"

Clint stood behind a chair and watched Madison as she talked. He shifted his weight from one foot to the other, clasping and unclasping the chair back with both hands.

Madison stalked to the other end of the balcony, jerking like a puppet with an unskilled puppeteer pulling her strings. "That's none of your business, Daddy… Well, I'll be eighteen in a few days."

The two glasses of Seven-Up waited for someone to notice them. I sipped my *Cuba Libre* and listened to one side of her family crisis. It felt as if I was watching a train wreck on TV and knowing I couldn't help the victims. This time, the victim was a guest in my home.

Madison tossed her hair back with a practiced motion as she bounced on her toes. "No, Mother, I won't come home. Not tonight anyway. I can't stand any more of your crying and Daddy's yelling…"

She clenched and unclenched her fist. "Clint said I could spend the night…"

Clint's face made a fleeting expression I couldn't describe. Longing, perhaps?

Madison stomped her foot so hard I felt a small vibration in the tile floor. "For God's sake, Mother, it's our first date. What kind of slut do you think I am?… I learned the word from you and Daddy. That's what you say when you gossip about your friends at the Wessington Club…"

The Wessington Club meant her family had *Money* with a capital *M.*

She spun to face me. "Of course, we'll have separate bedrooms. Chuck has a big condo." She smiled a little and winked at me. Perhaps she'd had this conversation before.

Madison stopped pacing, her back to me as she gazed over Seeti Bay. "I can't talk to you when you're like this…"

She paused a long time.

A heated voice was faintly audible from her phone.

"Ha!" Madison answered. "Fat chance. I'm turning my phone off now… No, I won't discuss it anymore tonight. I'll call you in the morning when you've calmed down."

She stuck her phone in her pocket. She faced me, eyes wide, fake smile painted on her face. "Isn't this too, too cozy for words."

She drew out a chair next to where Clint stood. Clint scooted her chair in and sat also.

Madison grabbed Clint's hand with one hand and her Seven-Up with the other. "Cheers."

Clint and I faced each other and lifted our glasses. "Cheers."

"Well, wasn't that special?" I said, just to say something.

"*Ugh*. Daddy makes me *so mad* with his racist jokes and superior attitude, and we're from *Boston*, for goodness' sake. You would think they would learn *something* living in the twenty-first century." She squeezed Clint's hand. "Mom's not as bad, but she lets Daddy walk all over her."

"How long until your eighteenth birthday?"

"August fifth," Clint answered with a grin.

"Since you're a minor, I'm surprised your mother or father didn't demand to speak to me."

Madison grinned. "Oh, they did. That's when I said, 'Fat chance.'"

"Should I expect the police to knock on my door?"

"I doubt it; they don't have your address. This isn't my first blow-up with my parents." She faced Clint. "Just the first time it was over a man."

"What will happen tomorrow?"

"I'll call my mother, and she'll come get me. She'll act as if everything is okay and go on with her routine. Daddy won't talk to me for a couple of days. By Wednesday, this will blow over." She sipped her drink. "Until next time." She put her hand on Clint's forearm. "*Please* tell me there will be a next time."

Clint placed his hand on hers. "You can count on it."

"Well then." My drink clinked on the glass top when I set it down. "I presume Clint showed you the guest room?"

She nodded. She lifted her Seven-Up and held it in front of her mouth. Tears formed in her eyes.

"You're welcome to stay as long as you want, Madison. I can find a big tee-shirt, maybe pajamas for you." Miyo's black silk pajamas were still in her drawer in my bedroom. I had not been able to get rid of them, and my breath caught for a second. No, I couldn't loan those. Or could I? The answer came in a flash. Miyo had had her own problems with her parents. She would want me to loan her pajamas to Madison.

"Madison, I have a pair of women's black silk pajamas that... a friend left here. Would you like to borrow them?"

"Yes, please."

"Clint, Miyo's old pajamas are in the bottom drawer of my chest of drawers. Would you get them for Madison and put them in the guestroom?"

Clint left.

I pushed the memories aside. "Is there anything else I can do for you?"

Madison shook her head. Tears spilled down her cheeks and dripped off her jaw line.

We waited in silence until Clint returned.

"You can talk or not," I said, "whatever makes you comfortable. Would you care for something to eat?"

"We stopped at a burger joint near the Falcon's Nest," Clint said. "That's what took us so long; the place was packed with concert people."

"I won't ask how you enjoyed the concert. It would be like saying, 'Other than that, Mrs. Lincoln, how did you enjoy the play?'"

Madison cracked a smile. "Other than that... That's a good one, Mr. McCr—, Chuck. I could use a few laughs."

"Madison, when I was a young man, I had my share of crises. When they happened, Mother and Dad would say 'Get a good night's sleep and things will look better in the morning.'" I stood. "They were right; things always look better in the morning. I will leave you two. I had a long day and I have another planned for tomorrow. If I'm gone before you wake up, Clint will fix you breakfast."

Madison smiled through her tears. She mouthed *thank you* although no sound came out.

SIX

The music rose to a crescendo. *Just like last night.* They were finishing the last song on the set list. Of course, it wasn't the final song; there would be an encore.

Spotlights flashed and pulsed on the audience, their wild colors changing as they raced across the stands. Theatrical smoke rose from cloud machines and spewed white columns toward the ceiling. Lights caught the droplets and transformed them into tiny rainbows that cascaded back toward the audience.

Cleo strummed her white and gold guitar harder, faster, her hand a blur. The red fringe on her cuffs waved like snakes on Medusa's head. It was the third costume she had worn during the performance. Spotlights reflected off her polished guitar to create bright sprites that danced across the stage and the audience in time to the pulsating music. The smell of flash powder from indoor fireworks hung in the air, even near the top where I sat.

During a key change, Cleo pushed her white cowboy hat back off her head and it hung on her back from the lanyard around her neck. It appeared to be a spontaneous gesture, but she had made that move at the same point yesterday. Despite being new at this, Cleo performed like a seasoned professional.

It was hard to tear my gaze away, but I needed to focus on 8,000 suspects. I felt nervous as a long-tailed cat in a room full of rocking chairs. True, nothing unfortunate happened the night before, but tonight I had more than 8,000 potential killers.

If I were the weirdo, I would have scouted the venue the previous night to do a dry run. Tonight, during the final Port City concert, I would take the shot. That would be during the so-called finale, or the encore. In other words, about now.

My heart rate increased as my glands pumped adrenaline into my bloodstream. It happened every time before action. The previous night passed without incident, and I felt the familiar letdown after the stage cleared and the maximum danger window passed.

My pattern was to aim my binoculars at each spotlight platform in turn, study the camera platforms, look across the crowd below, then turn my binoculars across the press box. Repeat as necessary. Nothing bad happened the night before. Of course, the nut job might not have been there that night.

Gunner did the same from his post ninety degrees to my left. Snoop was posted ninety degrees to my right. Pete was backstage.

From our positions on the top row of seats on three sides of the arena, we watched every part of the vast room. It wasn't enough to prevent a determined shooter, but it was the best I could do in that venue with the manpower the client could reasonably afford. Tonight was the crazy person's last shot—make that last *chance* to attack in Port City. *If anything happens to Cleo…*

Lester

Lester wiped the sweat from his forehead. Hundreds of tons of air-conditioning kept the seats and arena floor comfortable, but heat rose. He lay on his stomach and peered out at the crowded arena. Sweating as if he'd run a mile was a small price to pay for this view. There were 8,000 targets down there.

Lester peered through the telescopic sight. He rolled his left hand a millimeter to the right on its rest and aligned the crosshairs on a dimly-lit face. *I see you, McCrary. I misjudged the situation; you're more than just a bodyguard. You look like the picture I found on the internet. Why wasn't your picture on your website, hmm? Why did you make me work so hard to find your photo? Don't you want people to recognize you? After all, your name is well-known even if few people recognize you by sight.*

He held the crosshairs on the private investigator's forehead for a count of twenty while McCrary scanned the arena with high-powered binoculars. *You can't see me, McCrary. No one can. And, oh, how I'd love to take you down. Not yet... Not yet...*

Lester pulled the gun barrel back, crawled backward a few feet, rotated his position, and aimed at the stage.

He targeted each band member in turn. *Cleo's Kentucky Hillbillies, my ass! What a ridiculous name for a band.* He grew aroused as he placed the crosshairs between the eyes of each person on the stage. *You may be the hillbilly piano man, but you don't realize how close you are to dead.*

He felt powerful; he held an innocent person's life in his hands. *Mr. Hillbilly Drummer Boy, I can make a louder bang than your drums.* He moved the barrel a half-inch. *How well could you sing, Miss Hillbilly Backup Singer, with a bullet hole in your throat?* He toyed with the idea of shooting a hole in the bass player's acoustic bass violin. *You're a dinosaur, playing acoustic bass when the world has evolved to the bass guitar. Perhaps I'll do that another time. Maybe next week.*

He shifted the barrel one more time...

Carlos McCrary

Shifting the focus of my binoculars to the scoreboard, I heard a murmur rise from the crowd. A subtle change in timbre of the noise grabbed my attention and jerked my gaze to the stage.

Oh, geez.

Faye Toledo, a backup singer, sprawled on the stage, legs and arms akimbo. Godiva Simpson and Lisabeth Bonham, the other two backups, dropped to their knees on either side of her, knocking their microphone stands over. The microphones bounced on the floor, and *bangs* blasted from giant speakers that bookended either side of the stage. The keyboardist gazed to where the backups huddled but kept playing. The string bass player missed a note, peeked at the keyboardist, and resumed. A violinist positioned behind the backup singers ran from the stage.

Lisabeth Bonham held up a bloody hand and screamed. A microphone near her picked it up and the shriek shattered the pounding music to an uncertain stop.

It's happened; it's hit the fan.

Cleo pivoted to the fallen singer. "Oh, my God," she shouted. She took off her guitar, but the strap snagged on her hat lanyard. She grabbed the lanyard with one hand and lifted it over her head. Sparkles flashed from dislodged rhinestones as the hat fell behind her. She flipped the guitar strap from around her neck with a practiced move and knelt beside the fallen figure.

Sprinting for the exit, I barked into my walkie-talkie, "Get her out of there!"

SEVEN

My adrenaline-fueled race down the fire stairs and around the perimeter corridor took less than a minute, but it felt like an hour. I skidded to a halt at the emergency exit. Jerking the heavy door open, I sprinted across the backstage while Pete Martinez hustled Cleo toward her dressing room.

"I'll take it from here, Pete. Help the victim." I wrapped my arm around Cleo's waist and hurried her into the dressing room. I locked the door behind us.

Cleo threw herself onto a couch, sobbing into a throw pillow.

After I shoved the heaviest chair against the door, I sat in it. "I'll stay as long as you need me."

Her sobs sounded loud in the carpeted room with its sound-deadening drapes on the windowless walls.

A minute later, I heard a knock. "Port City Police."

Rotating 180 degrees, I put my knees in the chair, and leaned to look through the peephole.

I jerked to a stop when I remembered another peephole. I was transported back to my own condo where my fiancée answered the door.

Different circumstances, I told myself. *Well, not that different.*

Someone tried to kill *me* and believed I was behind the door. This time, a crazy shooter had attempted to kill Cleo and *she* was behind the door. So, not different. Nevertheless, I had no choice. I sure as hell wouldn't open the door without checking.

I put my eye to the lens. "Step back and show me your badge."

My heart pounded at this point of maximum risk. My eye was at the lens. *If he's going to shoot me through the door, this is how it happens...*

Two men in gray suits showed their badges.

I breathed again. "I'll open the door." My muscles shivered as I relaxed the tension I hadn't noticed before.

I'd never met the two detectives who stepped inside. "Are you all right, miss?" the first one asked while the second one closed and locked the door.

Cleo pushed herself upright from the couch pillow. Brushing back the hair that covered her face, she gazed at the cops through tear-reddened eyes. "How is Faye?"

"I'm Detective Beltran, Ms. Hennessey." The first cop edged between Cleo and me. "This is Detective Feldman. Are you okay?"

Cleo peered down at herself. "I'm okay. How bad was Faye hurt? Is she...?"

Beltran didn't say anything. The pregnant pause is a cop tool to soften the blow of bad news. "We don't know, ma'am. The EMTs are putting her in an ambulance. Is that blood on your sleeve? Were you hit?"

Cleo unbuttoned her cuff and slid the sleeve above her elbow. Turning her forearm to examine it, she studied the red mark on her skin. She rubbed it and it smeared. "It must be Faye's blood. I knelt beside her on the stage. Will she be okay?"

Beltran paused again.

Stepping closer, I said, "It's too soon to tell, Cleo. Detective Beltran doesn't know either. After these officers take your statement, two of my agents will drive you to the hospital so you can check on Faye."

There was a pounding on the door. "It's me, babe. Let me in."

The other cop peeked through the peephole. "It's LeMarvis Jones. I think he's Cleo's boyfriend."

"He is," I said. "He wants to make sure she's safe."

Beltran squinted an eye in thought. "Tell him she's okay, and ask him to wait outside while we interview Ms. Hennessey."

Office Feldman stepped out, pulling the door shut behind him.

Beltran stepped between me and Cleo. "You look familiar, but I can't place you."

"Carlos McCrary. I'm Ms. Hennessey's bodyguard. I'm a licensed private investigator and I carry a concealed weapon. You want to see my licenses?"

His eyes narrowed. "Nah. Now that you mention it, I recognize you. God knows, you been on TV enough. Bernard Beltran. Call me Bernie."

We shook hands. "Chuck McCrary."

"Could you babysit LeMarvis Jones while Feldman and I interview Ms. Hennessey? You were a cop. You know the drill."

"Sure. If I know LeMarvis, he's giving Detective Feldman a hard time. I'll hold his hand for you."

As I opened the door, LeMarvis marched toward me, eyes on fire. He wanted to barge past me, but stopped when I held up a hand. "Cleo's safe. I'm changing places with Detective Feldman while he and Detective Beltran interview Cleo." Putting a hand on LeMarvis's elbow, I tried to pull him aside. It was like tugging on a lamp post.

Feldman passed me and closed the door behind him.

I tugged on LeMarvis's arm again. "Let's sit over there where we can guard the door. We'll make sure nobody harms Cleo."

LeMarvis shook off my hand with a wordless snarl. "The way you made sure nobody harmed that backup singer? What the hell did I pay you for, McCrary? That girl was behind Cleo, and the freak missed. What the hell went wrong?"

My stomach knotted. If you reversed our positions, I would feel the same. The fact that nothing bad had happened the previous night gave no comfort now.

LeMarvis stepped closer, chest to chest, and glared down at me. The building's air-conditioning was set on *meat locker* to offset heat from the crowds, lights, and equipment, but sweat beaded on LeMarvis's face and neck. A drop of moisture hung on the tip of his nose. A vein in his neck throbbed.

Even though I was getting a crick in my neck staring up at him, I stood my ground. His nostrils flared with each ragged breath. His massive chest pumped like a bellows. I knew how he felt: fear, regret, relief—all the emotions stampeded through his mind, all fueled by adrenaline. I halfway expected him to grab me by the throat.

My hands hung at my side as I returned his glare with an expressionless face. His breath on my face smelled of toothpaste. Gradually, he regained control.

In my peripheral vision, I watched a crowd gather around us. Most held cellphones, videoing our every move. The others were paparazzi with sophisticated cameras. The spectators hoped for a brawl they could upload to the *Evening News*. Leaning closer to LeMarvis, I pitched my voice so only he could hear. "FYI, Marvelous LeMarvis, a dozen people are making videos. Don't do anything you don't want to see on the eleven o'clock news and on YouTube forever."

LeMarvis's chest deflated, his shoulders drooped, and his eyes closed as he blinked away the tears.

Two of my agents appeared and shooed away the onlookers, not without protest.

I nodded. "You're right; I blew it. If you fire me, I'll understand. I'll even refund your money."

LeMarvis spread his hands, searching for words. He shook his head. The bead of sweat flew off his nose and hit my shoulder. "You're not Superman. Even presidents get shot. Let's sit down."

Gunner Knutson jogged over, grabbed a folding chair from a stack, and sat facing us. "It's what I was afraid of. No one knows where the shot came from. The uniforms are gathering all the cellphone videos they can from the fans."

"Makes sense," I said. "Maybe they can trace the bullet's path if they cross-reference several camera angles."

I faced LeMarvis. "LeMarvis Jones, my associate Gunner Knutson. Gunner, LeMarvis."

The two men shook hands without standing.

LeMarvis was still pissed. "What's happening in Cleo's dressing room? Why won't those cops let me in?"

"Standard police procedure," I replied. "They interview witnesses separately so the recollections of another witness won't taint their memories. Don't worry, they won't take more than a half-hour or so. Cleo's safe with them inside and us outside."

I faced Gunner. "You see anything?"

"I saw squat. I was scanning the press box across from me when the crowd noise changed. I eyeballed the stage, and the girl was down. I didn't hear any shots because of the music. I ran down as fast as I could. You see or hear anything?"

I waffled a hand. "Samey-samey. We got *bupkis*. What about you, LeMarvis?"

"I stood in the wings, watching Cleo. The backup singer—her name is Faye—she collapsed. At first, I figured she fainted. Faye and I chatted before the show, and she told me her stomach felt queasy. She said she gets nerves before every show. I couldn't see her after she fell because the piano player and the drummer were between us. Then another girl saw Faye, and she screamed. All hell broke loose, so I ran out to grab Cleo, but your guys beat me to it. Another man, he grabbed me and pushed me back into the wings. By the time I shook him off, Cleo had disappeared. I came to find her, and I ran into you."

"Did you see the shooter?"

"No. I didn't realize Faye was shot until Cleo stood up and I saw blood on her sleeve."

"Did you see a muzzle flash? Anything out of place?"

"Nope. Nothing. Where did the shot come from?"

"God only knows," I replied. "The cops will search for clues, a spent cartridge, or even the weapon. He would have used a rifle, so he might have left a shell casing. He might have abandoned the weapon so he could leave the building without attracting attention."

Gunner stood up. "I'll poke around topside. There are a thousand places to hide up there and the cops may not know what to look for. Hand me your keys."

EIGHT

Gunner Knutson

Gunner stepped off the elevator on the top floor. The ring corridor was deserted. Tickets had been sold for the upper bowl, but they were for the lower rows closer to the stage. The concert stopped after the shooting, and the upper bowl had quickly emptied.

A quick U-turn brought Gunner to the walkway behind the top row of seats. He peered down at the Crime Scene Unit processing the stage area. Voices and photo flashes emanated from the CSIs.

As the shot or shots were fired, Gunner was watching the arena from where he now stood. The rows of chairs that waited in military precision earlier now lay in disarray. Panicked concertgoers had shoved them away or thrown them aside in their stampede to the exits.

Gunner swept his gaze around the arena. It was easy to see the floor and lower bowl of grandstands now that the huge lights which hung from the girders were lit. Four workers in purple uniforms with gold trim, the school colors, roamed the floor, stacking chairs on dollies in the areas police had cleared. The clatter of folding metal chairs echoed in the vast room.

A dozen other purple-clad men and women pushed brooms among the permanent seats. They swept debris left by thousands of people ahead of them and down to the row below to collect at the bottom.

Gunner didn't approve of the sweeping. If the gunman had fired from the rafters, an ejected casing might fall on the seats below. If so, the crew was sweeping and dumping crucial evidence. The CSU should have established control of the whole arena, not just the stage.

He shook his head in disgust.

Nestled in its niche in the girders that supported the roof, the scoreboard was barely visible in the glare of the surrounding lights. From his position, the huge video screens, now dark, were just above eye level.

Gunner paced to his right and studied the catwalks that accessed the service areas overhead. Everything was purple, and the dark color absorbed the light. The catwalks were hard to see in the gloom above the lights. Of course, that was the point. The metal maze above their heads should not distract the patrons. Thirty yards along his walk, he found it—an access to the catwalks.

Gunner noted the code painted in small gold numbers on the purple door and selected a matching key from the ring of keys Chuck had given him. He flipped on the light in the access room. Electrical panels were mounted on the left wall. To the right, a steel ladder led to the catwalks.

Gunner fitted a dust mask over his nose, pulled on a pair of crime-scene gloves, and climbed to the catwalk. From there, he could access the area between the girders and the roof.

He checked both ways. *Must be a half-mile of catwalks.* He sighed. *Only way to search it is to search it.* He switched on a Maglite and gazed down as he walked the narrow metal deck.

Carlos McCrary

Cleo's dressing room door opened and LeMarvis jumped to his feet. Detective Beltran came out and spotted us. He headed our way, Feldman behind.

LeMarvis pushed his way past the cops, darted into Cleo's dressing room, and slammed the dressing room door behind him.

Beltran gestured to Feldman. "Jerry Feldman, Carlos McCrary."

"Call me Chuck."

Beltran pulled out his notepad. "Let's sit. This may take a while."

"I wish," I replied. "I don't have much to tell."

Beltran unwrapped a stick of bubble gum, stuck it in his mouth, and stuffed the paper in his jacket pocket. "God, I miss my cigarettes." He loosened his tie and unbuttoned his collar. "Let's do this." He spent twenty minutes asking, writing, and asking again.

I filled him in on the emails, the concert schedule, my agents' locations, and what I did before and after the shooting. "My computer expert went to Cleo's place to trace the sender's IP address, but the bad guy used two anonymizers with each email. That's a dead end."

"Anything to add?" Beltran closed his notebook.

"Nope."

"Snoop available? I want to interview him next."

"He's searching the skyboxes and press box."

"He have a set of master keys?"

"The manager gave us two sets. Snoop has one and Gunner Knutson has the other. Gunner is climbing in the rafters searching for the shooter's perch."

Beltran frowned. "Snoop knows not to mess with my crime scene. What about this... Gunner, you say?" He blew a small pink bubble. It popped before it grew bigger than a marble. "God, I miss my cigarettes."

"Erik Gunnar Knutson." I spelled it. "He's former Special Forces. Gunner won't mess up any clues, either. If he finds something, he'll call me first."

Beltran craned his neck. "He's up near the roof? Oh, yeah, I see a flashlight. Gotta be miles of catwalks up there."

"Yep, and Gunner will check every foot. Unless you'd rather do it."

"I'd sooner have a root canal than climb up there. Too dusty. I would sneeze my brains out for two weeks." He popped another bubble. "He can be my guest."

He checked his watch. "Call Snoop for me, will you?"

I punched Snoop's number. "I have Detective Bernie Beltran here. He wants to interview you." Putting the phone on speaker, I handed it to the detective.

"Snoop, Bernie Beltran. How the hell are you?"

"Hey, Bernie. Last time I saw you, you drove a patrol car and did a piss-poor job of that. You a detective now?"

"I got promoted after I learned how to read and count to twenty without taking off my shoes, same as you. You putting this McCrary kid through his paces?" He winked at me.

"Taught him everything I know."

"That must've took all of ten minutes."

Snoop laughed. "Maybe fifteen."

"Where are you?"

"Skybox 721. I started with 701 and I'm working my way around. I have fifteen more to go, plus the press box. Should I come down?"

"Nah. Find anything?" Beltran asked.

"Some crap behind a trash can that the cleaning crew missed. Nothing of interest yet."

"So far, nobody saw shit. What about you?"

"No joy. Too much noise, too much confusion," Snoop said. "All the action was on stage. The shooter could have run around stark naked, waved a flag and shouted 'Look at me,' and nobody would have noticed. Maye we'll find his brass. It had to be a rifle from the distance he shot from."

"Yeah, if he was close enough to use a pistol, he would have been in the audience and someone would have seen something. Even with loud music, you can hear a gunshot next to you. You keep doing what you're doing. Call me if you find anything." He handed the phone back to me.

"Snoop, you there?" He wasn't. The phone vibrated. Odds were, Snoop had texted me. He had something to say that he didn't want Beltran to hear. "What do you plan to do now, detective?"

Beltran chewed his gum, blew another bubble, popped it. "Wait for the CSU to finish. We'll process the arena floor, but we won't find squat. Gotta do it though." He stood. "Perhaps the audience's cellphone videos caught something. Give me a heads-up if you find anything."

He and Feldman walked away.

The text was from Snoop.

Beltran couldn't pour piss out of a boot with the instructions printed on the heel. The man was a poor street cop and will be a worse detective. Don't trust him to do a decent investigation. Delete this text.

I deleted the text and walked toward Cleo's dressing room. I tried the doorknob. Locked.

I knocked. "Chuck McCrary here."

Just after LeMarvis let me in, my cellphone played *The Army Goes Rolling Along.* "Hey, Gunner. What you got?"

"I'm searching from the catwalk. Something between the seats below me reflects light. Might be a shell casing. Cleanup crew hasn't swept there yet. If I leave this spot, I might lose sight of the reflection and not find it again."

"Where is it?"

"Top level, north side, the walkway behind Section 58."

"I'll come. Be there in five."

I called Snoop. "You finished searching the suites?"

"Two more to go. Thank God Jackie and Ramona came to last night's concert instead of tonight. I'd hate to see them involved in this craziness." Jacqueline and Ramona were Snoop and his wife Janet's two teenage daughters.

"Yeah. You called Janet?"

"I told her I'd be late. She watches everything on the news."

"Then she won't worry about you. After you finish the suites, come to Cleo's dressing room. She wants to go to the hospital to check on Faye. That's the victim's name. Cleo and LeMarvis need an escort. I'll have Pete drive the four of you."

I called Pete Martinez. "Pete, what you doing?"

"Watching the CSIs and shaking my head."

"Are they that bad?"

Pete lowered his voice. "If I didn't see their uniforms, I would think they were amateurs who trained watching *CSI* reruns. If the shooter left clues, we'll have to find them ourselves."

"We're in Cleo's dressing room. You and Snoop drive her and LeMarvis to the hospital." I glanced at the couple. They nodded. "Stay with Cleo until she's ready for y'all to take her home, or wherever she wants."

The shooter was out there, but I didn't have to remind Pete or Snoop, and there was no need to spook Cleo more than she was.

"Snoop Snopolski and Pete Martinez will take you to the hospital. They'll stay with you, Cleo, until they take you wherever you want."

"That first call from Gunner," LeMarvis asked, "what did he find?"

"Something for me to look at. Don't get your hopes up. It might be nothing. We mine a ton of ore to find one ounce of gold. Even then, the gold can turn into fool's gold. Most of the stuff we find leads nowhere. It goes with the territory."

A knock sounded on the door, followed by a voice. "It's Pete Martinez."

I opened the door. "Snoop will be here soon. Take good care of Cleo."

NINE

"Can you see me, Gunner?" I had my phone on speaker.

"Yeah," Gunner replied. "The aisle to your left... walk down two rows... no, one more row... turn right, five or six seats ahead on the floor. Look under the edge of the seat."

"I see it. Good work. It's a 5.56×45-millimeter NATO casing. Snap my picture from there to show the position while I call Detective Beltran."

"A 5.56 millimeter, say, from an AR-15 carbine?" Beltran asked.

"Maybe we got lucky. We'll keep searching while you come up. There could be more than one."

Beltran arrived in ten minutes. "I had the arena crew stop sweeping the floor in case there are other casings."

"Good idea, Bernie," I said.

"What you got?" He blew a small bubble and popped it with his mouth.

"My guy, Gunner Knutson, found this shell casing."

"Has anybody touched it?"

"No. That's where we found it. Gunner spotted a reflection. He's moved on to look for others."

Beltran raised his voice. "Wave at me, Gunner."

Gunner shined his Maglite across Beltran and me. "Right here, folks." He was twenty yards farther down the catwalk.

"You see any sign of the shooter?" Beltran asked. "Disturbed dust, footprints, handprints, anything such as that?"

"No, sir. I searched a thirty-foot radius from the casing. All four catwalks I could reach. No other evidence, and there's something fishy concerning this whole scene, detective."

"What?"

Gunner looked around. "There's no suitable shooting position anywhere within fifty feet of that casing. It didn't come from the shooter's gun."

"What about that spotlight platform?" Beltran pointed. "It has a good sightline to the stage."

"Bernie," I said *sotto voce*, "that works only if the spotlight jockey was the shooter."

Beltran's face turned red beneath his tan. "Gunner said there was not a suitable shooting position. I meant there was a suitable shooting position, not that the shooter used it. Of course, with the spotlight operator there, he couldn't shoot from there. I never meant that."

"Right." I'm agreeable with cops, even dumb ones. My grand-pappy Magnus used to say, "Never make an enemy by accident."

Beltran rotated back to Gunner. "My CSIs will process the casing."

"Okay," Gunner hollered down.

My cellphone signaled a text. It was from Gunner.

Boss, I'll finish searching the catwalks. Maybe I'll find the shooter's position.

Ten minutes later, Gunner called. "There's another casing down there."

"Where?"

"Section 29, eight rows from the top."

"On my way."

Trotting around the perimeter to Section 29, I located the casing. "It's another 5.56 NATO."

In ten minutes, Beltran arrived. "This is too far away to have been fired from where you found that other brass."

"Yeah. Either the shooter moved, or this guy drops cartridges like breadcrumbs, having a laugh at our expense."

Twenty minutes later, Gunner called me again. "I'm inside the scoreboard. There's an M4 carbine up here."

I showed Bernie Beltran to the access room door. Gunner had left it unlocked.

The detective stepped inside and stopped six feet from the ladder. I would let him go first; he was the detective even if my man had found the shooter's hiding place.

Squeezing in beside him, I shut the door. "After you, detective."

He regarded the ladder, his jaw clenched. He stood rooted to the spot as I waited.

"Should I go first?" I asked.

"Yeah, you do that."

I pushed past him and climbed the ladder. I paused on the catwalk landing.

Beltran hadn't moved. His eyes were the size of golf balls. His gaze darted from the base of the ladder to me at the top, never fixing on one spot. His lips trembled. Was Bubble-Gum Bernie afraid of heights?

"You coming, Bernie?"

He clamped his mouth shut and backed toward the door.

"Is something wrong, detective?"

"No, no, you go ahead. The CSIs will be here in a minute. I'll send them after you." He opened the door. "I'll see you later." He left and slammed the door behind him.

The catwalk rang with my footsteps as I crossed over to the giant scoreboard stowed above the arena. I squeezed into the interior. Four giant video screens formed the walls. Wiring in various colors snaked behind the screens and to the center, strapped to steel supports. The cables disappeared through a gap where support beams came together in the center. Light leaked through the corner gaps between the screens.

Gunner squatted to my left. "Where's Beltran?"

"Changed his mind. He'll send the CSIs. What do you have?"

He gestured at the rifle near his feet. "Shooter left his rifle. Figured he could escape quicker if he didn't stop to disassemble it."

"He abandoned a firearm that cost over a thousand bucks. He ain't poor."

Gunner stood. "Notice anything strange concerning the weapon?"

The black steel rifle seemed ominous and lethal in the dim light. "M4 carbine with no gunsight and no magazine." Another 5.56-millimeter casing gleamed in the faint light. "At least he left his brass."

TEN

Lester

Lester glanced both ways and closed the steel door behind him. A handful of people straggled out to their cars. The expanse of pavement was virtually deserted; the lot was ninety percent empty.

His heartbeat throbbed in his ears like a drum, pulsing in his throat like a metronome.

By God, I did it. After all the practice and dreams and fantasies, I by God did it. I got to kill someone.

Willing himself not to run, he crossed to the far side where the employees parked. A half dozen cars remained, but they were empty.

Still, you can never be too careful.

Lester unlocked the pickup and opened the driver's door. When he had parked hours earlier, he'd switched off the interior lights so the cab remained dark. He set his toolbox behind the seat, careful not to make noise.

Excellent, all according to plan. No one to see. No one to notice.

He slipped behind the wheel, closed the door, and cranked the engine. The headlights switched on. High beams reflected off two cars in the next row like a beacon to alien spaceships.

Oh, my God.

Lester cursed and fumbled in the darkness to find the headlight switch. He twisted the switch to manual. The outside lights extinguished and the truck again became anonymous, unexceptional.

He pounded his fist on his knee in frustration.

Stupid, stupid, stupid mistake. You're too smart to make mistakes. You're smarter than all of them. Always keep the headlights on manual. Next time, he fumed, *next time...*

He set the air-conditioning to *max* and aimed the vents at his face and chest. The cold air fought to dry his sweaty body faster than his pores produced more. He hadn't realized that strong emotions would heat his body that way. The armpits of his purple uniform felt clammy and wet from perspiration. Even an hour after the kill, he felt stretched tight as a drumhead.

Oh, crap, no wonder I sweat so much; I'm still wearing the wig.

Lester pulled the wig off and tossed it on the passenger floor mat. He ran his fingers through his hair and they came out wet. He wiped his hands on his purple pants. So much he had not anticipated. He would do better next time.

He waited for his heart to slow. He stared at the arena and relived his triumph.

The loading dock door slid upward to reveal the brightly-lit backstage area. In front of the dock, a dark blue Escalade pulled to a stop. A man in a valet parking uniform exited the SUV and walked inside.

A minute later a different man came out and scanned the parking lot. Three more people walked into view.

Two of them, a man and a woman, towered over the third figure. Lester grinned in recognition. He put his pickup in gear and pulled closer to see what was happening.

Cleo Hennessey

Cleo Hennessey clenched LeMarvis's elbow harder and hunched her shoulders, making a smaller target as they scurried through the backstage toward the vehicle doors. Her tears had stopped, but her eyes burned and she couldn't stop shivering.

The killer could be lurking anywhere, waiting to take another shot at me. Anywhere...

She had no idea who the killer was or what he looked like or if he was a *he* instead of a *she*. She choked back another sob at the idea that someone wanted her dead.

LeMarvis patted the hand that clutched his arm. "Easy, babe. You're safe. I'm on one side and Snoop's on the other and Pete's in front."

Snoop placed his left hand protectively on the small of Cleo's back and guided her and LeMarvis toward the exit. "Everywhere you go, Cleo, two of us will be with you—one in front and one behind. If anyone tries to get to you, it will literally be over our dead bodies. You can count on that."

Snoop stopped as they approached the exit. "There's the parking valet. Our Escalade is outside, folks. We'll stop here while Pete checks the surroundings. He's in front; I'm behind like I promised." He nodded at Pete, who accepted the key fob from the valet, slipped him a few bills, and stepped outside.

Pete scanned the pavement. He signaled *stop* while he eyeballed a pickup truck approaching from across the lot. "Hold on. Someone's driving this way without lights."

Cleo shivered. A vehicle without lights sounded ominous.

The pickup's lights flicked on as the truck reached the circle road that curved around the arena. It turned toward the exit.

Pete nodded as the truck headed away. He moved toward the Escalade and opened the back door. "Okay, let's get you guys to the hospital."

Cleo slid into the back seat. LeMarvis and Snoop got in on the other side.

"Buckle up, please," Pete said as he took the driver's seat. He adjusted the rearview mirrors. "Snoop, what hospital did they take her to?"

"Port City Baptist Hospital. It's on—"

"I know where it is."

Cleo's throat tightened when she saw three television news vans parked in view of the hospital. A television reporter framed by TV lights spoke to a camera.

They're reporting on the shooting at my concert. Omigod, I don't want no one to interview me. Not until I learn what happened to Faye.

Her stomach ached. She tapped Pete's shoulder. "Avoid the reporters, Pete. I... I won't talk to no strangers. Not until I learn how Faye is doing."

"No problem. They can't come onto the hospital property. Too much congestion if they do."

Pete stopped the Escalade under the *porte-cochere* and let the other three out. "I'll park the car and join you inside." He flashed a smile to reassure her. "Snoop's in front... and I'm right behind."

Cleo stopped short when the double glass doors to the emergency department opened and frigid air spilled into the humid night. Hospital smells assaulted her nostrils and invaded her mind, conjuring images from the past.

LeMarvis grabbed her arm. "You okay, babe?"

Shaking her head, she followed Snoop inside. "It's nothing, honey. I'll be okay." She hoped she spoke the truth. Maybe she would be okay. Too soon to tell.

Snoop stopped at the reception counter. "We're here for Faye Toledo. Can she have visitors?"

The receptionist checked her computer screen. "Ms. Toledo's in surgery. She'll be there for some time. Why don't you take a seat over there?"

"What can you tell us regarding her condition?"

"Are you family?"

"She don't have no family," Cleo said. "We're the closest thing she's got. She's a singer in my band."

"I can't discuss a patient's case with anyone but family without a healthcare directive or the patient's permission. Sorry."

Cleo squeezed LeMarvis's hand as they sat in adjoining institutional chairs. "We can pray and hope for the best."

Snoop sat with his back to the wall. He scanned the waiting area.

Pete Martinez walked through the doors. "Any news?"

"She's in surgery," Cleo replied. "That's all they'll tell us."

A door marked *Authorized Personnel Only* opened and a woman in hospital uniform came out. "Are you Ms. Toledo's family?"

Cleo stood. "No, ma'am. Faye's an orphan. I'm Cleo Hennessey. Faye sings with my band."

"She has no family? None?"

"No. We're it."

The woman considered for a moment. "I'm Nurse Eva Wagner. Would you follow me to the surgery waiting area?"

Cleo grabbed LeMarvis's hand and followed Nurse Wagner. She prayed Faye would recover. If Faye died... No, she wouldn't think about that now. Like Scarlett O'Hara, she would think about that tomorrow.

Nurse Wagner held a magnetic card to a sensor beside the door. The door clicked and she held it for Cleo. She raised a hand as Snoop tried to go first. "Sorry, family only."

"Nurse Wagner," Snoop said, "we are Cleo's bodyguards. Someone tried to kill her tonight and shot your patient by mistake." He flipped open the leather wallet with his PI license and concealed weapon permit and shoved it under her nose. "That man back there is Pete Martinez, an off-duty Miami cop. He's with us. We don't leave Cleo's side."

The glass-walled waiting room was crowded with four people in it with two of them as big as Cleo and LeMarvis. The air-conditioning struggled to keep the temperature comfortable. Cleo shivered even though she felt warm. The sight of Snoop's concealed weapon permit reminded her of the threat to her life. She grabbed LeMarvis's hand again.

He smiled at her, but she didn't feel reassured.

A man in a light-green surgical gown walked down the hall, a surgical mask hanging around his neck. He opened the waiting room door and the group stood.

"I'm Doctor Levine. Are you Faye's family?" He sat across from them.

"We're not blood relatives or nothing. She don't have no family. How is she, doctor?"

The doctor didn't say anything.

Cleo's face sagged like wax under the summer sun. Her lips quivered.

LeMarvis wrapped his arm around her shoulder and she leaned into his embrace.

The surgeon shook his head. "We did everything we could. She lost a lot of blood. The bullet hit two arteries and a lung. There was too much damage to repair. I'm sorry."

Cleo moaned and clung to LeMarvis.

ELEVEN

Carlos McCrary

LeMarvis answered the door to Cleo's apartment. "Come in, Chuck. Cleo is pretty upset."

Cleo had returned to collect the last of her equipment and furniture since she had moved in with LeMarvis. The front door of the modest apartment opened into a combination living room/dining room. An expensive music and recording system filled the space intended as a dining area. That much tonnage would require professional movers.

Cleo sprawled on a couch. Her eyes were red, her face was blotchy, and her makeup was a mess. Good thing no paparazzi were there to snap a candid photo.

I dragged a chair closer to the coffee table. "How are you feeling?"

"I could use a bourbon and branch."

Before I could stand, LeMarvis laid a hand the size of a catcher's mitt on my shoulder. "Let me. I'll get it, babe." He left the room to the kitchen I saw through an archway.

I gave her my don't-worry-everything-will-be-all-right smile. It didn't feel convincing. "Do you feel up to telling me what you saw?"

Cleo wiped her eyes with a tissue. "It was horrible. After the key change, I have this favorite guitar riff I play before the final chorus. After I began to play, I heard two or three big booms—like someone dropped a microphone. Once in a blue moon, someone does drop a microphone, but not twice or three times... I knew something was wrong, so I twisted around to see what happened. That's when I seen Faye lying on the stage..." She paused as if seeing the singer sprawled on the stage again. She ran her fingers through her hair. "I remember I couldn't get my guitar strap over my head."

LeMarvis handed her an Old-Fashioned glass filled with amber liquid and ice cubes.

She smiled her thanks. She took a long pull of the drink and held the glass in both hands in her lap. She gazed into the glass as if mesmerized. Perhaps she was gathering her thoughts from wherever they had escaped.

She moved a coaster and set the glass on it, then patted the couch beside her. LeMarvis sat and held her hand. "Anyway, I managed to get my guitar off, and I knelt beside Faye and felt for a pulse. That's how I got blood on me." She was wearing a tee shirt now, but she glanced at her arm.

In her mind, did she still see the blood on her sleeve?

"Your man grabbed my arm and pulled me to my feet. Next thing I knew, I was in my dressing room. How did this happen?" she asked. "You were supposed to protect us from this crazy man."

"It was my fault. I'll resign. I'll even refund your money."

"LeMarvis told me you offered to do that." She barely smiled. "He said even presidents get shot, and they have more men in the Secret Service than you have. At least your security worked last night. I mean, the night before. I didn't get no sleep last night. I'm kinda mixed up on what day it is."

"It's Monday morning."

My security worked because the shooter didn't try anything Saturday night. I didn't say that out loud.

LeMarvis took Cleo's hand. "Babe, we should cancel the tour."

"You invested twelve million dollars, honey. If we don't make the tee-shirt sales, album sales, and DVDs—not to mention refunding tickets—you'll lose a pot full of money."

LeMarvis scoffed. "Babe, how many times I have to tell you? I don't give a crap about the money. I have more money than we'll ever need, and I can play basketball for ten or twelve more years. If I help you develop your career, it's not to make money. It's because I love you and I want you to be happy."

He pushed the coffee table aside, sloshing Cleo's drink, and got on one knee. He held Cleo's hands in his. "Babe, let's blow off this whole tour. Say you'll marry me right now, today. We can fly to Vegas this afternoon and be married tonight. We'll have tall, beautiful children and build a house in Kentucky with a picket fence and forget this madman. Just say the word."

Tears spilled down Cleo's cheeks. She leaned over and kissed LeMarvis softly and stroked the back of his head.

It was embarrassing to watch, but moving would call attention to myself, and I didn't want to intrude further on an intimate moment.

She pulled a cluster of tissues from the box and sopped up her spilled drink. I don't believe she was aware she did it. It was an automatic reaction.

"I want the big fancy wedding we discussed. I want all my family and all your family there to cheer and wish us well and throw rice and everything we dreamed about."

"You realize that some in my family won't approve or attend. They… they don't want me to *date* a white girl, and as for marrying one…"

Cleo almost smiled. "I have cousins like that too." She kissed him again. "Get off your knees, honey." She stood and pulled him to his feet. She hugged him. "As for those who don't understand…" She gazed into his brown eyes and smiled.

"Screw 'em!" they said together.

"We meet in a couple of hours to discuss the tour," LeMarvis said. "If we proceed, we'll rent metal detectors if the venues don't have them."

"My key people and I will attend the meeting. I'll look into metal detectors," I said. "Cleo, did you notice anything unusual?"

"Unusual how?"

"An audience member acting funny. Someone in the crew doing something flaky. A band member or singer who acted a little off. Anything out of place."

Cleo's forehead wrinkled. "No, nothing. With the lights and smoke and all, I wouldn't even know there was anybody out there if it weren't for the applause."

She leaned toward LeMarvis. "What about you, hon? You were in the wings. There wasn't no light in your eyes. Did you see anything?"

"I always look at you, babe." He patted her knee. "I didn't see anything until Faye fell."

"Did you talk to the cops?" Cleo asked me.

"Yeah. They asked me the same things they asked you."

"Do they have any clues, or evidence, or whatever you call it?"

"No, but the investigation has just begun. You can't expect them to know much yet. Wait until we all finish searching the arena."

"You search it too?" LeMarvis asked. "Why?"

This was awkward. It wasn't good to undermine any citizen's confidence in their police, but I wouldn't lie to my client either. I decided to go with the truth.

"I don't have any confidence in Detective Beltran."

TWELVE

C leo paced from one end of Tank Tyler's conference room to the other, which was quite a hike. The conference table seemed as big as an aircraft carrier flight deck.

She must have logged three-quarters of a mile in the thirty minutes the rest of us sat around the table. From sixty-one floors up, the view across Seeti Bay was breathtaking. Rainy-season thunderstorms usually form over the Everglades and move east. Today, they gathered offshore and wafted with the trade winds over Port City Beach, spoiling the tourists' beach afternoon. On the mainland where we were, the sun shone like a Chamber of Commerce ad.

Half the population of Port City was in Tank's conference room. Cleo's entourage consisted of LeMarvis Jones, Avery Harper, Tank Tyler, and Cleo's musical director Hound Dog Hannigan. Detectives Beltran and Feldman represented Port City's finest. My team included Snoop, Gunner, Pete Martinez, and, of course, me.

Cleo and LeMarvis had scheduled the meeting to discuss whether to perform the remaining concerts. They talked about Faye Toledo's murder and the progress (or lack of it) on the murder investigation. They debated the risk to Cleo, her band, and to concert attendees if she did perform. They considered the risk to LeMarvis's money if she didn't perform. They brought up the state of the nuclear disarmament negotiations in Geneva— I'm kidding about that last one.

Everyone had an opinion and everyone except Tank and me expressed their opinion. Repeatedly. Tank was the strong, silent type that day. I was the hired gun.

I kept a small scorecard on my notepad. Cleo said she wanted to perform so LeMarvis wouldn't lose money, but I think she was getting a bad case of stars-in-her-eyes.

LeMarvis didn't care about the money; he wanted to cancel and elope with Cleo to Las Vegas. Then they would buy a house in Kentucky with a picket fence and raise enough children to field a basketball team.

Avery Harper argued that Cleo owed it to her fans and his fifteen percent agent's commission to perform, although he tactfully never mentioned his fifteen percent.

Hound Dog Hannigan had "dope" ideas for improvements to the music list and arrangements to turn the next concert into a *Live from Tampa!* best-selling CD album, maybe even a Netflix program.

How corrupt is a culture when "dope"—slang for street drugs or for a stupid person, which are bad—had come to mean "good?"

Tank Tyler reserved judgment until we had more information on the murder investigation.

"We should cancel the concerts, babe," LeMarvis stated for the fifth or sixth time—I'd lost count. "Not only for the risk to you with that nutcase out there, but the risk to anybody else on the stage. A stray shot could hit the audience too. It's too risky."

"LeMarvis, honey, we don't know that bullet was meant for me. Whoever this guy was, he hit Faye an inch from her heart. That don't sound like no stray shot to me. Besides, you invested millions of dollars in this tour." She stopped pacing. "Chuck, did he aim at me and miss?"

"No. The shooter meant to hit Faye. He staged it like a professional contract hit. He took the gunsight and magazine from the murder weapon. The mounting on the carbine was for a telescopic sight. From that distance, a skilled shooter could put a bullet into the target's left nostril. *If* he was a contract killer, he meant to hit Faye in the heart."

"Well then," said Avery, "Faye was the target, not Cleo. We don't know anything about Faye. There might be a list of people a mile long who want her dead. Hound Dog can find us a new backup singer and we'll proceed."

I raised my hand. "Not so fast, Avery. I said if he was a skilled shooter, he meant to hit Faye. I did not say Cleo wasn't the target."

"I don't get it, Chuck," Avery said. "You can't have it both ways. Either Cleo was the target or Faye was."

"Both women might be targets. Look, Cleo, I read the emails this nut sent you. His rage against you and LeMarvis is personal. He wants you to suffer, even if he sends only emails. If the shooter was the weirdo who sent the emails, Faye's murder was not a professional hit. Many amateurs are skilled shooters. Your weirdo might be one. Telescopic sights make it easy to hit a distant target. Contract hits are direct and to the point. All the killer wants is to kill the target. Suffering is irrelevant. But your emailer hates you and LeMarvis. Maybe he sent you a message that's more complicated than killing you. Perhaps he shot Faye to make you suffer."

"If that's his goal, God knows he succeeded. I didn't sleep a wink last night for worrying and feeling guilty about Faye. Detective Beltran, what do you think?"

Beltran cleared his throat and straightened his tie while he waited for every eye to focus on him. "Our investigation is in the preliminary stages. We took the weapon and the brass casing to our evidence technicians a few hours ago. We have just begun our investigation into Faye Toledo also. It's possible she has enemies we don't know about yet. Too soon to have an opinion."

"Cleo," I said, "you don't need to decide now. You put a week's slack in your schedule. Nobody got enough sleep last night, and it's best not to make important decisions when you're tired, stressed, and in a rush."

Cleo sat at the table. "Avery, can we wait a week to decide?"

"Sure. Hound Dog can hire a new singer and keep rehearsing as planned. We'll cancel later if necessary."

"Then it's settled," Tank said. "Let's see what the murder investigation produces. If the shooter wanted Faye dead, Cleo wasn't the target and her email nut wasn't the shooter. Maybe the email nut was blowing off steam like she said. I'll open an escrow account to deposit money from ticket sales. You announce to the public that the concerts have not been canceled, but if you do cancel, you'll refund everyone's money."

THIRTEEN

At his request, I met Bernie Beltran in the Southwest Precinct squad room. "You want a bagel, Chuck?"

"I never say no."

Bernie didn't pick a bagel. Maybe because his mouth was full of bubble gum. "God, I miss my cigarettes." He blew another bubble.

He led me to his cluttered desk. *Chaotic* was a more apt description. I held my coffee in one hand and my bagel in the other. There was no place to put either on Beltran's desktop. Hopefully, his jumbled desk wasn't an indicator of a disarranged mind.

I choked down a bite of stale bagel without comment. The bad coffee was adequate to wash down a bagel, but that was all. Perhaps that's why Beltran preferred bubble gum to bagels. *Note to self: Do not accept bagels and coffee in the Southwest Precinct again.* "You have something for me, Bernie?"

"First, the bad news. The M4 carbine was one of eighteen assorted weapons stolen from a gun show in Orlando last year." He blew a bubble.

"Any leads on the thieves?"

Beltran popped the bubble before he replied. "Surveillance video of the theft shows a masked gang of four people hit at 2:30 a.m., in and out in two minutes. No leads."

"The carbine might have changed hands a dozen times since then. You have any good news?"

"I got a hit on the fingerprints on the shell casings I found at the Nest."

It was my man who found the casings, but I didn't correct Beltran. "Anybody we know?"

"Prints belong to an ex-dogface named Jeffrey Oscar Wister. Did twenty years in the Army. Honorable discharge as a Master Sergeant. Desert Storm veteran. Awarded a Purple Heart for a shrapnel wound in Iraq. Forty-nine years old. Marksmanship medal. That could be significant."

"You're not a veteran are you, Bernie?"

"*Nah.* Why do you ask?"

"Everybody in the Army earns a marksmanship badge after they pass a weapons qualification course. It's as exclusive as graduating from high school. If he received a marksmanship *competition* badge or qualified as a sharpshooter or an expert, that might be significant."

He gestured to the monitor. "This doesn't say anything about those... other qualifications."

"It would have been a long time ago. What did Wister say about this?"

"We haven't found him. I called him and his wife says he's fishing in the Florida Keys with army buddies."

One basic Snoop taught me as a rookie cop was never to warn a suspect you were coming. Surprise them at their home or work. Telephone a suspect and you gave them a chance to destroy or hide evidence or even skip town.

"You didn't go to his house?"

"*Nah.* We telephoned. The wife said he left last Friday."

Beltran was stupid *and* lazy.

"The day before the first concert," I said.

I attempted to bite off another chunk of bagel. I was afraid I'd chip a tooth. Maybe if I set down my coffee and pulled at the bagel with both hands, I could disassemble it. "Can you make a space on this corner for my coffee cup?"

"Oh, sure. Sorry." He scraped a pile of files into a higher, but more compact mound on his desk.

I set my cup down and tugged at the bagel. "Thanks. What did you learn about the victim, Faye Toledo?"

"Huh? The victim? Why, nothing. I haven't run her through the system... yet."

Snoop was right—this guy couldn't detect his way out of a wet paper bag. I managed to break off a small piece of bagel. If I broke one small enough, I could swallow it whole.

"Did you look at Wister's credit cards, bank accounts, stuff like that?"

"Uh... We're working on it."

Sure you are, Bernie. I didn't say that either. I could not express most of my thoughts concerning Detective Beltran in polite company.

"You know what to do, Bernie. You'll run a background check on the victim to see if she has enemies. To make sure Cleo was the target and not Faye, right?"

"Right. Should have results this afternoon. And that other thing you asked... about Wister..."

"Credit cards and bank accounts."

"Right. We need a warrant to search those too. Should have it tomorrow."

Snoop had nailed it: Anything we found to help the case, we would find by ourselves. I gave up on the bagel and dropped it in a trashcan. "Nice talking to you, Bernie. Keep in touch."

"Yeah, you too."

No way, Bernie, baby. No way.

FOURTEEN

The shooter was smart enough to take the gunsight and magazine from the rifle he left behind, but he left a brass casing in plain sight. In fact, he had scattered them all over the place to make sure we would find at least one. With fingerprints, no less. He had made this so easy that it had to be a false trail, but I had to follow it up.

The internet is a wonderful thing for private investigators and other nosy people. In fifteen minutes, I learned where Jeffrey Oscar Wister and his wife Luisa lived and worked and what cars they drove.

I drove to the furniture store where Jeffrey had worked the last three years. Their two-year-old silver Ford F150 pickup was not in the lot, nor their red nine-year-old Toyota 4Runner. Telephoning the store, I asked for Jeffrey. He was on vacation and could someone else help me? I said it could wait until he got back.

Five o'clock. I swung by the fabric store Luisa had managed the last six years. Bingo. Her Toyota 4Runner was parked on the far side of the lot. The sun had faded the Toyota's paint to a color that reminded me of rust. That told me the car spent most of its life parked in a driveway instead of a garage. Could be a clue.

I decided not to bother her at work.

I parked up the street from their conventional house in a conventional neighborhood in a conventional Port City suburb named Humbolt Springs. They had bought it with a VA loan five years earlier after Wister served twenty-five years and retired from the Army on 60 percent pay. Their credit report showed they had made every payment on time.

Jeffrey Wister's online footprint didn't indicate he was a deranged killer.

At 5:45, the Toyota pulled into the driveway. Luisa Wister walked in her front door.

I gave her five minutes to unwind before I parked in front.

The Wister home had a wireless video and audio doorbell. I rang the bell.

"Yes, who it is?"

I held my PI license next to my face where the camera would see it. "My name is Carlos McCrary. May I come in?"

"What do you want?"

"Detective Bernard Beltran called you yesterday looking for your husband Jeffrey. I have a couple of questions to ask. Would that be all right?"

"Sure." The dead bolt clicked and the door swung open. "Come in. Are you a detective?"

"Not anymore. I'm a private investigator helping Detective Beltran with a case." I stood in the tiny entryway and waited.

"What case?"

"Did you hear about the shooting at the concert Sunday night?"

"Yes, I saw it on the news. It was horrible. A girl singer was killed, wasn't she? If this is about that, we didn't go to the concert."

"Yes, ma'am. Can we sit somewhere?"

"Oh, where are my manners? Would you care for tea? I put the pot on the stove."

"Yes, ma'am, tea would be nice."

She led me to a tiny living room filled with furniture from Wister's furniture store, no doubt. White imitation leather couch and two identical side chairs with coordinating mahogany end tables and a coffee table.

The tidy living room didn't resemble a lair for a deranged killer either.

I stopped next to the side chair that seemed less used. I didn't want to sit in her favorite seat.

"Have a seat, Mister… What was your name again?"

"McCrary, but please, call me Chuck. Everyone does." I handed her a business card.

She set it on the table. "Chuck, then. How do you take your tea?"

"Lemon, no sugar, if it's no trouble. Otherwise, plain is fine." I waited for her to leave before I sat. Always the gentleman. Mom and Dad would be proud.

Family photos covered one wall. The traditional photo of Wister in uniform posed with Old Glory, and another beside it of a young woman, not Luisa, also in uniform. The Air Force Academy? There were pictures of Luisa and Jeffrey and the young woman at the beach and standing at the Matterhorn in Disney World.

In two minutes, Luisa returned with a lacquered Chinese tray with a Chinese tea service on it.

As she entered the room, I stood.

"Oh, you're so polite. No need for that, Chuck. Make yourself at home." She set a napkin, teacup, and saucer with lemon slices on the table.

"Yes, ma'am." I sat and fixed my tea. "I notice you take your tea with milk."

"I learned to drink it that way when Jeff was stationed in Japan. That's where I bought the tea service."

"It's beautiful." Okay, the tray was Japanese, not Chinese. Mom would recognize the difference at a glance. She's into stuff like that. On the other hand, Mom couldn't tell a Glock 19 from a Glock 17.

"Thanks." She sipped her tea and set the saucer on the mahogany table. "How can I help you?"

"Detective Beltran wanted me to talk to Jeff. Where might I find him?"

"He's fishing off the coast of Cuba. He and some friends go there once or twice a year."

"I thought he was in the Florida Keys."

"One of Jeff's buddies lives on Big Pine Key and he owns a sport fisherman that sleeps four. They take his boat to Veradero. See that sailfish?" She pointed at a trophy mounted above the couch. "He caught that on their first trip to Cuba."

"It's impressive."

"I told the detective that Jeff went to the Keys to fish. He misunderstood."

"Can I reach Jeff by phone?"

"Are you kidding? In Cuba? They barely have electricity and running water. And they're fishing offshore."

"When will he be back?"

"Friday night. He promised to mow the yard Saturday, and he works Sunday. Why does this detective want Jeff? Is he in trouble?"

"No, ma'am, but he may have information to help us find the shooter."

"What information?"

"Does Jeff own a gun?"

She laughed. "He served twenty-six years in the U.S. Army. Of course, he owns a gun. In fact, we own several."

"May I see them?"

"Now you're making me nervous. Do you have a search warrant?"

"No, ma'am, but Detective Beltran can have one tomorrow if necessary. I hope it won't be necessary."

"You can't believe my husband shot that girl. I told the detective; he's fishing off the coast of Cuba."

"Yes, ma'am, but I want to see Jeff's guns, if it's not too much trouble. Can you show me?"

Luisa Wister pursed her lips. I could practically hear the wheels turn in her head. I waited.

She set her cup down. "We have nothing to hide. There's a gun safe in the guestroom closet. Come with me."

She led the way past two other bedrooms. One had an Air Force Academy pennant on the wall above a queen-sized bed. The other was the master bedroom.

While she entered the combination, I stood across the room. She opened the safe and flipped on the light. "We own an AR-15, a 12-gauge shotgun—Jeff uses it to hunt birds—and that S&W LadySmith belongs to me. Jeff took a Colt .45 with him."

Two shelves in the safe held boxes of ammo for the weapons. "Can I poke around a little?"

She stepped back. "Help yourself."

I opened a Federal ammo can designed to hold 420 rounds of 5.56-millimeter bullets. It was half-full, or half-empty if you're a pessimist. Two more Federal cans sat beside it. I hefted them by their latches; both were full. Most homeowners buy one or two boxes that hold 20 rounds each; Wister bought his by the hundreds. *Hmm.*

The shelf above the Federal cans held three boxes of 12-gauge shotgun shells, a half-dozen 20-round boxes of .45s, and one 25-round box of .38 specials for Luisa's revolver. Another shelf held AR-15 magazines in various sizes up to thirty rounds.

"Okay if I look at the AR-15?"

"Was the girl shot with an AR-15?"

"You'd have to ask Detective Beltran. Can I see the AR-15?" I used a cloth handkerchief to grab the barrel. That was the last place most people would grab to carry a gun so I wouldn't ruin any fingerprints. I smelled the muzzle. A faint gun-oil scent. It hadn't been fired recently, and it hadn't been cleaned in a while. The AR-15 wasn't the murder weapon. Bubble-Gum would check it anyway. No stone unturned.

Using another handkerchief, I removed the magazine and ensured the chamber was empty. Studying the weapon, I saw why Wister bought ammo by the case. "This weapon was converted to full automatic."

She put her fists on her hips. "Okay, that's enough. Tell me what the hell is going on. Do I need a lawyer?"

I set the carbine back in the safe. "We found 5.56-millimeter NATO brass casings at the crime scene Sunday night. The kind that comes in those Federal ammunition cans."

Luisa scoffed. "I know guns and ammo. Lots of rifles use the 5.56. Why are you pointing at my Jeff?"

"We found his fingerprints on the casings."

Luisa Wister stepped back and brought her hand to her chest. "That… that can't be right. There must be a mistake."

"No, ma'am. They're his prints."

70

Luisa closed the gun safe and spun the dial. "I need to call my daughter. Please wait in the living room."

"Yes, ma'am."

As I returned down the hallway, I glanced into the daughter's room. A Humbolt Springs High School Hurricanes pennant hung on the opposite wall and a volleyball jersey with *Wister* on the back.

Five minutes later, Luisa came back.

I stood.

"Please sit. Anna wants to talk to you." She set the phone on speaker.

"Mr. McCrary, I'm Anna Wister. I'm a cadet at the Air Force Academy. Mother says you found Dad's fingerprints on shell casings at a crime scene?"

"Yes, ma'am. We need to figure out how his fingerprints got there."

"I have an explanation."

"Great. Let's hear it."

"Dad loves three sports: hunting, fishing, and shooting. He shoots at a local range once or twice a month. It's simple to collect spent cartridges."

"Good point. Do you know where he shoots?"

"Sure. I shoot with him whenever I'm home from the Academy. The Everglades Gun Shop and Range. Bruce Lewis owns it, but he's a privacy advocate. He won't talk to you without a warrant."

"Detective Beltran can obtain a warrant, but it'll be trouble and the media might get hold of the story. Did your mom tell you there was a shooting at the concert Sunday night?"

"Oh, yeah."

"It's front-page news in Florida. If the news sharks learn about the warrant, and if your father's name comes up, it might look bad for your parents."

"Bruce is a gun nut and big Second Amendment defender. He won't care. He thumbs his nose at the government—*any* government: federal, state, or local."

"Perhaps there's another way. Does Bruce know you?"

"Sure. We've lived here six years. Dad and I have been shooting there since I was thirteen years old. Bruce says I remind him of his granddaughter."

"Would he talk to me if you asked him?"

"He might. Tell you what, I'll call Bruce and call you back. Mom, you and Mr. McCrary hang out while I call him."

"Sure, honey. Chuck and I will have another cup of tea."

Fifteen minutes later, Anna called back. "It took some convincing, but Bruce will see you. I'd go before he changes his mind."

FIFTEEN

M y GPS told me it would take twenty minutes to drive to Bruce Lewis's range that time of day.

I punched my Bluetooth. "Call Flamer." Flamer21 did my internet research. I had met him in person a handful of times, but I never knew his real name or where he lived. We communicated via phone, text, or email. He made a rare personal appearance after he agreed to visit LeMarvis's house to check Cleo's computer. Turns out Flamer loves country music.

"What do you need, Chuck?" No hello, how-you-been, or how's-it-hanging. Flamer was all business most of the time. The traffic cleared and I pulled onto the highway.

"I have an appointment to see Bruce Lewis at the Everglades Gun Shop and Range. Tell me all you can about him and the gun range in the next fifteen minutes."

"Which way does he spell *Lewis*?"

I spelled it.

Flamer replied in seconds. "The gun range's website claims it's 'Disneyland for shooting enthusiasts.'"

"Do you suppose Walt Disney knows a shooting range is using the Disneyland name?"

"I doubt it. Anyway, it has four indoor ranges and four outdoor. Each range has twelve shooting lanes. The outdoor ranges are 100, 200, 300, and 400 yards. The indoor ranges are from ten yards to fifty yards. Parking for 150 cars. You need to hear this crap?"

"*Nah*. That's enough about the range. What do you have on the gun shop?" In front of me, all three lanes had packed up with rush-hour commuters. The first green light cycled ahead of me as I waited stuck in the jam. That's why everyone loves city traffic.

"They sell enough kinds of pistols, rifles, and shotguns to make a Democrat's skin crawl. Ammunition to match. Oh, get this: They have facilities for birthday parties and corporate meetings."

"You're kidding." The light turned green and I inched three car-lengths ahead before the light changed again.

"Nope. Hand to God, the website says 'birthday party facilities.' If it's any consolation, no alcohol is allowed on the premises."

"What kind of person throws a birthday party at a gun range?"

"Sounds fun to me, Chuck. Grown-up Whack-a-Mole at a kid's party."

"Aren't most of these gun people anti-gay?"

Flamer is gay; that I do know. Perhaps he picked his handle to take ownership of the anti-gay slur, but we have never discussed it. People are strange and Flamer is no exception.

"You'd be surprised, boss. Some of my best friends are Republicans. Even gay ones."

Finally, I worked my way forward in the traffic queue and was the last vehicle through the light. It turned pink as I darted through the intersection. *I swear, officer, it was pink, not red.*

"What about Bruce Lewis?"

"Very private about his personal life with a very public *persona* about the gun shop. Viet Nam vet. Decorated twice. Loves the Second Amendment, NRA, Don't-Tread-On-Me, yada-yada-yada. No criminal record although he was busted once for parading without a permit. DA dropped the charges. Sounds like he would be a fun date."

The Everglades Gun Shop and Range abutted the Florida Everglades. It occupied the last stretch of habitable land west of Loop I-895.

The freshly striped parking lot was nearly full in the evening twilight. I pushed through double glass doors into the shop. Rows of showcases for shotguns, rifles, pistols, and accessories filled the store. Behind the counter, shelf after shelf of ammunition for every firearm imaginable. Security cameras covered every inch.

My regular shooting range had a modest gun shop and two indoor ranges: twenty-five and fifty yards. Compared to this, it was a high school football team versus the NFL.

The young woman behind the counter wore a red, white, and blue tee shirt with the range's name embroidered on the chest. The tee shirt fit her like a second skin and showed off her assets. Both of them.

"I'm here to see Bruce Lewis. I'm Carlos McCrary." I handed her my card.

"Do you have an appointment?"

"He's expecting me."

She smiled and picked up a phone. "Is Bruce in? Carlos McCrary is here."

She listened and nodded. "Yes, ma'am. I'll send him back." She pointed across the store. "See that blue door over there near the Don't-Tread-On-Me flag?"

"Yes, ma'am."

"Through there. Bruce's office is the third door on the left."

As I opened the blue door, I heard faint gunfire through double-paned windows overlooking the indoor ranges. More security cameras. The left wall held framed copies of the U.S. Constitution, Declaration of Independence, and Bill of Rights. The first door had a red, white, and blue sign which said *Party Room*. The second door was marked *Conference Room*. The third door held a simple sign: *Office*.

Bruce Lewis's gatekeeper was an elderly woman whose salt-and-pepper hair was more salt than pepper. Her skin appeared as if she had spent years in the sun, and it had sucked all the moisture and fat from her body, leaving a prune-wrinkled husk. Her red, white, and blue tee shirt didn't fit like the young woman's who greeted me in the store.

At first glance, she seemed as frail as a wet tissue, but something in the way she spoke told me she was as tough as my old army boots. "You Carlos McCrary?" she demanded.

"Yes, ma'am. At your service." I felt tempted to salute. Instead, I handed her a business card. Maybe I should add a US flag logo on the card.

"Are you armed?"

"Yes, ma'am. You want to see my concealed weapon permit?"

"Nope. Hand over your weapons."

"All of them?"

"Look, smart guy, you want to see Bruce or not?"

I pulled my Glock 17 from its belt holster and my Browning .380 from the ankle holster and laid them on her desk. I didn't volunteer the knife stowed up my left sleeve. While I didn't assume that Lewis bore me any ill will, or at least no more than he bore the public generally, you never know.

"Give me the knife too."

Busted. I slipped the non-magnetic knife from its sheath and set it beside the pistols.

She lifted the phone. "A Glock 17, a Browning .380, and a composite knife... Right." She disconnected.

"You can go in."

As my hand touched the doorknob, she pressed a buzzer beneath her desk to unlock the inner sanctum.

I'd seen Lewis's picture on my phone before I left my minivan in his parking lot, but he seemed different, older. His skin was pale and his face resembled a concentration camp victim. He struggled to stand and reach across his desk.

"Chuck McCrary." I handed him a business card. We shook hands; I could tell he once had a strong grip, but he couldn't manage it anymore.

Lewis was ill with a wasting disease. I hoped it wasn't contagious.

"Sorry about the frosty reception. There have been attempts on my life, and I'm ill. Agent Orange. I got sprayed in Viet Nam. The VA does what they can, but..." He waved vaguely. "My illness is no secret, but I don't publicize it. News media jackals, you know. I'm not real popular."

"You're popular with Anna Wister. She said nice things about you." That was true if you consider *gun nut* a compliment.

"Anna is a fine young lady. She's near the top of her class at the Air Force Academy."

"She didn't tell me that."

"She's modest. Her Daddy is a fine man. Twenty-six years he served his country. Are you a veteran, Mr. McCrary?"

"Yes, sir. Please, call me Chuck."

"Iraq or Afghanistan?"

"Both."

"What unit?"

"Alpha Company, Third Battalion, Seventh Special Forces Group (Airborne), Team 7."

"Green berets. You have the look."

He broke into a coughing spasm.

I wanted to do something, but what? "Can I help you with something? A glass of water?"

He waved me off and took a water bottle from a desk drawer. He took a sip and brought his cough under control. "I don't have long. One of these times, my heart will stop like a light burned out. *Click*, I meet my Maker. While I'm on this earth, I try to make it a better place. How can I help Jeff Wister?"

I explained about the murder and the brass casings with Wister's fingerprints. "Does he shoot his AR-15 here?"

"Sure. Lots of guys shoot the AR-15. They hang out at Range One, so the regulars all know each other. It's a popular weapon and fun to shoot." He pointed at the array of security monitors on the wall behind him. "Not much happens that I don't know about." He grinned. "Like the weapons you carry."

"Could another customer gather someone's brass without anyone noticing?"

"Sure. We encourage our shooters to police their brass, and most use brass catchers. Jeff told me he likes to see the brass fly. We pay customers for empty casings and sell them to reloaders. Nothing goes to waste. At any given time, dozens of casings litter the floor."

"So, someone could save Wister's brass. Might you have that on security video?"

"We keep security video one week." He punched the intercom. "See what date Jeff Wister was last here."

"June 17th," the voice on the intercom responded.

"Okay, thanks." He checked a calendar on his desk. "More than ten days ago. If the security camera did capture it, it's been deleted."

SIXTEEN

When I walked into Bernie Beltran's squad room, he had his feet propped on a desk drawer and he blew another bubble, green this time. He popped it and dropped his feet to the floor. "Have a seat, Mac. I got what you asked for."

I don't like people to call me *Mac*. I have a nickname; it's *Chuck*. I decided not to grab him by the throat and beat him senseless. Wouldn't have been prudent. But I might spank him after we closed the case.

Bubble-Gum slid a manila folder across his desk. "Background check on Faye Toledo."

I lifted the folder but didn't open it. "Give me the abridged version."

"Full-time drug user, part-time drug dealer to support her habit, and works as an irregular call girl between singing gigs."

"Did you find anybody who wanted her dead?"

"You believe she was the target and not Cleo?"

I shrugged. "We can't know who the shooter aimed at. He took the gunsight with him. It was likely a telescopic sight, maybe laser-guided. That's what I would use. If he had the skill, he would hit where he aimed."

"He used a laser-guided scope," Beltran said.

"You know something you haven't told me yet?"

"We collected videos taken by people who attended the concert. My tech gurus pieced them all together using the time stamps and sound track on each video. It's a little choppy because we spliced nine videos together. Watch this." He rotated his monitor where I could see it.

The screen filled with a wide shot of the band. Music played, then Beltran paused the video.

"Look at the bass violin."

A red dot showed on the round lower part of the bass violin's body. Beltran played the video again. The dot moved across the tailpiece then slid up to the fingerboard. The dot moved to the bass player's forehead. The picture jumped to another viewpoint and the red dot moved to the drummer, then to the bass drum. The drumhead pulsated beneath the dot as the drummer beat time to the music.

The view jumped again, and the dot passed across Cleo's chest and tracked down to her guitar.

Beltran paused the video. "Long story short. The shooter aimed at every member of the band." He resumed the video. "The next segment is where the shot came. It takes a strong stomach to watch."

Another jump of the picture and the dot tracked across the backup singers' throats, lingering on each one. The red dot reached Faye Toledo and tracked from her throat to her heart. It paused on her heart for five seconds. The dot disappeared in a flush of blood as the bullet hit her chest.

Faye fell to the stage.

Beltran paused the video again. "The video shows the aftermath until your people scooted Cleo off the stage, if you want to see it. Nothing you don't already know."

"I don't need to see it now. Can you give me a copy of the whole video to study later?"

"Sure. I already made you one." He handed me a stick drive.

Lester

Lester logged into YouTube. He found three Cleo Hennessey videos he hadn't seen. He clicked on *Cleo Hennessey plays 5 instruments*. Cleo played a medley of country classics with her singing and playing piano, guitar, banjo, steel guitar, and harmonica. *Bitch thinks she's so goddam smart and talented. When I knew her, she only played guitar. Does the oh-so-great Marvelous LeMarvis know her story? He might look at her with different eyes if he knew.*

SEVENTEEN

Carlos McCrary

G odiva Simpson sang alto in the trio that accompanied the Kentucky Hillbillies. The band members called them *girl singers*, but I couldn't consider them as *girls*; it wasn't politically correct. Of course, since Donald Trump, it was politically correct in some circles to be politically *in*correct, but it felt... disrespectful.

Cleo's agent gave me Godiva's address and phone number. She lived at a small residential hotel near the studio where Cleo's band rehearsed. The address was in an artsy-craftsy neighborhood on Port City Beach.

The three-story Art Deco hotel built in the 1930s had no elevator. Godiva's suite was on the third floor.

Exercise is good for me. Thunder rolled in the distance as I climbed the exterior stairs. Summer in South Florida. I rapped on the freshly-painted turquoise door. Turquoise is popular in South Florida, although some people call it aqua.

A curtain on the window moved, and the door opened.

"Come in, Chuck."

Godiva held the door. Standing next to her, I saw she was over six feet tall. Watching them sing on stage, I never noticed the backup singers' heights because they were all tall. The three of them standing on stage behind Cleo reminded me of the Supremes with Godiva playing the role of Diana Ross. I'd watched old videos of their greatest hits.

"Sit down. I made coffee. You want some?"

"I never say no."

Godiva had already placed a coffee pot, two mugs, a cream pitcher, and a sugar bowl on the table between the loveseat and two tasteful side chairs. "Help yourself."

I filled my cup. "Shall I top yours off?"

"Please."

I did.

"How you holding up?" I splashed cream in my mug.

Her shoulders rose and fell. "Faye was next to me, hips touching, as the bullet hit her. As she fell, she nearly pulled me with her. I was that close."

Mentally, I saw the video of the laser dot targeting the backup singers. The red dot had lingered on Godiva's throat. How had the shooter decided which of the three backup singers to kill? Eeny-meeny-miney-mo? Or was Faye the target all along?

"That must have been awful." Helpful Chuck, available for anyone to cry their eyes out with.

"You have no idea."

She was wrong. I knew how it felt to lose someone close to you. In Godiva's case, she was close physically; in mine, I was close emotionally. Of course, Godiva might have been close to Faye emotionally also. That was one thing I wanted to find out.

I stirred my coffee. "Tell me about Faye."

"I didn't know her that well."

"How long had you known her?"

"Three weeks. Cleo introduced us after Faye came down from Nashville to rehearse for the tour. That's how I met Lisabeth also."

"Did you hang out with Faye or Lisabeth?"

"We didn't have much in common, other than singing on Cleo's tour. They were white; I was black. They came from blue-collar backgrounds; my family has money. They attended the school of hard knocks; I attended Julliard. Different worlds."

"Surely you had interactions other than in rehearsal. How about breaks or meals?"

"We had coffee a couple of times during rehearsal breaks, and Cleo and I took Faye and Lisabeth out for pizza once."

"You said you and Cleo took Faye and Lisabeth out. How close are you with Cleo?"

"Very close. I met Cleo a year ago at a party the Peregrines threw for LeMarvis to celebrate extending his contract. LeMarvis brought Cleo and we hit it off, despite our different backgrounds. Perhaps it's a case of opposites attract. Did you realize that Cleo never had a music lesson? She taught herself to play all those instruments."

"I read that when I Googled her."

"She plays piano, guitar, banjo, harmonica, and perhaps other instruments. I busted my ass to develop one instrument—my voice. Cleo is a freaking musical genius. Did you realize she writes all her own songs?"

"No, I didn't. She's a woman of many talents."

Godiva gestured to a keyboard on a stand against the wall. "She's teaching me to play the keyboard. She's smarter than people give her credit for."

"You said Faye went to the school of hard knocks?"

"Faye had a rough life. It's difficult to earn a living singing, and it's harder if you're that tall. Lead singers and Broadway leading men want to be taller than the backups. Also, there's heavy competition among singers of any height."

"Everybody is born with a voice, and everybody believes they can sing?"

She nodded. "Every club, lounge, cruise ship, and community theater—they're full of singers who believe they're good enough for the Grand Old Opry if they could catch a break. That's the whole appeal of shows such as *American Idol* and *America's Got Talent*. Most people don't understand the difference between singing professionally and singing well enough to solo with the church choir."

"And Lisabeth Bonham? How well do you get along with her?"

She waggled a hand. "Okay, I guess. We don't hang out socially. She'll screw any man who gets on her radar. And she does drugs. I don't do drugs, and I won't hang around for other people to do them. That's another thing Cleo and I have in common. Lizabeth is a good singer though. She has a great set of pipes."

"Was Faye good enough to sing professionally? Or good enough for the church choir?"

Godiva smiled. "If you repeat this, I'll deny it, but she was marginally good enough to sing professionally."

"She didn't have the right... *chops*?"

"Wrong word. *Chops* refers to jazz musicians. Faye had looks, personality, and an adequate voice. Plus, she slept with anyone who might help her career—man or woman."

"Who did she sleep with to land Cleo's concert gig?"

"Avery Harper, the agent."

She had answered without hesitation. "You know this for a fact?"

"Puh-leeze. I have eyes."

"Did she sleep with Cleo too?"

"Not a chance. Cleo is as straight as a kite string in a high wind. Besides, Cleo only has eyes for LeMarvis. I wish I had a relationship that strong." She sipped her coffee. "I'm pretty sure they're secretly engaged."

A lightning flash lit the room, followed a split-second later by thunder that juddered the windows. Godiva jumped. "I swear I'll never get used to Florida thunderstorms."

"Where are you from originally?"

"I was born in New York City, of course. My parents decided to live there full time so they wouldn't have to take me out of school every year."

"Full time as opposed to...?"

"Living in Florida during the off-season."

Why would anyone with money live in Florida during the hot and humid off-season? The answer wasn't germane to my investigation, so I didn't to pursue it.

"So Faye had a rough life and you didn't?"

"My parents sent me to Julliard to study voice. With the connections I made there, I got roles off Broadway and in chorus lines on Broadway. Enough to make a pretty good living." She smiled and sipped her coffee. "And, of course, there are my parents..."

"Your parents?"

"You don't know who my father is, do you?"

"Simpson is a fairly common name."

"My father is Hendry Simpson. He played nineteen years for the Knicks."

I set down my mug. "You're 'Hatchet Man' Hendry Simpson's daughter?"

"Hatchet Man" Hendry Simpson earned his nickname as the best rebounder in the NBA for more years than I could count. During his Hall of Fame career, he was all elbows and knees under the basket, yet he was seldom penalized.

Godiva smiled demurely. "You got it, sport."

"That explains your remark about the off-season. You didn't mean the *tourist* season; you meant the *basketball* season."

She smiled. "You should be a detective."

I pointed at my chest. "This is me, being embarrassed. Your father owns ten percent of the Peregrines NBA team."

"Twenty percent now. And he's good friends with LeMarvis Jones. In fact, he talked LeMarvis into signing with the Peregrines originally."

Lisabeth Bonham sang soprano. Avery Harper told me she lived with Andy Stanley, the drummer in Cleo's band.

Like Detectives Beltran and Feldman, I try never to interview witnesses together. Other witnesses could taint their memories.

I arranged for Beltran to invite Stanley to the precinct for his interview. Snoop attended the interview to make sure Beltran covered all the bases.

I watched outside Bonham and Stanley's apartment until Stanley left.

The front doorbell was a cheap *ding-dong*. After a minute, I pushed it again. The peephole went dark as someone peered out. A chain rattled on the other side of the door and a deadbolt clicked. The door opened six inches.

"Hi. I'm Chuck McCrary, in case you forgot. Avery Harper said you were expecting me."

She pulled the door open and yawned. Her hair gave the impression she had just gotten out of bed. "I couldn't forget you, Chuck. You're the sexy private detective who guards Cleo's body. Sorry for the delay answering the door, but I was asleep." She regarded me up and down and smirked. "I'm glad Avery sent you over. At least you're easy to look at. Come in and let's get acquainted."

Lisabeth stood as tall as I did, and she was barefooted. Another Amazon. She wore loose-fitting shorts and a loose tee-shirt from some concert tour of yesteryear. She might have slept in them. It was three o'clock in the afternoon.

She grabbed my hand and led me to a linen couch. She rubbed the back of my hand before she let go. "Relax, sit. Give me a minute to get decent."

She walked toward the hallway, gliding like a dancer across a stage. She peered over her shoulder and winked. "Don't go anywhere, handsome; I have plans for you. Big plans."

I suspected her plans were different from mine.

She left the room.

I leaned over and sniffed the couch. The faint, acrid scent of marijuana clung to the fabric.

In the distance, the toilet flushed. After that, the shower ran. Then a hair dryer. Twenty-five minutes later, she reappeared in a different shirt and white short shorts, which left nothing to the imagination. She posed like a model—or a centerfold. The new tee shirt fit like shrink-wrap. She didn't wear a bra. She had fixed her hair and applied makeup.

To my chagrin, she was seductive as hell. *Courage, horny guy, you have a job to do.*

She sat beside me on the couch. "Can I fix you a drink first?" Her breath smelled of toothpaste and mouthwash.

"Coffee would be good, or a diet soda. Whatever's easy."

Lizabeth smiled, eyes half closed. Without seeming to move, her thigh touched mine. "I have whiskey, beer, and wine. Or, we could have a party. I have some high-quality blow. In my bedroom." She laid a hand on my thigh. "You can guard my body. I'm more fun than Cleo; you'll see."

"Don't you and Andy live together?"

"So what? Doesn't mean we're exclusive. Don't be so twentieth-century. Andy's at an interview with the sheriff. He won't be back for two hours. Plenty of time for us to have a party." She stroked my arm.

"On second thought, I don't need a drink. Thanks, anyway. I'm here to ask you about Faye."

Her eyes flew open. "Faye? Didn't Avery send you here to get your ashes hauled? Hell, I even put clean sheets on the bed for you."

"I'm investigating Faye's murder."

"Crap. Avery said you were coming to see me, and I figured he wanted me to show you a good time. What about Faye?" Again, without visible motion, she magically slid a few inches away.

"What was Faye like?"

Lizabeth stared at the ceiling and her eyes unfocused. "She sings contralto—I mean, she *sang* contralto. We met three weeks ago at rehearsals for Cleo's tour. We had drinks once or twice."

"Tell me what you know about her. What you talked about."

"I didn't pay attention. We were high."

"Which time?"

Lisabeth's eyes widened. "*Every* time, of course. I have a prescription for medical marijuana. To help me sleep."

Just what every PI wants—a brain-damaged junkie to interview.

"I know three or four girls named Faye. One was a stripper in Vegas… or a topless dancer in a chorus line? The Faye you're talking about was a singer, not a dancer. She said she auditioned for *American Idol* years ago. Made it to Hollywood Week or Las Vegas Week, or whatever the hell they call it. She lasted four days before they cut her." She gazed into the distance. "I think that's what she said."

Lisabeth viewed me with lidded eyes. "Chuck, you and I could have more fun than discussing Faye. Why don't you use those sexy muscles and carry me to the bedroom and bang my brains out? Or we could do it here." She lifted her tee-shirt and flashed me. A rhinestone ring sparkled from her left nipple. She waggled her twin peaks. "Don't you want a taste of these?"

"Any man would, but I have a job to do so I must reluctantly pass." I softened the message with a smile. She wouldn't be too disappointed. Probably propositioned every pizza delivery guy who came to the door. A man with less character than I would have succumbed to her charms.

"Andy says I give the best head he's ever had, and, believe me, he's had plenty. How about after Cleo's Summer Fun Concert Tour is over? You and I can have our own summer fun. You want a rain check?"

"Sure, I'll take a rain check." That was not a lie. Taking a rain check doesn't mean you'll redeem it.

"Well, if we're not gonna fuck and we're not gonna get high, I'll make coffee." She stood and tugged her tee shirt down. "Let's talk in the kitchen."

She grabbed my hand again and led me to the kitchen. I perched on a stool at the breakfast bar. I was safe there as long as I didn't let her corner me.

Lisabeth opened a cabinet door and took down a coffee grinder. "Ask your questions."

"How did Faye come to live in Port City?"

"She's from Chicago, you know." She opened another door and selected a bag of coffee beans.

"Yes, I heard that."

"That's where she auditioned for *American Idol*, in Chicago. Before she bombed out of Hollywood Week, she got glitter in her blood." Lizabeth set a bag of beans on the counter. "Or was it Vegas? I suffer from CRS." She grinned and waited for me to ask the obvious question.

The CRS gag was an old one, but my role was to play straight man to junkie humor. "What is CRS?"

"Can't remember shit." She laughed at her own joke and dumped coffee beans in the grinder.

"Faye loved the vibe out there in Vegas. Or Hollywood." Her forehead creased. "Both have glitter and glitz, don't they? Anyway, she liked wherever it was, and she cashed in her return airline ticket and her travel advance from *Idol*, and she hung around L.A. Or was it Vegas? She tried to be a movie star or a singer or practically anything. Maybe she was a topless dancer in Vegas." She grinned. "We were kinda high when we discussed it. I might have her confused with someone else."

She pushed a button, and the grinder roared to life. "Can't talk while it grinds." She opened another cabinet and took down two mugs.

Lisabeth smiled at me until the grinder stopped. "She got a couple of gigs singing or stripping or something. Wait, I remember. It was L.A. because she claimed all she could get hired for was country music."

She set the mugs on the island.

"Funny thing is: She didn't care for country music at first. She sang heavy metal rock for *American Idol*. She has that deep, gravelly voice. Perfect for heavy metal."

"Perfect," I agreed.

She dumped the ground coffee in the brewer. "L.A. has a heavy metal rock band on every street corner, but they didn't have many female country singers. Money talks." She rubbed her fingers in a show-me-the-money gesture. "She reinvented herself as a country singer. Not many girl country singers with a husky voice. Or did she dance topless in Vegas? I didn't pay attention. Andy was with us, and me and him spent the time making out."

She punched another button and the coffee maker gurgled. Lisabeth sat on the barstool next to mine. "Takes seven minutes to brew." She rubbed my thigh. "It's better if we let it steep awhile. I'll bet I can get your rocks off twice in ten minutes. Want to try?"

I grabbed her hand and set it on her own thigh. "Tell me how Faye came to be in Port City."

"She sang at clubs in L.A. and everybody told her to go to Nashville or Austin to make it big in country music. She loved the glitter, so she wouldn't leave at first."

"What changed her mind?"

Lisabeth peered at me a long time. Her eyes roamed across my face as if she wanted to memorize it or read my mind. Or my soul. Tears filled her eyes. "She's dead, isn't she?"

Of course, she was dead and Lisabeth knew it. But the way she said it... I didn't dare break her train of thought, so I nodded.

"I knew in my head she was dead, y'know, but I now know it in my heart. She's dead. She's not gonna walk through that door."

No kidding. I nodded again. If the drugs hadn't fried Lisabeth's brain, maybe she would say something useful.

"They can't hurt her, can they?"

"No. No one can hurt her."

"She had to leave L.A. For her health, you know?"

90

"Was Faye in danger?"

Lizabeth's forehead wrinkled. "She fell in with some bad people. I'm vague on the details."

The coffee maker sighed and finished dripping. She stood and the barstool toppled over backward.

I caught it before it fell.

"Ooh, you're good with your hands. I respond to a man who's good with his hands."

I ignored the hint. "Coffee's ready."

She dimpled. "How do you take yours?"

"A touch of milk or non-dairy coffee creamer, if you have it. Otherwise, nothing."

"Look in the fridge."

I moved to the refrigerator.

Lizabeth moved to the coffee maker as a swan glides across a pond. She picked up the carafe and poured.

"What trouble was she in?"

The fridge held a pint of half-and-half, two days past the expiration date. It smelled okay, so I splashed some in my coffee. It didn't curdle, so it was fresh enough. Life is full of risk.

"Faye did drugs, y'know. Hell, we all do—everyone in the band except Miss Pure-as-the-Driven-Snow Cleo."

"The autopsy report said she had traces of heroin, cocaine, all kinds of crap in her blood."

Lisabeth smirked. "Welcome to the music business."

"Did she tell you what trouble she was running from?"

Lisabeth held her mug in her hands as if trying to warm them. She pressed her hands together and flexed her breasts. Her nipple ring moved under the tee-shirt. She winked and raised an eyebrow.

I ignored it and waited for her to answer.

"Faye stole some drugs in Vegas. From very bad people."

"I thought that was in L.A."

She scanned me as if she hadn't heard.

"How much did she steal?"

"Enough that somebody out there wanted her dead."

"Did she tell you who?"

"The name was something Italian, or Greek."

Wow, that sure narrowed the field of suspects. I stirred my coffee to see if she added anything. "Is that why she changed her name?"

"How did you know?"

"Faye Toledo materializes in the last six years. Her identity originated after she arrived in Nashville. Did she tell you her real name?"

"No. She said if they found her, they'd kill her. The Italians, I mean. Or were they Greek? She said it was better if I didn't know her real name."

"Why pick Nashville to disappear in, and not Austin?"

"Nashville was closer to Chicago? She sold the drugs for enough money to establish a new identity and live on while she developed a new music career. Nashville is where she met Cleo."

EIGHTEEN

S noop munched on a bagel. "I never appreciated your bagels, bud. Not
until I visited the Southwest Precinct. Bagels at Beltran's squad room
taste like cardboard. Stale cardboard."

"You noticed, eh?"

We sat in my conference room. Betty had brought us a tray of bagels, a
pot of coffee, and a tub of cream cheese. We had skipped breakfast to get
an early start.

"And don't mention their coffee. Warmed-over dishwater." He held his
cup under his nose and inhaled. "It's great to drink a good cup of coffee."

"What did you take from Andy Stanley's interview?"

"Andy's a Good Old Country Boy. Born in West Virginia, learned to
love country music at his daddy's knee—or his momma's. Both parents
play the fiddle, but they're amateurs. His parents wanted Andy to go to
auto mechanic school like his dad. Andy dropped out of vocational school
and came to Nashville to be a drummer, do drugs, and get laid. In that
order."

I sliced open another bagel. "Pass the cream cheese."

I spread a dollop on my bagel. "Bright lights, big city, huh?"

"You got it, bud. The boy has the IQ of a picket fence, but he's a hell of

93

a drummer and the ladies consider him good-looking. He bragged that he gets laid a lot."

"Did he see anything useful?"

"Nope. He dove for cover the instant he saw the blood on Faye's chest. He hid behind his drums, then crawled off the back of the stage."

"Perhaps he's not dumb as you think he is."

Snoop set his half bagel on a napkin, wiped his mouth, and drank some coffee. "No one could be as dumb as I think he is."

"What does Andy know about the victim?"

"He and Lisabeth, his live-in, did drugs with Faye and the piano player a couple of times. Claims he didn't know her well, but he knew her well enough to have sex with her at least twice that he remembers and with her and Lisabeth together one time. He remembered that threesome in exhaustive detail."

"Did Andy know Faye's real name?"

"Faye Toledo wasn't her name? I wondered why everything in the file Bubble-Gum gave me was less than six years old."

"Lisabeth Bonham said Faye had to run from some bad guys in L.A. She stole a sizable amount of drugs and ran to Nashville to begin a new life. That's where she met Cleo."

"Maybe the bad guys in L.A. found her." He finished his second bagel.

"That's what I suspected."

"Beltran and Jerry Feldman, his partner, ran her fingerprints. Cops in Nashville busted her for prostitution five years ago."

"Did Beltran or Feldman check IAFIS?"

Snoop scoffed. "That dickhead stopped looking after he found a match in Nashville. He didn't notice that nothing in her background check was more than six years old."

"What about Feldman? Is he as bad as Beltran?"

"Hard to say, bud. He doesn't talk when Bubble-Gum is in the room."

"Did you notice the gap before six years ago?"

"Sure, but I didn't mention it to Bubble-Gum head or Feldman."

"You should. The Port City PD has more resources than we do to identify the victim. If she's not in IAFIS, there's another clue. She's from

Chicago and she competed on *American Idol*. They can identify her from that."

Bubble-Gum Bernie Beltran didn't grasp what I said.

"You mean Faye Toledo is not Faye Toledo?"

"The woman we knew as Faye Toledo adopted a stage name when she came to Nashville," I explained again. "She adopted the new identity and her old identity disappeared." I had already told the detectives this once.

"How do I check that out?" Beltran asked.

"Run her fingerprints through IAFIS. Contact the television network and ask them to check their records. We want a woman who auditioned in Chicago seven or eight years ago, made it to Hollywood Week, then was cut. That will narrow the field."

"I used to watch *American Idol*. They auditioned thousands of people in every city. That was when they were on the Fox network."

"Tell you what, Bernie. Tell them this: Female, auditioned in Chicago, made it to Hollywood Week, got cut. Find out how many people fit those criteria. Then call me and I'll tell you what to do next. Okay?"

"It's Saturday, Mac. No one will be there."

Don't call me Mac. I held my tongue. Bubble-Gum would live another day. Maybe. "Try. At least you can find out who to ask for when you call back on Monday."

Beltran regarded me as if I had tried to sell him a timeshare. Jerry Feldman sighed and made notes. Maybe Jerry could figure out this complex, graduate-school-level problem: how to telephone the Fox TV network.

At least I hoped so. If not them, someone at Fox network would be smart enough to figure this out once we told them we were investigating a murder.

NINETEEN

"You're looking sporty this afternoon, bro." Clint wore his blue and gold plaid Bermuda shorts with a Gator golf shirt. He carried a straw beach bag he bought when we took my boat, *The Gator Raider Too*, to Bimini.

"I'm taking Madison to the beach."

"Are things better with her parents?"

"Not yet. She asked me to pick her up at her gate."

I researched Madison's parents after the dust-up the night of Cleo's first concert. Both were college graduates, and he was an insurance company CEO. They owned a waterfront home on the bay side of Port City Beach which the tax assessor valued over seven million dollars, and they belonged to a liberal Episcopalian church. Not people I would expect to be racist. I chalked them up as one of life's small mysteries and hadn't given it any further attention.

Until now.

Racism is bad enough to contemplate in the abstract. Clint was family, which made it personal. "You mean her parents won't let you on the property?" I felt my eyes narrow with strong emotion. I relaxed my face and calmed myself with an effort.

Clint laughed. "Chill, big bro. You don't have to fight this battle. It's her father. Madison and I will handle it. If we need you to step in, I'll tell you. Like you said, this isn't the first time I've faced this crap, and it won't be the last."

He headed for the door. "Wish me luck."

He grinned. "And yes, I'm carrying."

TWENTY

The original *American Idol* television producers came through.

Beltran called. "I sent you the file on the victim."

"What's her name?" I asked.

"Fortunata Torelli. She wasn't from Chicago, but she auditioned there. She was from Gary, Indiana. We located her parents and they're coming down to identify her body."

"I want to talk to them. When do they arrive?"

"Their flight lands tonight. They'll meet me at the morgue tomorrow morning."

"Hell of a way to spend Independence Day, identifying your daughter's body."

Frank Torelli and his wife Sophia acted 95 years old though I knew they weren't old enough for Social Security. Pain and grief do that to you.

The family resemblance to Fortunata was obvious. She had her mother's coloring and her father's height. He was taller than I am, but he stooped as if something weighed him down, which I guess it did. Sophia was five-nine.

It seemed as if Frank and Sophia weren't quite there, as if their life force had faded. Their appearance made more sense to me after they said Fortunata was an only child. With her dead, they had no one. Nieces and nephews, but that's not the same as having grandchildren.

We met in an interview room at the Atlantic County Morgue: the dead girl's parents, Detectives Beltran and Feldman, and I.

Tears ran down Sophia's cheeks. She held her husband's hand while he told me their story. "Everything was all right at first. Fortunata was a grown woman, twenty-five years old when she went to Hollywood with *American Idol*. We expected great things from her."

He patted Sophia's hand. "Sophie always said Fortunata was destined for great things."

Sophia nodded. "Great things. She had a husky voice like Stevie Nicks, that girl singer from Fleetwood Mac. Sounded just like her."

Frank Torelli nodded. "Exactly. Anyway, after *Idol* cut her, she bounced back. Always had a positive, optimistic attitude. She and another girl from Chicago stayed in L.A. to build singing careers there. They shared an apartment for a while, roommates, y'know?"

Beltran wrote something on a notepad. "The other girl got cut also?"

"Yeah. She came from North Dakota or Minnesota—maybe Wisconsin. Someplace in the Midwest, but she auditioned in Chicago. She and Fortunata, they hit it off when they got to Hollywood. They was the same age and liked the same music."

"What was her name?" Beltran asked.

Frank regarded Sophia, who shrugged. "We don't remember. Dorothy? Dotty? I remember it started with a D. It don't matter none, since she quit Hollywood after a couple of months and went back to wherever she come from." He patted Sophia's hand. "That was the beginning of the end, wasn't it, honey?"

"Why is that?" I asked.

"Without Doris—that's it, her name was Doris." He eyed Sophia, who nodded. "Without Doris to share the rent, Fortunata couldn't afford her apartment no more. She got evicted. Everything pretty much went to shit—you'll pardon the expression—after Doris left."

I wrote *Doris-North Dakota-Minnesota-Wisconsin? Call Fox TV network about her.*

"Every time she called us," said Sophia, "we offered to send a ticket for her to come home, but she was stubborn. She gets that from his side of the family." She elbowed Frank.

Frank wiped his eyes with a tissue. "She finally stopped calling altogether."

"Until the end," said Sophia. "She called home one last time before she disappeared. She said she was in big trouble and somebody wanted to kill her."

"Did she say why?" Feldman asked, "Or who was after her?"

"She owed $50,000 to some bad men over drugs that went missing," said Frank. "Me and Sophie, we don't do drugs and we didn't raise our daughter to do no drugs. She got in with a bad crowd in California."

"You know what California people are like," said Sophia, "they're all into drugs. The drug people, they threatened to kill our baby girl if she didn't pay. She was desperate."

I handed her a tissue, and she blew her nose.

"Desperate," added Frank. "If we had that much money, we would have sent it. We offered her enough for a ticket back to Gary. But she said she couldn't come home."

"Why not?"

"Her friends in L.A. knew she was from Gary. That was the first place the drug dealers would look. Me and Sophie, we're Italian. We was both raised in Chicago before we moved to Gary. We lived near the Mafia all our life. From what Fortunata said, these guys was Mafia. You don't mess with them guys."

Sophia wadded the tissue into a ball and stuck it in her purse. "Fortunata said if she came home, we would be in danger."

Frank nodded.

I gave Sophia another tissue. "That must have been tough to hear."

"Thanks." She dabbed her eyes. "You have no idea... To have the Mafia after our daughter..."

Fortunata's parents hadn't answered the question about who was after her. I waited for Feldman to ask again.

"So we wired her what money we could," Frank said, "and told her to call us after she got settled."

I handed him a tissue also. *Note to self: Carry more tissues in my coat pocket next time.*

"She never called. Six, almost seven, years, we didn't hear *bupkis*. Until Detective Beltran called..." his voice broke, "...and asked if our daughter was missing." He put his arm around his wife's shoulder.

Sophia sobbed. Silent tears tracked down one side of Frank's nose and disappeared into his gray mustache.

Bubble-Gum still hadn't asked who Fortunata owed the $50,000 to.

"I'm sorry for your loss." The cliché sounded hackneyed and banal, but I didn't know what else to say.

Frank nodded.

I offered them each another tissue.

Frank blew his nose. "How soon can we take her back to Gary for her funeral?"

"Soon," Beltran replied. "There's a little paperwork to sign and we'll release her body to you."

I lifted my hand. "Frank, I'd like to ask a few questions to help us find the man who did this."

"Sure, sure. Whatever we can do."

"Did Fortunata tell you names of people she knew in L.A. or the names of the people she owed money to?"

Frank's eyes opened wider. "Two names. The first one is a boyfriend, name of Sam, or Sammie, or Samuel, maybe Samson—something like that."

Sophia said, "In that phone call, though, I got the impression that Samson, or whatever his name was, he provided the drugs to her."

"Yeah," Frank said. "The other name was Sarducci."

"Sarducci?"

"Yeah, like Father Guido Sarducci."

"Father Guido Sarducci?" I asked.

"You're too young. Father Guido Sarducci was a character done by a comedian on *Saturday Night Live* before you was born. He used to crack me up. We're Catholics, and that comedian, he reminded me of this priest I knew in Chicago when I was a kid."

"And who was Sarducci?"

"He was the guy she owed the money. He was the Mafia *capo*. Never heard his first name. She called him 'Sarducci.'"

I noted the name. "Did Fortunata send either of you any letters or postcards from Los Angeles?"

"No." He gazed at Sophia. She shook her head. "Nothing. She telephoned now and again.

"After she left L.A., did you receive any communications from her? Letter, Christmas card, email?"

"Nothing. If she had disappeared without that last phone call, we would have figured she was dead, but we knew she was alive… somewhere."

"Knowing she was alive…," Sophia said, "We kept the faith all these years… Until Detective Beltran called."

"Even then," Frank said, "we hoped when we got here, it wouldn't be our baby." Silent tears streamed down his cheeks.

I felt my eyes fill. I blinked tears away. Bad for my tough guy image.

Feldman spoke for the first time. "We haven't figured out how a mobster from California discovered your daughter was in South Florida. You have any ideas on that?"

"After you called and told us the name she used, I Googled her and that Cleopatra Hennessey girl she worked for. I found our daughter's picture on Cleopatra's website for her tour. It wasn't a great picture. I mean, she was singing in the background, but I recognized her even though she changed her hair. Of course, I'm her father. Even then, I prayed the girl in the picture wasn't Fortunata. Maybe Sarducci saw her picture?"

"It's possible," Feldman replied.

I doubted he and Beltran believed it. It was a stretch to suppose a Mafia hitman would search internet photos for seven years.

It didn't make sense. But maybe Sarducci was the kind of guy who held a grudge.

TWENTY-ONE

C lint gazed up from his book as I walked into the den. "You sure you won't come with us tonight, bro?"

Plopping on the chaise, I kicked off my shoes. "I just met two middle-aged parents who lost their only child to a murderer. A child they hadn't seen in more than seven years. This is the lowest I've felt since Miyo left us. I wouldn't be good company for you and your friends. Y'all have a good time. And bring back my boat in one piece."

After he had returned from the beach the previous Saturday, Clint asked me my plans for Independence Day. The previous two years we took *The Gator Raider Too* into the Atlantic and watched fireworks the Chamber of Commerce shot off from a barge anchored offshore. Clint had demonstrated good seamanship on a trip we took to Bimini. I had offered him the *Raider* and suggested he take Madison and some friends out instead.

I didn't have to offer twice.

"It might cheer you up to watch fireworks while the symphony plays patriotic music on the beach. What about it, big bro?"

"How are things with you and Madison's parents?"

Clint waggled his fingers. "So-so. I took her home last Saturday night, and she brought me into their living room unannounced. We sang a chorus of *Ebony and Ivory* to her parents. Her mom smiled a little, but her dad threw me out."

He grinned. "I'm still banned, but Madison says her mom will come around."

Lester

Lester smiled as he watched the television news anchor read from a teleprompter. *Pretty Boy thinks he's cool, but he has trouble following his script.*

"Port City Police Detective Bernard... Beltran said yesterday that alleged Los Angeles crime boss Carmelo Sarducci is a person of interest in the investigation of the murder of... Fortuna—Fortunata Torelli. Ms. Torelli was shot by a sniper ten days ago during a music concert... a *country* music concert where she sang with rising star Cleopatra Hennessey. Ms. Torelli assumed the name Faye... Toledo after she left Los Angeles seven years ago after telling her parents she feared for her life."

What a stupid prick. He should practice the names before he reads them on the air.

The stupid detective proved a marvelous stroke of luck for his campaign of terror against the bitch. He hadn't sent Cleo any emails since the shooting. Should he send Cleo one to tell her the idiot detective was wrong? Or let the bitch relax and imagine she was safe? Then pounce again with another near miss, perhaps at the concert in Tampa. *Yes, that would be delicious—give her time to unwind, let her guard down, then hit her again in Tampa.* Did he have time to plan something new? Of course, he did. He was brilliant. He could plan anything. He licked his lips. *That's it: Let her relax... Then BAM! hit her with something else.*

He would sleep on it. Yes, he would have more dreams about how to drive Cleo into his arms.

Hmm. Today is Independence Day. I wonder if any fireworks stands are still open.

Lester thought of another way to make Cleo's life hell on earth.

After what she did, she deserves it.

TWENTY-TWO

Carlos McCrary

Tank splashed more water on the hot rocks. Steam sizzled into the heated air of the cedar-lined room, obscuring the opposite wall. That was okay, the other people in the steam room were Tank Tyler and an old man who must've weighed 250 pounds. He hadn't moved in a while. I hoped he wasn't dead.

My last sight of Teresa Kovacs in her sweaty workout clothes had filled my mind's eye as I toweled off the leg press and headed to the steam room. Every time I glanced back, my eyes swung like a compass needle to the body I had known so well.

Terry had waved and smiled; she wanted to talk.

Talking to Terry was the last thing I wanted; my wounds from the time she dumped me were still raw.

Terry wore shorts tight enough that you knew she wore thong underwear. Her old gray tee shirt over a sports bra, both dark with sweat, revealed her athletic figure. That hadn't changed.

I was surprised, but not astonished, when she showed up at Jerry's Gym after Tank and I got there. I suspected Kennedy Carlson, the gym's owner, gave her a heads-up that I was there. I hadn't seen Terry in over a year. Ken believed it was time I got back in the game.

Eleven months had passed since Miyo had left me. Terry dumped me after the cops arrested me for murder. She said she couldn't take "this" anymore—whatever "this" was—and wished me good luck with the trial. A first-degree murder charge was no fun for me either.

Now she had shown up here. Rule Seven: *There is no such thing as a coincidence—except when there is.*

Everyone in Atlantic County knew I worked out at Jerry's Gym. After Terry dumped me, she changed gyms. Now she had changed back. It didn't take the world's greatest detective to figure out why: Terry was back, and she was open to my approach.

My nerves were raw and Miyo breaking our engagement tore my guts. Still… Terry looked good. Very good.

Tank Tyler groaned and ended my reverie. The fat old man shifted his weight. Good, he was still among the living.

"Easy there, sport," Tank said. "If you stick more steam in here, I'll dissolve into a puddle like that Wicked Witch of the East in *The Wizard of Oz.*"

"You mean the Wicked Witch of the West. Steam will do us good, big guy. We worked out longer than usual. You don't want to feel sore later on your date with Tameesha."

"She won't keep me out late. She has a game tomorrow. Besides, we did an extra-long workout because you wanted to ogle Terry. She exerts a magnetic force you can't escape."

"You noticed, huh."

Tank smiled with his eyes closed. "She looked pretty good." He opened his eyes. "You think Ken called her?"

"You know Ken. The eternal romantic."

"He's right; it's time you got back on the horse."

"Can we change the subject, big guy?"

Tank scoffed. "What's happening with the murder investigation?"

"I met the victim's parents yesterday."

"Hell of a way to spend Independence Day."

"That's what I thought, but they insisted. Frank and Sophia Torelli, from Gary, Indiana. Nice people with nothing left to live for."

"Torelli? Oh yeah, I heard on the news last night. Must have been tough on them."

"Yeah. Faye Toledo's real name was Fortunata Torelli, and she was their only child." My eyes stung. I hoped it was from the steam. The Everly Brothers had a hit from the oldies channel on my satellite radio, *Crying in the Rain*. First, the distraught parents, then Terry reminding me that Miyo left me too. Was I fated to remain single my whole life? Was I crying in the steam room? That would make a lousy song title.

"I called the producers for *American Idol* and learned another name— Doris Taylor from Duluth, Minnesota. She auditioned with Fortunata on *American Idol* and they shared an apartment in L.A. I sent Pete Martinez to Duluth to interview her."

"The snow should have melted by now. I have this one client, he made a fortune from iron ore in Duluth and moved to Port City to enjoy it. He said they have two seasons in Minnesota: winter and July."

"I told Pete to pack a sweater."

Tank moved from the upper bench to the lower one. "Too hot up there."

The old man left without a word or a wave.

Tank readjusted his towels. "Hendry Simpson called last night. He's worried his daughter is in danger with this killer on the loose. He wants Godiva to quit the tour, but she told him the killer was after Faye Toledo. She assumes she's safe. Hendry asked me how good a bodyguard you are."

"Ask Fortunata Torelli how good I am. Oh wait, you can't. She's dead."

We lapsed into silence.

Tank let me stew in my own juice a minute. "Don't be so tough on yourself. Hell, somebody got to John F. Kennedy. Somebody got to Ronald Reagan. How long you gonna beat yourself up over this, bro?"

"Protection duty is a bitch. I have to play defense the whole time and be 100 percent perfect. The bad guy has to get lucky once, like at that concert."

"I loved playing defense. You did your job, you got the ball back after four plays and turned it over to your offense. You earned a small victory each time you got the ball back." He grinned. "Plus, I got to hit guys."

"In my business, playing defense sucks."

"Yeah, and you don't get to hit anybody very often either."

We sweated a while.

"Was Godiva right?" Tank asked, "Is the danger over?"

I waggled a hand. "Beltran and Feldman believe so, but I reserve judgment. The shooter targeted his laser on every person on the stage before he shot Fortunata. A professional hitman wouldn't take the risk that someone would notice the laser and raise the alarm. Toying with the laser is something a nutcase would do. If the shooter is the nutcase who sent Cleo those emails, he's out there, and he's still a threat."

"The television news reported that Cleo Hennessey wasn't the target. They say a Los Angeles mobster named Carmelo Sarducci is a person of interest in the murder."

"They reported what Bubble-Gum Beltran told them. They don't realize that Beltran is dumber than a mud fence."

"You don't believe it was Sarducci," Tank said.

"I've seen no evidence either way. Maybe Fortunata Torelli wasn't the target, no matter what Bubble-Gum told the media. How did a *mafioso* in California find a singer from Gary, Indiana in Port City, Florida seven years after she went into hiding?"

"The internet?"

"The internet isn't magic, big guy. TV thrillers make it look easy to find out anything about anyone, anywhere in the world. Don't buy it. Fortunata kept a low profile under either name. No Facebook page and no Twitter handle. No social media presence at all. That's unusual, almost unheard of, for her generation."

"You don't have a social media presence either, bro," Tank said, "and you're the same generation."

"And, like Fortunata, I have enemies I don't care to run into."

Tank waved dismissively. "We put $7,450,000 of ticket sales for Tampa in escrow and $8,950,000 for Orlando and $8,400,000 for Jacksonville. And there will be souvenir sales too. If the tour continues to completion, LeMarvis will make a profit. A small one to be sure, but a real one. Has Cleo decided to perform in Tampa?"

"I go from here to a conference at her agent's office. That's the main item on the agenda."

I stood and rewrapped my towel. "Bubble-Gum Beltran might be right, but my gut tells me this weirdo is still lurking out there."

TWENTY-THREE

Two new pictures of Cleo were displayed on the wall of Avery Harper's office: one of her with LeMarvis and one in her red, white, and blue costume for the Summer Fun Concert Tour. Harper wasn't LeMarvis's agent, but that photo let him bask in the reflected glory of the NBA superstar.

It was the Wednesday before the Tampa concerts, time for the go/no-go decision.

Cleo, LeMarvis, Snoop, and I gathered around a small conference table with the beaming agent. "We're sold out in Tampa and advance sales in Orlando and Jacksonville look strong. Cleo, honey, you're a superstar. I'm real happy for you, sweetheart, real happy."

"The shooting didn't scare people away?"

"Obviously not. That California mobster was after Faye—I mean Fortunata—and he got her. So that nightmare is over. Hound Dog has rehearsed the new backup singer on the songs in your set. You and the band rehearse with her this afternoon. Things look good."

Cleo eyed LeMarvis, who kept his mouth shut.

"Then we're a go," she said.

"My team and I leave for Tampa this afternoon to examine the venue and plan our security," I said.

The Tampa Bay Tepee arena once served as home court for the Tampa Bay Timucuas, a minor league professional basketball team named after an ancient Indian tribe that lived in Florida. Since the last known Timucua Indian died in 1767, it was poetic justice that the basketball team went extinct soon after the arena was built.

The Tepee was revived three years later to host a short-lived indoor football team named the Tocobaga—another local tribe that went extinct in the 18th century. After the football team failed, a local sports columnist nicknamed the Tepee the *Zombie Arena*, filled with the ghosts of dead minor-league sports teams.

The Tepee woke from the dead to host concerts, boat shows, and political conventions. Its most recent resurrection was for a Donald Trump rally during his campaign for reelection. The local newspaper reporters delighted in pointing out that Trump was speaking to the ghosts of dead sports franchises in the Zombie Arena.

Snoop and I sat halfway up the grandstands. He peered at the scoreboard hanging above us. "The shooter wouldn't use the scoreboard again, but we have to cover that base regardless."

Carpenters were building the concert stage and I raised my voice over the din of nail guns, circle saws, and cordless drills. "Gunner will search the rafter area the morning of the concert, then seal all access doors. Before the concert starts, we'll confirm all seals are intact."

"These old door locks aren't very secure," Snoop said. "If I were the shooter, I could pick an access door lock in less than a minute. He could close the door behind him, bud, and we can't see the perimeter corridor from here. After the concert starts, the corridors will be empty. No one would see him."

"I'll assign two rovers to patrol the perimeter corridor during the concert. As I walked the circuit earlier, I timed it at seven minutes. Allowing for crowds heading to the restrooms and concessions, our guys will make one circuit in, say, ten minutes. With two guys, even if the shooter picks a lock and gets to the rafters, one rover will lay eyes on every door seal every five minutes."

Lester

Lester carried his toolbox to the security scanner and set it on the conveyor. He unbuckled his tool belt and dumped it on the conveyor, then emptied the pockets of his olive-drab work clothes into a plastic bin and placed it behind the toolbox.

The guard at the metal detector motioned him to proceed.

Lester waited until the conveyor carried his toolbox into the X-ray machine, then stepped through the rented metal detector.

What a pathetic excuse for a metal detector. It looks like it's built from Tinker Toys.

The detector beeped and both guards gazed over. "You have more metal on you?' the first guard asked.

"Steel-toed boots," Lester responded, holding the X-ray guard's gaze as his toolbox passed through the scanner. "I'll pull them off." He unlaced his boots and dumped them on the belt. "Sorry about that."

"No problem," the second guard replied, "happens all the time."

He hid his inner smile as he passed through the detector. He laced his boots, grabbed his toolbox and tool belt, refilled his pockets, and sauntered into the arena.

One more trip tomorrow, with the timer hidden in the false bottom.

He made his way to the lower service level, donned a pair of work gloves, and walked halfway around the empty corridor. Glancing over his shoulder, he made sure the transparent tape he had stuck on the metal door the previous day was undisturbed. He peeled off the tape, unlocked the door, and entered the storeroom, locking the door from inside. He wiped each tool with a soft cloth. He lifted the toolbox's false bottom and extracted the wiring harness and detonator.

Lester shoved a five-gallon can of paint aside and placed the wiring harness and detonator beside the plastic explosive he had hidden on the bottom shelf the previous day. *A little at a time, a little at a time. Even if the guards see something, they won't recognize it as part of a bomb. Everything is explainable.*

On his first trip to the Tepee, he had searched three different storerooms. The old doorknobs were worn and loose, and they yielded to a thin screwdriver. Lester selected the one with the thickest layer of dust on the equipment.

No one's used this room for months.

The room stored the scissor lifts and scaffolds used to access the high ceilings in the corridors.

He had snapped a picture of the doorknob, driven to a hardware store, and bought a similar knob. The next day he replaced the original doorknob with the new one with a new lock. With the storeroom under his control, he brought in the bomb components one at a time. He left the door unlocked on the long odds someone might want to use the equipment stored inside. Even if they used the equipment, they wouldn't notice the block of plastic explosive on the bottom shelf. If they relocked the door, he had the key.

He shoved the heavy paint can back in place. The dust on the bottom shelf showed scuff marks where he moved the paint. He debated what to do. He couldn't dust the shelf because that would stand out like one clean window in a deserted house. Dusting all the shelves would flag the whole set of shelves.

Lester climbed the scissor lift to the light fixtures on the ceiling. He removed one four-foot fluorescent tube from each fixture which cut the light level in half. Laying the fluorescent tubes on the scissor-lift platform, he peered at the shelf. The marks in the dust were scarcely noticeable. *Still…* Climbing down, he scooted objects around on the other shelves so each shelf seemed untidy. *No one will notice the bottom shelf.*

Lester took a clipboard from his toolbox and repacked his tools. He left the toolbox and tool belt in a corner behind the door. He locked the door as he left. Sticking the clipboard under his arm, his shoved his work gloves in a back pocket.

Carlos McCrary

"I'll use the press box for my command center, Snoop. I'll put you and Gunner at 90 degrees to me like last time."

"It didn't stop the shooter last time, bud. Can't you think of anything better?"

"I'm open to suggestions, Obi-Wan. Perhaps we can access the Force."

Snoop chuckled. "Hey, you're the one who makes the big bucks. I'm the hired help. You do the thinking; I do the legwork."

"I'm serious about suggestions, Snoop. If you see anything I overlooked, don't be shy. A spaceship full of Jedis could secure this place, Obi-Wan, but I'm fresh out of light sabers."

Lester

Lester fastened kneepads across his pant legs, pulled a Maglite from a loop on his belt, and dropped to his knees. He started to crawl under the stage.

"Hey, who are you?" a carpenter asked.

"Safety inspector." Lester rolled onto his backside and sat on the concrete arena floor. He flashed a badge he bought at a novelty shop. "Need to make sure the stage is safe." Flipping back to his knees, he crawled a few feet and spanned the distance between two joists with a tape measure. He wrote something on the clipboard. "Twelve inches on center with three-quarter-inch plywood," he spoke loud enough for the carpenter to hear if he was listening. He waved at the carpenter. "Code allows sixteen inches. Why did you put yours at twelve inches?"

"Them musicians, they jump up and down. We don't use no subfloor; we use three-quarter-inch plywood with twelve-inch spaces and two-by-eight-inch joists instead of two-by-six."

"Yeah, I was gonna ask about the two-by-eights. Better to err on the side of safety. Looks good... You can go back to work while I finish the prelim."

And the eight-inch joists give me two more inches to hide my surprise.

Lester crawled farther under the stage, stopping every few yards to measure and write on the clipboard. A few minutes later, he crawled from under the platform. "When you guys gonna be ready for final?"

The carpenter motioned to the other side of the stage. "Guy in the Bucs hat. That's Steve, the foreman."

Steve regarded Lester and the carpenter, one eye squinted.

Lester nodded to the carpenter and waved at the foreman. He walked around the stage, removed his kneepads, and hung them on his belt. He raised his clipboard and pen. "You the foreman?"

Steve nodded and frowned. "Yeah. Who're you?"

"Safety inspector. Checking the stage for safety. What's your full name?"

"Esteban Oviedo. We never had no inspector before."

Lester spread his hands. "What can I say? New rules took effect July 1. When you gonna be ready for final?"

"We should finish by noon tomorrow."

"I'll be back then, after you finish. Who's gonna be here if I require changes?"

"Depends on if you get here before we finish. The union never mentioned no new rules. We finish, we out of here. Nobody told us there would be an inspection."

"Don't get your panties in a knot, sport. I'll be here at 11:30 tomorrow."

TWENTY-FOUR

Pete Martinez

Pete Martinez pulled his sweater tighter around his chest. It was 60 degrees with bright sun in a cloudless sky. It felt like a January cold snap in Port City. Why on earth would people live in Duluth? Sunshine was wasted this near the North Pole. Hell, he could hit a pitching wedge and the golf ball would land in Canada. Okay, a driver anyway.

Pete had felt cold since he landed the previous night after flying all day. He changed planes in Chicago and missed his connection because of pop-up thunderstorms. He hated to change planes in Chicago in the summer. Thunderstorms bloomed every afternoon and wreaked havoc across half the flights in the Midwest. After the airline canceled his flight, his mood plummeted. The airline put him on standby and squeezed him onto the day's last flight. He arrived at the hotel, tired and hungry, to learn that the restaurant was closed. Then he discovered the hotel had switched off the heat for the summer, and he had slept under two blankets. He hated to sleep under a blanket.

Pete knocked on the door of the neat brick house in the middle-class neighborhood. He stepped back to let whoever was inside see him. Women alone often feel nervous around strangers, so he kept his hands visible.

The door opened wide. A pretty girl, fresh-faced, early thirties, wearing shorts and a tank top, stood in the door.

Are people in Duluth always so trusting? Pete could be a robber, a rapist, a killer, and she opened the door without looking.

"Doris Taylor?" he asked.

What was she, an Eskimo? Who wears shorts and a tank top on a day this cold? She must have antifreeze in her veins.

She smiled and the day felt warmer. "It's Doris Poteet, but it used to be Taylor. Are you Pete Martinez?"

Was everybody in Duluth this nice?

Pete handed her a business card. "Yes, ma'am. I called yesterday from O'Hare Airport."

Doris stepped back and pulled the door open. "Come in. There is a fresh pot of coffee and some sticky buns."

Pete wiped his feet on the welcome mat.

Doris poured Pete's coffee and her own. "I was sorry to hear about Fortunata. I hadn't heard from her in years, but we roomed together for four months and it's sad when someone you know dies, especially someone young. Cream and sugar?"

"No, ma'am, I'm good with black."

"How can I help you?" She added half-and-half from a paper carton and one spoon of sugar to her coffee.

"We're following up on something Fortunata's parents told us. They mentioned a man named Carmelo Sarducci?" He let the question hang in the air.

Doris's smile froze. "Sarducci? How do you spell that?" She tasted her coffee.

Pete spelled the name. "What do you know about him?"

Doris set her cup down. "I don't recognize the name. I'm sorry you came all this way for nothing." She stood. "Now, if you'll excuse me, I need to pick up my daughter from preschool."

Pete was a Miami-Dade deputy sheriff too long not to know a witness was lying. He took a bite of sticky bun. "This bun is delicious, Doris. Thanks for baking these. Now I understand why Minnesotans are famous for hospitality." He set the bun on a small plate and wiped his fingers with a napkin. "About Carmelo Sarducci, did you and Fortunata sing at his parties? Or have a date with him? Or buy drugs from him? What was your relationship?"

He leaned back on the couch and waited.

Doris stood like she was cast from cement.

Pete watched for two slow breaths. "Anything you tell me stays between us. It won't get back to your husband or your daughter because of me."

Doris fell into the chair. "I... I... I can't."

"Sarducci is a dangerous man. That's why Fortunata left L.A. and changed her name. That's why he'll never know you talked to me. Someone murdered your friend. He hid in the scoreboard where she was performing and used a telescopic sight on a sniper rifle... and he shot her through the heart."

Doris held her coffee cup in her lap. She gazed into the cup.

"We want to catch the guy who did it. Her parents, Frank and Sophia Torelli, they need closure. They deserve to have her killer caught. You can help."

Doris lifted her cup and slurped. "Carmelo Sarducci threw big, expensive parties for his so-called friends. One of his... I don't know what to call him. Not an employee—that's an honorable term. Call him a gangster. His gangster saw Fortunata and me on *Idol* and then saw us on the show that covered Hollywood Week. I got a gig singing at a politician's fiftieth birthday party in Beverly Hills and this... person... was one of hundreds of guests. He recognized me from *Idol* and he wanted to hire me to sing at another party."

She lifted the coffee pot. "Want a refill?"

Pete extended his cup. "Please."

Doris refilled his cup and added a smidgeon to hers.

Pete waited while she sipped and nodded her approval.

"His name was George Papadopoulos. They called him Georgy Pops, that or Pops for short." She shuddered. "Such an innocent nickname for a cold-blooded thug. Of course, I learned that later. He was Carmelo Sarducci's personal assistant. Personal *procurer* is more accurate. After Sarducci's first party, Pops introduced me to Carmelo. Carmelo and I did a couple of lines of cocaine and he... I... We..." She studied her hands in her lap. "Later Georgy Pops asked if I knew another singer to sing backup for a major pop star at another party."

"And you brought in Fortunata?" Pete asked.

"Right." She sipped coffee again. "This stays between us?"

Pete made a zipper motion across his lips. "Yes, ma'am."

"The party was held around Carmelo's pool. The caterer set up a huge tent and a stage and everything. After the party, Carmelo invited Fortunata and me into his house—a mansion actually. We did a few lines of cocaine and he wanted a threesome with me and Fortunata. It was bad enough to sleep with one man. I wouldn't degrade myself further, but we were miles from home, and Georgy Pops was our ride back to our apartment." She sipped coffee and regained her composure. "Afterward... The next day I decided to move back to Duluth. I've never regretted coming home. I've lived a normal life since I got back."

"Did you stay in touch with Fortunata?"

"We texted and emailed for a while. That's how I learned she got in deep with Carmelo." She bit off a piece of sticky bun. "She developed a pretty bad cocaine habit. Before she disappeared, she emailed me that she had an idea how to get enough money to escape L.A. and start a new life somewhere else." She licked her fingers and wiped them on a napkin. "That's the last I heard of her until you called."

"Do you remember any names other than George Papadopoulos?"

"No. Carmelo didn't want either of us to learn about his operation." She sat back. "I feel better telling you. I didn't even tell my priest."

"I'm no priest, but your secret is safe with me."

TWENTY-FIVE

Lester

Lester set his toolbox on the conveyor belt, followed by his tool belt and the bin with his pocket items. He unlaced his boots and set them on the belt.

"I thought you guys was finished," the metal detector guard said.

Lester chuckled. "It's always something, ain't it?"

The guard grunted as Lester passed through security.

Careful not to hurry, Lester returned to the storeroom, dumped his tools, and retrieved the clipboard that gave him instant credibility. He checked his phone: *11:27 a.m.*

The carpenters had disassembled the table saw and stacked the sawhorses. Two carpenters carried equipment away while a uniformed arena employee ran a push broom across the stage. Sawdust flew into the air and drifted to the concrete floor. An industrial vacuum cleaner with *Tampa Bay Tepee* stenciled on its canvas bag waited at one side.

Lester knew from the procedure followed at the Falcon's Nest that the crew would nail a black curtain around the stage that hung down to one inch above the floor.

Steve the foreman still wore his Bucs cap. He and a man in khakis and a sport shirt stood behind the stage.

Lester fastened on his knee pads. He walked over and interrupted the two men.

Better show them who's boss. "You guys ready for final inspection?"

Steve regarded Lester like he had farted. "This here's my union rep. He says there ain't no new ordinance about no inspections for temporary facilities like this stage."

Les's breath caught in his throat.

The man with Steve said, "Well?"

Lester blinked and swallowed. "I didn't say it was a city ordinance. This is a policy of arena management. Their liability insurance carrier insists on safety inspections since that stage collapsed at that West Coast concert last year. Hey, don't get your bowels in an uproar. Based on what I saw yesterday, this stage will pass final inspection with no problem. Let me do my job and everybody's happy. *Capisce?*"

Without waiting for a reply, Lester moved behind the stage. He squatted and scooted under. He crawled a few yards, flashed his Maglite on the joists, and emerged from beneath the stage. "You pass. Nice job, fellows. I gotta go back underneath for pictures and final documentation, but I'm finished as far as the insurance company is concerned." He smiled, warmly he hoped. "Have a nice day."

Steve and the union rep eyed each other and shrugged.

Lester crawled under the stage again, looking for the perfect spot.

The vacuum cleaner fired up. The noise of its powerful motor echoed between the floor and the stage, deafening him. *Hard to think with that racket, but I shall persevere. It will be worth it when I make a fool out of McCrary. As for Cleo... she'll never have a good night's sleep again... until she sleeps with me.* He grinned.

He found the spot. He scanned either direction; it was under the middle of the stage. He stuck out the tape measure. *Ten feet back. She'll stand over this spot. Kentucky Hillbillies indeed.* He emerged from beneath the stage and stepped to the exit.

He watched as the worker finished vacuuming. His stomach growled.

He'd missed lunch. Sacrifices must be made. He would wait in the storeroom for the workers to fasten the curtain around the stage. Then he'd sneak back. With his surprise.

TWENTY-SIX

Carlos McCrary

The day of the first Tampa concert, I slept late because my crew and I had worked the night before to search the arena. We ensured no one was hiding there. Gunner searched the rafters and catwalks and sealed all access doors before we left. We locked all doors so no one could get in and I got to bed after three a.m. I planned to control everyone who entered on concert day. I also planned a last-minute search for bombs.

Before I arrived at the Tepee, someone with an extra key had already opened the entrance and service doors and the security scanners had not arrived. The employee lot held a dozen cars. So much for our controlling access to the venue. *If you want to make God laugh, tell Him what you have planned.*

We could do nothing about the security breach except begin from square one—starting with a search for any bomb.

Hound Dog Hannigan had Cleo and the Kentucky Hillbillies rehearsing on stage. The new backup singer was six inches shorter than the other two. Hound Dog hadn't had time to find another Amazon. The cuffs of her red, white, and blue pants hung to the floor, even in her four-inch heels.

I debated whether to hustle the band off the stage while I searched underneath it. *No point freaking everyone out. I'll search it while they rehearse.*

I began with Cleo's dressing room. It's amazing how many places someone can hide a bomb in a dressing room. Two couches, three side chairs, a chifforobe, a bar, catering locker, and, and, and... Snoop and I searched a half-hour in there. I stationed Desiree Clover, an off-duty Miami cop, on the door; no one we didn't know would get in.

Pete Martinez arrived back from Duluth. He pitched in and the other dressing rooms went faster.

The stage measured 25 by 50 feet. I learned a painful lesson at the Falcon's Nest as I searched under the stage on my hands and knees. This time I brought a mechanic's creeper to lie on my back while I scooted underneath the stage.

As soon as I slid under the stage, I knew it would be ear-splitting. The music boomed, which did wonders for my concentration, like working inside a bass drum. The stage joists were deeper than standard and spaced twelve inches apart. The beams were spaced five feet. That meant I had to get underneath each of the 250 alcoves to see anything hidden there.

Beginning at the front right corner, I worked my way across, fifty feet, ten alcoves. I revolved 180 degrees and scooted the other direction on the second row, like mowing a lawn. On my eleventh sweep, I saw something in my peripheral vision hidden in the twelfth row. Sliding sideways on the creeper, I found it.

The bomb was the size of an old-fashioned cigar box. A sand-colored brick of plastic explosive with a wiring harness and a cellphone attached with electrical tape. Staples on either side held the whole contraption against the floor above with silver duct tape found in a gazillion stores. No clues there.

I snapped pictures with my phone.

Carefully, I set the Maglite on its end with the light aimed at the bomb. The bomb squad would find it easily after they arrived.

I slid the creeper out the front of the stage and rose to my feet.

I decided not to shout, "There's a bomb." Starting a panic would not help. Someone might do something stupid and set the bomb off. Besides, I was competing against industrial-strength speakers which book-ended the stage.

"Stop the music," I shouted.

No one heard me.

I waved my arms over my head to grab Cleo's attention, but her back was to me. She faced the band and backup singers while they worked with the new singer.

I jumped up and down and waved my arms.

Hound Dog saw me and waved back.

Vaulting onto the stage, I drew my finger across my throat in a *cut* motion.

The drummer stopped and signaled by pointing his drumsticks at me.

Cleo saw me. She smiled, until she noticed my expression and *cut* motion. She stopped singing. The other musicians fell silent.

"Cleo, there's a dangerous structural problem with the stage and there's a risk it will collapse. Everyone, please exit the stage *smoothly* and *quickly* while we fix it. Don't cause unnecessary vibration while you get off the stage. It's shaky."

That worked. They moved, but not fast enough for my peace of mind.

"Leave your instruments, but set them down *gently*, please."

I shooed the band down the steps. Soon they milled behind the stage, safely on the concrete floor.

Climbing to the top of the steps, I said, "May I have your attention, please? I lied to you. There's a bomb underneath the stage. Exit the arena as fast as you can while I call the bomb squad."

That worked like a charm.

The Tampa Bay Regional Bomb Squad arrived as I finished shepherding the last person outside.

It was raining off and on, and the band and building crew huddled under the building overhang. The bomb's kill radius was small enough that they were safe if it went off.

The head of the squad pulled to the service entrance of the Tepee. He ducked his head and trotted through the shower. "Are you Carlos McCrary?" His name badge read *Sergeant Robert Leonard*.

"Yes, sergeant. I called you." I handed him a business card.

Leonard glanced at my card. "Private Investigator, huh?"

"I was on the job in Port City before I was a PI. The building is evacuated. Everyone's out."

"What did you find?"

"An IED." I showed him the picture on my phone. "Plastic explosive with a cellphone detonator. It's fastened under the stage."

"You sure it's a bomb and not a fake?"

"Check out the picture. I was Special Forces in Iraq and Afghanistan. I recognize an IED when I see one. If it's fake, it's a good one. Didn't stick around to find out."

He peered at the phone again. "Looks real. Where is it?"

"Underneath the stage, in the middle, maybe ten feet from the front. My Maglite is under the stage shining on the bomb."

"The rain has stopped. Move these people farther from the building."

"Right."

Leonard waved his team closer, five men and a woman. "Suit up. We have a hot one."

The rain stopped as suddenly as it started.

LeMarvis stood as close as the police would let him. A gaggle of television reporters shouted questions that he ignored. The reporters had shouted and clamored for a comment since they arrived. Now they talked among themselves. Old home week with the media sharks. Perhaps they could interview each other and let the rest of us alone? Not likely.

I stayed inside the crime scene tape, but the news vultures shouted questions in my direction.

Leonard and his team disappeared inside. LeMarvis waved me over to the yellow tape and asked the uniformed officer, "Can I cross that police tape and talk privately with my security expert? We won't go inside; we'll stand over there."

The cop gazed at the assembled mob of media folks and raised the yellow tape. "Sure thing, Mr. Jones."

We stepped a few yards away.

"What happens now?" LeMarvis asked.

I showed him the picture on my phone. "Did you hear my conversation with Sergeant Leonard?"

"Yeah. Do we need to cancel the concert?"

I checked my watch. "The concert doesn't start for six more hours. After the EOD finishes—"

He interrupted. "The what?"

"Sorry. EOD means Explosive Ordnance Disposal. In the army, we call a bomb squad an EOD unit. After they finish, I'll search every square inch with my own team. The police do that also, but we'll make our own search. To be sure."

"To what purpose?"

"If we don't find anything, you can hold the concert, assuming you still want to."

"You mean if Cleo wants to." LeMarvis stroked his chin. "We'll offer anyone a refund, but, yeah, if the arena is clear, we could do that."

The EOD unit worked for two hours. Sergeant Leonard walked out the rear door followed by two technicians carrying a bombproof box. He came over to me. "It's real, but something's funny with this thing."

"Funny?"

"Show me the picture on your phone again."

I found the picture and handed the phone to him.

Leonard pointed to the cellphone attached to the bomb. "See that cellphone? The battery was dead as a dog in a well. No way he could detonate this bomb."

"Did he wire it correctly?"

"Near as I can tell at first glance, yeah. We'll learn more after we get it to the lab, but it appears the bomber did everything right, except the cellphone detonator had a dead battery."

"That's seventeen kinds of weird. If the perp knew enough to build a bomb, you would figure he could charge the battery, right?"

Leonard handed my phone back. "Maybe he didn't intend it to go off.

Or it could be a decoy. You had any union troubles? Maybe Mafia wanting protection money? Could it be a warning?"

"No, nothing like that. This is Florida, not Chicago or New York."

Leonard scoffed. "You wish. We have troubles like that in Tampa Bay."

We finished our second search before five p.m. We cleared the Tampa Bay Tepee—again. No bombs—again. Gunner searched the area beneath the roof again and resealed the doors the bomb squad and Tampa cops had unsealed during their sweep.

Avery Harper sent a group text to the cast, most of whom had returned to the hotel.

Arena has been cleared and is safe. No more bombs. We have permission to perform. Am meeting with Cleo, LeMarvis, and security team to discuss. We perform tonight as scheduled.

The TV news crews breathlessly broadcast live feeds, flogging the bomb threat on local news.

Harper called a meeting in Cleo's dressing room. Cleo and LeMarvis were there along with Snoop and me. And Hound Dog Hannigan.

I never knew who invited Hound Dog to these meetings. He just appeared. Some people have that knack.

"Okay, people," said Harper, "we need to make a decision."

Cleo cleared her throat. "Whatever happened to 'The show must go on?'"

"Cleo, honey," Harper responded, "I'm with you. We should put on the show these folks paid for."

LeMarvis stood, towering over us. "You all think I'll vote to cancel." He smiled at us. "You all know I want to marry Cleo and take her away from all this. But I say we should put on the show, because that's what Cleo wants. She *wants* to be a star, and she *deserves* to be a star, and if there's anything I can do to help her *be* a star, I say let's do it."

"Are we safe, Chuck?" Cleo asked.

I nodded. "The arena is clear."

"Avery, tell the TV people, and the social media, and the radio, and that stuff."

Avery Harper stood. "I'll hold a news conference outside."

Cars began to arrive for the concert two hours before the scheduled start. All tickets were reserved seats, so no one came early for a front-row seat. Maybe they came to tailgate.

Hound Dog Hannigan insisted Cleo delay the concert until nine p.m. "Since your goldarned private detective interrupted our goldarned rehearsal, I ain't had time to get things the way I want. You gotta give me an extra hour with the band." That was why he charmed his way into the meeting.

We opened the doors at eight-thirty. By eight-forty-five the arena looked full. Around 1,500 people asked for refunds. Practically all the concession employees showed.

It appeared that the concert would come off without a hitch—or, at least, without *another* hitch.

Lester

"Hey, guys," Lester said, "would you fellows like to make a hundred bucks each for five minutes' work?"

The high-school-age boys eyed the space around them to make sure the older man was talking to them. "You mean us?"

"Yeah." Lester showed a window envelope he had obtained from a local bank. The envelope said *Happy Birthday* in festive red letters on the front. Ulysses S. Grant's picture showed through. "A hundred bucks each for five minutes' work. There are four 50s in this envelope. Two for each of you."

The first kid stepped closer, then stopped. He eyed his friend and shot back at Les. "Wait a minute. You're not a weirdo, are you?"

Lester laughed. "Nope. After you get home, tell your parents how you earned an easy hundred. Nothing bad, nothing illegal. Five minutes work to pull a practical joke on a friend of mine. You guys won't miss the concert."

The boys moved closer. "What's the job?"

"Do you see that man walking away? The man in the navy-blue sport coat and khaki pants?"

Carlos McCrary

I sat in a desk chair on the front row of the darkened press box with my binoculars to my eyes. Alternately, I scanned the floor, scoreboard, grandstands, and parts of backstage visible from my perch. Folding chairs filled the arena floor. Music fans nearly filled a horseshoe-shaped section of both upper and lower bowls. The few empty seats did not stand out in the crowded arena.

The curved grandstands behind the stage sat empty. The arena couldn't sell those seats because they lacked a stage view. The overhead lights were off and the dark blue seats draped with dust covers were barely visible in the dim light spilling from the occupied sections. A potential assassin dressed in dark clothes would be invisible in the darkness and would have a good shot at Cleo from behind. I scrutinized that area with the binoculars.

The opening act finished their set and took their bow amidst warm applause. Budding stars of tomorrow, the opening act for today's new star.

The stage lights faded and the musicians left the stage in semi-darkness. Some fans left their seats for the restrooms, souvenirs, and concession stands. They would be busy as the stagehands rearranged the equipment for Cleo and her band.

Fifteen minutes later, the overhead lights flashed once, twice, then went dark. Fans streamed back into the arena.

The LED banner that circled the arena flashed red, white, and blue like a giant waving American flag, pulsing in time to a recorded drum cadence. Any moment, I half-expected a marching band to enter.

The careful part of me noticed the drummer was loud enough to drown out a gunshot, but Cleo was still backstage.

On the stage, Cleo's band took their places as they had in Port City. The speakers clicked, hummed, and popped as musicians synced wirelessly with their amplifiers. A thump and a bump as the backup singers tapped their fingers against the microphones to test.

The drum cadence ended. In the expectant silence, the overhead lights pulsed, first dimly, then brighter.

A guitar riff like a trumpet flourish played from the speakers and the crowd quieted. "Ladies and gentlemen," Hound Dog Hannigan's voice boomed, "from the Appalachian Mountains to the Sunshine State, Port City Productions and musical director Hound Dog Hannigan are proud to present the Kentucky Hillbillies and..." he paused, "the Kentucky songbird, Miss Cleopatra Hennessey!"

I had heard it in rehearsal and twice before at the Port City concerts, and I was still impressed. Hound Dog was a born cheerleader. Or maybe a circus ringmaster from the Twentieth Century, reincarnated in the Twenty-First.

Spotlights flashed and swept the crowd into a frenzy. Music thundered from giant speakers. The stage lights brightened to reveal the Kentucky Hillbillies in their blue costumes as they played the intro to their first piece.

The stage lights dimmed again. The spotlights turned white and swung upward to a spot in the girders above the stage. The beams focused on Cleo waving from a red velvet swing trimmed with gold braid. The rhinestones on her white costume flashed sparkles of light across the crowd.

The fans jumped to their feet and cheered, taking videos as Cleo descended, waving at her people.

My cellphone screen flashed on the desk and played *Reveille*, the special ringtone I programmed for my security team. I had set the phone on the desk since I would never hear it ring and wouldn't feel it vibrate in my pocket, what with the giant speakers filling the arena with ear-numbing sound and vibrations. I snatched it and hurried to the soundproof broadcast booth.

Stepping inside, I shut the door and welcome silence greeted me. "Yeah, Snoop, what you got?"

"The seals on the access doors to the rafter area were cut."

"Which door? Call a team. I'll be there."

"It's all of them, everywhere."

"All of them?"

"Our rovers called. They caught two boys who followed them and cut every seal behind them. The kids broke over half the seals before our men caught them."

Oh, geez. Just what we needed. "Vandalism or something else?"

"I'm on my way to Section 63 to question them," Snoop said.

"I'll call Gunner, then meet you there. Don't scare the kids. We can't legally hold them. Offer them a bribe if they'll stick around and talk to us. Then call the cops on site."

"How much you willing to pay?"

"Hell, Snoop, money isn't an object. Keep them there, whatever you need to do." Then I had an idea. "Offer them an autographed copy of Cleo's CD after the show."

I disconnected and texted Gunner.

The catwalks are compromised. Numerous access door seals are broken. Assume the shooter is up there. Take three men, one for each quadrant. Get topside and search the catwalks. Trap this guy.

I locked the press box behind me and jogged to the ring corridor on my way to Section 63. Naturally, it was on the other side of the arena.

After two minutes jogging around the perimeter, I reached my two rovers and Snoop standing with two skinny boys near the big blue *63* sign.

One boy stood five-foot-six and weighed a hundred pounds if he carried bricks in both pockets. He had bushy blond hair and a scraggly beard, which he kept scratching. His eyes darted back and forth as if he expected my men to attack him any second. He chewed on his lower lip. *A stoner? Not a reliable witness.*

The other boy was my height. For a high school boy, he had a red mustache and goatee that Svengali would have been proud of. He seemed to enjoy the attention.

I stopped a few feet away to catch my breath.

Snoop had his notepad out. "What did he hire you to do?"

Svengali gestured at the nearest access door. "He told us to follow this guy," he nodded at my rover, "and slit the door seals after he passed. I told him I didn't have a knife, and he said to use a key."

It must be the shooter.

"Can you describe the man?" Snoop asked.

Svengali frowned. "A guy. I didn't notice, y'know?"

"What race was he? White, black, Latino?"

"He was white."

"Yeah, white," Stoner echoed. "Like he didn't get out much."

"What color hair?"

"Brown," said Svengali.

"Yeah, brown," Stoner agreed. "Real long. Almost covered his ears."

"Eyes?"

The boys glanced at each other. "Who notices that shit? Brown? Hard to tell behind the sunglasses."

"He wore sunglasses?"

"Yeah. Cheap ones you would buy on the corner from a street dude."

"Yeah, cheap," Stoner agreed.

"Okay," said Snoop. "How tall was he?"

Svengali said, "Lemme see... He was taller than me."

"Yeah, and taller than me," Stoner added.

"How tall are you?"

"Six-two," Svengali said. "Five-six," Stoner said.

Snoop repressed a smile and recorded the information. "What was he wearing?"

"I didn't notice," Svengali said.

"What about you, son?" asked Snoop. "Did you notice his clothes?"

Stoner scratched his beard. "I think they was long pants, kinda gray maybe? You know, Dickies work pants like my dad wears. White sneakers, sorta, but kinda dirty. The dude didn't care what kicks he wore."

"Do you remember his shirt?"

Stoner chewed his lower lip. "His shirt?"

Snoop waited. Svengali waited. I waited.

"Oh, yeah. He didn't have no shirt. He wore one o' them, whatchacallit, sweatshirts."

Snoop took a note. "What color?"

"Old-fashioned sweatshirt. Gray, y'know. One that says XXXXL but it's not, y'know? The dude was real tall, but he wasn't no XXXXL size at all. Sorta beefy, like a normal guy who works out."

My cellphone signaled a text from Gunner.

We're in position and beginning the sweep. If he's here, we have him cornered.

Snoop finished asking them about the money.

"Where are the 50s?" I asked.

They each reached for their pockets.

I raised my hands. "Don't touch them. We need to check them for fingerprints. I'll give each of you two one-hundred-dollar bills in exchange for the two 50s. Deal?"

"Sure, dude. I'll take that deal any time."

I slipped on evidence gloves. "Step over here. I'll reach into your pocket..." I did. "And get the bills." I plucked out a wad of cash and fished through it. "These the only 50s you have?"

"Yeah."

"What about you?" I asked Svengali.

"Only the ones he give me, man."

After stuffing the bills in a paper evidence bag, I repeated the procedure with the other boy.

I peeled four 100s from my money clip. "How did the man hand you the bills? Like this?"

"No, man. They was in an envelope—one that says Happy Graduation or Happy Birthday. I remember 'cause Grant's picture was in the window. He held out the envelope with the top open. He said, 'You each take two.' And we pulled them out of the envelope."

That would avoid leaving fingerprints on the bills.

"What did he do with the envelope?"

Two more shrugs. "Didn't see, dude. We were busy sticking the money in our pockets. We followed the dude in the blue jacket and slit the seals with our car keys." Svengali pointed at my rover. "Then this guy turns around and yelled at us."

"Where were you and your friend standing when this man gave you the money?"

"Around that bend," Svengali replied. "Our seats are in Section 49. Say, man, we're missing the concert. This isn't fair. We paid good money to hear Cleo."

"If you'll show me to where you two were standing to talk to the man,

I'll give you each another hundred. Then you can go."

Svengali and Stoner showed Snoop and me where they talked with the shooter. "Thanks, guys. After the show, come to Cleo's dressing room. Hand this business card to the guard and he'll let you in to meet Cleo. She'll give you each an autographed CD." I handed them each a business card along with another hundred-dollar bill. I made a mental note to record $600 for bribes on my expense report. Make that "witness fees."

I sent for Pete Martinez and Desiree Clover. "Two witnesses described our suspect as having brown hair long enough to cover his ears and wearing a gray sweatshirt with XXXXL stenciled on the front. The long hair might be a wig. Maybe he dumped it and we can find DNA. He would have dumped the sweatshirt also. Pete, you go clockwise and search every trashcan on the right side and every men's restroom. Desiree, search trashcans on the left side of the corridor and all ladies' rooms. Then move down one level and search it. Continue until you reach bottom."

Lester

Lester took the stairs down one level. Heart pounding, he walked to the men's restroom behind and two levels above the stage. *They can't sell seats behind the stage. This end will be deserted.*

Lester checked both ways. The old arena had no security cameras in the corridors. Muffled music echoed in the empty passage, which curved out of sight both directions. *Nobody home. If this tree falls in a forest, there is no one to hear it. Or to see it.* Smiling, he entered the restroom.

He flipped on the lights, closed the door behind him, and leaned his back against it, shivering even though he was sweating. Soon this night would be over. He took a deep breath. Another. Another. He felt his pulse through the clear vinyl gloves he wore. *I thought of everything. No fingerprints on the money, the envelope, not on anything.*

He locked the door to the handicapped stall behind him and stood at the mirror. *By God, I did it again.* He removed the sunglasses and grinned at his image before sticking the shades in his pants pocket. He slipped off the brown wig and inspected the wig cap inside. Clean, no sweat this time, thanks to the rubber skull cap he wore. He had burned the last wig to destroy any DNA from his sweat which soaked through the wig cap and into the hair. Not this time. The cops would not find DNA in this wig.

He pulled off the rubber cap and felt cool air on his sweaty scalp. The inside of the cap dripped from his sweat. *Christ, this sweaty cap is full of my DNA. I can't let it spill.* He folded the cap with the sweaty side in. *Can't be too careful.* He rinsed the cap under the faucet and washed it again with hand soap. He dried it with the air dryer and stuffed the cap in another pocket.

He pulled the sweatshirt over his head. *Oh Christ, I should have left the skull cap on while I removed the shirt. My own hairs might come off on the fuzz inside the sweatshirt. Dumb, dumb, dumb. You're too smart to make a mistake, Les. You're smarter than the cops, smarter than that damned McCrary, smarter than the bitch for sure. Don't make that mistake again.* He turned the sweatshirt inside out and scrutinized every square inch. *Yes, there is a hair.* He pulled it off and stuck it in his pocket.

Lester had shaved his arms. Nothing to come off inside the sweatshirt. He was left wearing a tee shirt. *Maybe next week, I'll wear a tee shirt from the bitch's concert tour. What a delicious irony that would be.*

He considered his bare arms. With arms exposed, someone might notice the clear vinyl gloves. He would make changes before next week. Next week he would wear a long-sleeved western shirt under the sweatshirt. *Unless I wear a Summer Fun Concert Tour tee shirt. No, bad idea. Stick with what works, Les.*

He peeled off the gloves and stuffed them into his pants pocket. Good thing he wore loose pants.

He had thought of everything. Okay, nearly everything. *Nobody's perfect, but with practice… with practice… Practice makes perfect. When the bitch brings her hillbilly tour to Orlando, I will be perfect.*

Carlos McCrary

Gunner and his men did not have the weirdo cornered after all. Weirdo wasn't there. He was toying with us.

Gunner's team finished searching the catwalks before the first intermission ended. They resealed the access doors and resumed their rounds. I returned to the press box.

My cellphone rang again. It was Pete Martinez. "What you got, Pete?"

"We found the wig and the sweatshirt. Third level men's restroom, Section 3."

The good thing about this fiasco was that nothing interrupted the concert.

TWENTY-SEVEN

S unday was no day of rest. We had clues to work.

The Tampa police put a rush on testing the $50 bills. They had dozens of fingerprints on them, most smudged beyond use. I got fingerprints of Svengali and the Stoner for comparison when they came to collect their autographed CDs from Cleo.

All the readable prints on the 50s came from the two boys and one set from a cashier at a convenience store in Largo, a town near Tampa.

The cops interviewed the cashier that afternoon. He remembered one man asking for 50s.

We reviewed the C-store's security video and found a muscular tall man buying four 50s from the cash register with ten twenties. It was our guy, but he wore a hat, a wig like the one we found, and sunglasses.

Since we didn't have photos or mugshots for the cashier to look at, I felt as worthless as an expired fast-food coupon.

The police lab examined the sweatshirt and wig with a microscope. That's how they found the rubber residue from a skull cap. No DNA. Weirdo had made no mistakes. Yet.

I took consolation from the fact that nobody bats a thousand. If Weirdo stayed active, he would make a mistake. Eventually.

But would Cleo be alive by the time that happened?

I wished Bubble-Gum Beltran and Feldman were as thorough as the Tampa detectives.

I sent Pete to investigate Carmelo Sarducci and George Papadopoulos, the gangster's name he learned from Doris Poteet. He took off for Los Angeles.

I drove back to my Port City condo, kicked off my shoes, and pretended I knew what I was doing. Everywhere I turned, I hit dead ends.

Then the next email arrived, addressed to my business email address from *white-mans-burdun* at a free email site I had never heard of.

The bitch has a secret, McCrary. Ask her about Uncle Henry Lynch and Cousin Chester Lynch. Ask her why she claims to be from Kentucky when she was born in Tennessee. You can't protect the bitch forever. I'm watching you, McCrary. Let your gard down one time, and the bitch is mine. Maybe you to.

Was the bad grammar and misspelling intentional? Perhaps Weirdo wanted me to underestimate him.

Clicking *reply*, I typed my own message:

You forgot to charge the battery on the cellphone, Weirdo.

I hit *send*.

A minute later I received an error message saying the email address was bogus. No, Weirdo wasn't stupid. He had batted a thousand, but at least he gave me a clue. Two clues, in fact.

One of my own clients had tried to kill me a few years earlier. I learned the hard way to run background checks on new clients and their key employees. I had done that after Cleo and LeMarvis hired me.

LeMarvis had lived in a goldfish bowl since his sophomore year at Duke University after the Blue Devils made it to the Final Four. A female student who had a drunken sexual encounter with him claimed she was too drunk to consent to sex. LeMarvis counter-claimed she was the assailant, and *he* was too drunk to consent to sex with *her*.

Reading the report, I wondered if they raped each other. Since the alleged encounter happened in her dorm room instead of his, and she hung a scarf on her doorknob to signal her roommate not to interrupt, the DA dropped the case. LeMarvis didn't press charges against the girl. Nothing else bad happened to LeMarvis his junior year. Then he left Duke early and was a first-round NBA draft choice.

Cleo was different. Cleopatra Hennessey appeared in public records for the last three years, since she began her music career in Nashville. Cleo was her stage name and she never told me what name she'd been born with. Despite her having left no evidence before three years ago, I accepted her as a client based on Tank's recommendation, LeMarvis's reputation, and my gut feeling that she was okay.

But what else had she not told me? I decided not to tell her that I knew, but I told Flamer to do a deep dive on her background.

The email put more pressure on me to uncover her history. Weirdo was no stranger. Was he an estranged family member? I sent both new names to Flamer. He would find something with these new clues.

I pondered the email's last two sentences: "Let your gard down one time, and the bitch is mine. Maybe you to."

It sucks big time to play defense.

"What did you find on Cleo?"

My internet guru Flamer21 had called my cellphone. "This was a bitch to find, hot shot. I searched for days to run this woman down. With the two relatives' names, I found her. Then I located a hard copy of a small college newspaper in Tennessee which interviewed her three years ago. The newspaper isn't on the internet in a digital format. I read screenshots of jpeg files of each page to find the interview. You should give me a medal for this, even with Uncle Henry and Cousin Chester's names."

"Nice work, Flamer. What did you find?"

"Her name's not Hennessey. She mentioned in the interview that she drinks Hennessey VSOP cognac on special occasions, and she considers it means high quality."

"What's her birth name?"

"Ironic that she's engaged to a black man. Her birth name is Lynch."

"So, her real name is Cleopatra Jane Lynch?"

"No, she changed everything. It's Katie Boone Lynch—not Katherine, but Katie, spelled K-A-T-I-E. I found her birth certificate. She told the college newspaper that she picked an exotic first name."

"Cleopatra is exotic for sure. Does Cleo have a criminal record under her birth name?"

Flamer paused. "Not exactly."

"What does that mean?"

"It means she comes from a generations-long line of moonshiners and bootleggers that began before Prohibition. That's the connection to Uncle Henry and Cousin Chester, both moonshiners. Chester served time for Federal Alcohol Tax evasion."

"*Hmm.* At our first meeting in my office, she asked for a bourbon and branch at ten o'clock in the morning."

"What's bourbon and branch?"

"In East Texas where I grew up, a creek is called a branch. They call it that in Tennessee and other parts of the South. Moonshiners use branch water to dilute their whiskey before they bottle it. It means bourbon and water."

"You had moonshiners in Adams Creek, hot shot?"

"Sure. When I attended Theodore Roosevelt High School, we bought 'shine when we partied. Moonshiners never ask for ID. People didn't call us *The Rough Riders* for nothing."

"There's more. The Lynch family has a feud going."

"The Hatfield's and McCoy's feud?"

"Yeah, except this one is between the Lynches and the Lynches."

"They had a feud within the same family?"

"Two answers to your question. First, it's not *had*, hot shot. They *have* a feud in the same family. It's still going on. Five Lynches were murdered in the last thirty years, including Uncle Henry and Cousin Chester. One feud victim was a woman. This is an equal-opportunity feud."

"Okay. What's the second answer?"

"It's two branches of the family."

"You mean they're distantly related?"

"No, they're close relatives. In rural Tennessee, the population is so small there aren't many choices for husbands and wives. First and second cousins often intermarry. It's been going on since before the Civil War."

"What about Cleopatra Jane Hennessey a/k/a Katie Boone Lynch?"

"Let me check her birth certificate… Mother's maiden name was Jane Boone, and she was born in Kentucky. No cousins there. Cleo used her mother's first name as part of her stage name."

TWENTY-EIGHT

My 1963 Studebaker Avanti, the *Silver Ghost*, hadn't been driven in a week, so I drove it to LeMarvis's mansion to knock the cobwebs off the engine.

Lowering my window, I punched *1125* into the keypad. LeMarvis Jones's high school jersey number was *11* and his college and NBA number was *25*.

The polished stainless-steel gate to LeMarvis Jones's waterfront mansion rolled open, and I bumped across the tracks into his outer courtyard. The gate slid closed behind me. I parked near the inner wall next to a blue Bentley with a personalized plate that read *MMONEY7*. I strolled through the pedestrian gate with my head on a swivel, admiring the flowers and tropical plants in the lush garden. I descended three steps, passed around the cast-stone fountain, and climbed five more steps to his front door.

As I approached, LeMarvis opened a carved wooden door that could have been commissioned for a Spanish monastery. "Thanks for coming."

He led me across an omigod foyer to a living room big enough to accommodate the entire Peregrines basketball team and their coaches. A wrought-iron chandelier hung from the twenty-five-foot ceiling with fake candles aglow five feet above my head. The light fixture must have come from the monks' dining hall in that same monastery.

"Cleo's upstairs practicing in her studio," LeMarvis said. "We have the downstairs to ourselves until she finishes. Have you eaten lunch?"

"I grabbed a pulled-pork sandwich on the way here."

"I wish I had remembered to tell you not to. My cook whipped up a bratwurst plate for Tank and me that would make your mouth water. Maybe next time."

"I'll look forward to it."

Tank Tyler sat at one end of a nine-foot sofa built for people as big as Tank and LeMarvis Jones.

I high-fived Tank and sat in a facing chair. "That must be your Bentley I saw in front. What happened to the BMW?"

"I still have it. I had three cars in a six-car garage. They were lonesome, so I bought them a Bentley to keep them company when I'm gone."

"*Silver Ghost* and my Caravan get lonely in my condo's parking garage. Maybe you should buy them a Ferrari to play with."

"Maybe you should take a long walk on a short pier."

Tank Tyler's mansion occupied a chunk of waterfront on Pink Coral Island in the north end of Seeti Bay. Until now, Tank's house was the most luxurious mansion I had personally seen. Tank managed with a cook, a butler, and a gardener, and his butler was a charity case; the old guy came with the house and was too old to find a job elsewhere. Tank was a soft touch. Good thing he was loaded, or he'd be broke.

LeMarvis Jones's mansion sprawled over four acres of bayfront on Magnolia Island, another private island in the bay's south end. It was the kind of place that needed staff to maintain. LeMarvis's mansion made Tank's look like a cookie-cutter three-bedroom bungalow.

LeMarvis plopped on the other end of the sofa. "You want something to drink?"

A tuxedoed butler who seemed Asian stepped up. "What may I bring you, sir?"

So much for having the downstairs to ourselves. LeMarvis doesn't count the servants.

"Diet Dr. Pepper with a lime wedge if you have it. Diet Coke with lime if you don't."

The butler seemed chagrined. "We have Diet Coke, sir, but I assure you: Next time you visit we shall have Diet Dr. Pepper."

The butler left. I felt confident he would order Diet Dr. Pepper for the mansion's pantry within the hour. He seemed that efficient.

LeMarvis pulled a folded sheet of paper from his shirt pocket. "I called you because I received another disturbing email this morning."

He unfolded the paper. "First half is pretty standard hate mail. Nigger-nigger this. Nigger-nigger that. Send the blacks back to Africa, etc. It's the last part that made me call you."

He handed it to me.

The fourth paragraph caught my attention. *The cops assume a California mobster killed the girl. They are stupid jews curs. That dago singer was NOT the target. I used her for practice and to send a message to you and to Cleeo. Maybe next time I'll kill the hillbilly. Or I'll kill the nigger-lover. Or I'll kill the nigger.* He signed it *Defender of White America.*

I set the paper down as if it burned my hands. Reading that crap felt yucky and putrid, like inspecting a cesspool.

"Is it the guy who sent those emails to Cleo?" LeMarvis asked.

"You had time to study it. What's your opinion?"

"I don't know what to think, Chuck. It's not the first email I've received like that."

"When you say 'like that,' do you mean from that sender, or that it's one of several pieces of similar hate mail?"

"Both. I've received four emails from this *Defender of White America* that I remember."

"Did you keep any?"

"Hell, I didn't even *read* any until this one. I deleted the others soon as I saw what they were. I never clutter my mind or my hard drive with crap." He gestured at the paper. "Life's too short to dwell on crazy people."

"Why read hate mail at all? Why not delete it as soon as you recognize it?"

"I do, but this email's subject line grabbed my attention. It said *The girl singer was not the target. Cleeo could be next.* Same misspelling of *Cleo.*"

"Why wait until now to call me?"

The butler appeared with my Diet Coke. He set a small stack of napkins on the table and a salad plate filled with lime wedges. "FYI, LeMarvis, I think Cleo is wrapping up her practice."

"Thanks for telling me," LeMarvis said.

The butler nodded and disappeared without a word.

"The earlier emails didn't mention Cleo. Or at least the subject line didn't. I remember the email address because I saw it on the subject line in my inbox. They were like other hate mails I get."

"This is the first one that ties to the threats to Cleo?"

"Right. I didn't tell Cleo, because I didn't want to worry her more than she already is. Should I tell her?"

"For now, no. She's spooked and she's already careful about security. Reading this email wouldn't make her more secure, but it could make her worry about you. Even though you deleted the other emails, my computer guy might be able to trace the sender. If it's the person who emailed Cleo, he used an anonymizer, but I want to try. I'll send him over to examine your computer."

"Anything for Cleo."

The mahogany stairs echoed with footsteps and Cleo walked in. "Hello, boys. I have to tell the gardener something. After that, would you like me to join you?"

Tank and I waved at her. LeMarvis blew her a kiss as she swept across the giant room. "Wonderful, babe."

I waited until Cleo left the room. "I'll send the guy I used to check out Cleo's computer. His name is Flamer."

LeMarvis stated to speak and I held up both hands. "I know, I know… It's a derogatory slang for gays, but it's the only name he gives me. He couldn't trace the emails on Cleo's computer, and the stalker probably hid his tracks on these emails too, but we'll try. He'll call you tomorrow and make an appointment. I have to see Cleo on another matter, so I'll come back tomorrow also, but not with Flamer."

"Is he gay?"

"Yeah. Why? You have a problem with that?"

"No. It just seems strange that a gay man would use a nickname like Flamer."

"You can ask him when you see him."

"No. I wouldn't do that. That would be intrusive. I was just curious is all."

I picked up the email and read it again. "Another thought occurred to me: Weirdo could be lying."

"What do you mean?" LeMarvis asked.

"Weirdo claims that he shot Fortunata, but that doesn't mean that he did. Consider the possibility that someone else did shoot her: Weirdo claims the credit so he can frighten Cleo more. Make her think that he's more dangerous than he is. I'm not saying that's what happened, but we shouldn't take this email at face value. Let's keep our guard up, but keep an open mind."

Cleo returned to the living room, kissed LeMarvis, and picked a chair facing the rest of us. "What were you three talking about?"

I said, "Tell me about your great-uncle Henry Lynch."

Cleo cut her eyes to LeMarvis then back to me. "Let's go outside, Chuck. There's a nice breeze off the bay."

Cleo opened an eight-foot glass slider which led to the pool. Port City in July feels sultry, steamy, and sweaty if there's no breeze. Trade winds off the Atlantic offset that most of the time and we were on an island. We sat at a poolside table under a green-and-white striped awning that flapped with the breeze. It felt comfortable.

A Latino man in a white guayabera and dark blue Bermuda shorts appeared at her elbow. "Something cool to drink, Miss Cleo?"

It must be nice to make more money than you know what to do with. At least LeMarvis's household staff payroll was good for the South Florida economy.

"Sweet tea, please, Danny."

"And for you, sir?"

"I'm good, thanks."

Danny left.

Cleo peeked back at the house.

"LeMarvis don't know nothing about my family. He read my website, but I told him most of that's puff stuff that Avery made up because it sounded good. LeMarvis said that our lives before we met wasn't important. After he proposed, I told him they were things about me he should know."

Tears gathered in her eyes. "LeMarvis, he said to me, 'My life began the instant I saw you, babe. Nothing that happened before I met you is important to me, and nothing you did before that is important to me either.' Isn't that the most romantic thing ever? I woulda told him if he wanted to know, but he never asked." Tears spilled down her cheeks. "Now I'm kinda afraid to bring it up."

I handed her a tissue and waited while she pulled herself together. This case had me dispensing tissues by the bucket full.

Danny brought Cleo's drink out on a small tray. He placed a white cloth napkin on the table and topped it with her drink. He peeked at Cleo as he finished but didn't say anything.

"Thanks, Danny," Cleo said.

Danny gazed at Cleo and back at me.

I shook my head and he left.

"How did you find out about Uncle Henry?" Cleo asked.

"I'm a private investigator. Finding things is what I do." Perhaps I should put that on my business cards: *McCrary Investigations—We find out stuff.*

"What do you want to know?"

"Everything, but let's start with why you claim to be from Kentucky when you're from Tennessee?"

"What does my family have to do with this case?"

"Maybe nothing. The way I work is to find out everything I can. It's like panning for gold: You scoop up a ton of gravel from the river bed and sift it for the few ounces of gold. Your family history may be gravel, or it may be gold. I won't know until I catch Weirdo. I will keep anything you tell me confidential. Fair enough?"

Cleo's left eyelid fluttered. "I guess that's okay. The reason I pretend to be from Kentucky is that, in Nashville, most folks are from Tennessee. I figured being from Kentucky made me stand out. Made me more, uh, *distinctive*, as Avery says. He says words like *distinctive* and *marketable* a lot."

"Weren't you afraid for your reputation if you got caught in a lie?"

"What reputation? When I started singing professionally, nobody knew me from any other hillbilly singer. I didn't have a reputation. Besides, Pine Hollow, Kentucky ain't far from Thornburg, Tennessee, where I was born. And my mother hails from Kentucky. I did an internet study on Pine Hollow in case anybody asked. And no one did."

"Okay. Tell me how Uncle Henry died."

"ATF agents shot him during a raid on his still in the holler between Thornburg and Grapevine Hill. That happened before I was born, but Maw-Maw, she told me about it."

"Could Uncle Henry's family consider you or your family to be responsible for his death?"

Her left eyelid fluttered. "Couldn't have been me. I wasn't even born. Could have been Grand Mama or Grand Poppa, or maybe Maw-Maw or Paw-Paw."

"Who are Maw-Maw and Paw-Paw?"

"They's Grand Poppa's parents—my great-grandparents."

"You call your grandparents Grand Mama and Grand Poppa?" I asked.

"Only Daddy's parents. Mom's parents in Kentucky, I call them Grandpa and Grandma. That's how I keep them straight. We have a big family, you know."

"What do you call your great-grandparents?"

"I only had the two—they was Grand Poppa's parents. Everybody called them Maw-Maw and Paw-Paw."

"Do any family members—a cousin, aunt, or uncle—any of them want to harm you?"

Cleo's left eyelid jumped as she peered at Seeti Bay. I don't think she focused on anything but the inside of her own head, constructing her next lie. I noted that she took my question seriously. Perhaps the family feud wasn't ancient history after all.

"Do you know about Cousin Chester?"

"Assume I don't. Tell me everything." I knew almost nothing about Chester. Perhaps she would let slip more information.

"Cousin Chester was killed after Uncle Henry. They can't blame me for what Grand Poppa did."

"Did Grand Poppa, your grandfather, kill Cousin Chester?"

"He swore he didn't, but my Momma, she believes he did it."

"What did they fight over?"

"They were fighting over Grand Mama. Cousin Chester, he courted her before she married Grand Poppa, and she favored him too. Grand Poppa feared she was about to marry Cousin Chester. Then Cousin Chester, he died sorta mysterious-like. My Momma figures Grand Poppa killed him. But nobody could blame me. It happened before I was born."

"Most people would agree that no one *should* blame you, but that doesn't mean someone *doesn't*. Five people are dead, so some folks blame somebody for lots of things."

Danny materialized at the table. "Anything else for either of you?"

Cleo smiled at him. "We're good, Danny. Thanks."

Cleo waited until Danny moved out of earshot. "I'm not used to servants. Don't know if I ever will be. LeMarvis, he calls them *staff*. It's strange to have other people in our home. I moved in four weeks ago. Danny, he tends to the garden and pool area. LeMarvis has a cook and a maid and Danny, the gardener."

"A butler too."

"That's Chan. I forgot about him."

Cleo was stalling. Some people sneak up on revealing secrets.

"When I first told LeMarvis about the scary emails, he got upset. He insisted I move in with him because I didn't have no security at my apartment. This house is so big I don't know if I even seen all the rooms. If LeMarvis hadn't given me a spare bedroom upstairs for my studio, I probably would never even visit the second floor. That's our bedroom over there." She pointed across the pool where an identical set of outdoor furniture sat under a similar awning. A wall of floor-to-ceiling glass reflected our images back.

She giggled. "Of course, he'd been after me for weeks, wanting me to move in with him. These emails were a pretty good excuse."

"About your Great Uncle Henry…"

The telltale eyelid signaled another lie. "I ain't seen Uncle Henry's kin since Paw-Paw's funeral ten years ago. Maw-Maw, she asked everyone to get along at the funeral. She was awful upset after what happened at Cousin Chester's funeral. Even though it was before I was born, but I heard about it my whole life. Maw-Maw, she told everybody she would die of a broken heart if anything bad happened at Paw-Paw's funeral. Uncle Henry's kinfolk and Grand Poppa agreed to set the feud aside for the funeral. I don't believe no one's been feuding since." Another lie.

"Three members of your family were killed in the last twenty years."

"That don't have nothing to do with the feud," she lied.

"Your family still make moonshine?"

"The Lynch family, we been making whiskey since before the Civil War. It's in our blood. Moonshine is dangerous business. That's why them cousins got killed. Didn't involve no feud."

"How do you know there isn't another Cousin Chester in the family?"

Her eyes darted to me and back out to sea. "I don't know if there is or there ain't, and I don't care." She swirled her iced tea with jerky motions. Ice cubes tinkled against the glass. "I left home the day after I finished eleventh grade. I didn't want nothing to do with moonshine, and bootlegging, and feuds. I moved to Nashville, changed my name, and never regretted it."

As I drove away from Cleo's and LeMarvis's mansion, I knew more than when I got there. Weirdo's email had given me the key to a unlock bunch of thought-provoking family history on Cleo. I wasn't sure what value the info had, but there is always Rule Five: *You can never have too much information.*

TWENTY-NINE

"How did the July Fourth boat trip go?" I had arrived home the same time as Clint.

Clint was grilling hamburgers on the balcony. We sat on the shady side, away from the setting sun and the smoke.

"We had a great time except for Alonzo and Jasmine. They went below to make out in private, and they got seasick."

"How many kids did you take with you?"

"Four plus Madison. She invited her girlfriend Montserrat and Montserrat's boyfriend. I invited Alonzo and his girlfriend Jasmine."

"Madison's girlfriend's name is Montserrat?"

Clint grinned as he rotated the burgers. "I didn't ask, but I bet there's a great story behind that name. Hand me the squirt bottle."

I did. "Did Madison get seasick?"

Clint put out a grease fire which flared on the coals. "Thank God, no. Only 'Zo and Jasmine. I warned them not to stay in the cabin long. I told them if they can't see the horizon, it's easier to get seasick."

"They didn't believe you."

He laughed. "They lasted fifteen minutes. Don't worry, I cleaned the boat."

"But Montserrat and her boyfriend have good sea legs?"

"Don't know. They didn't go below. They weren't shy about making out. They used the sunbathing bench on the bow to play huggy-bod-kissy-face.

"I'm glad you had a good time. How're things with Madison's parents?"

Clint rocked his hand palm-down. "So-so."

He stacked the cooked patties on a tray and turned off the gas. "Let's eat in the kitchen. This balcony is hot as the hinges of hell."

Clint finished his first burger and started to build his second. "I'm glad we both had the evening off, bro. Something I need to discuss with you."

I was halfway through my first hamburger. I lifted a finger while I swallowed a bite. "Let's hear it."

He spread mayonnaise on one half of his bun. "You, of all people, realize I never had a normal family."

"I know."

Clint didn't know his father, and his mother was a drug-addicted prostitute. All his other relatives were dead, in jail, or didn't care.

"I have no father to talk to, not even an older brother."

"I imagine myself as your older brother or a cool uncle."

"Like your Uncle Felix. Yeah, he's cool." He slathered mustard on the other half of the bun and stacked lettuce, tomatoes, and an onion slice. "I told you about our July Fourth boat trip with Madison and our friends."

"Yeah. Two seasickness casualties."

He slipped a patty off the spatula onto the onion slice and laid cheese on it to melt. "After 'Zo and Jasmine went below and Montserrat and her boyfriend were making out on the bow, Madison pulled me off the captain's chair, led me to the back bench, and sat on my lap."

"Way to go, Romeo," I said to let him know I heard.

He flipped the other bun on top and pressed it down with his palm. "I'm embarrassed to discuss this, y'know."

"Yeah. When I was your age, I felt the same way."

"Madison asked me if I had ever had sex on the boat."

"How did you answer the question?"

"I told her I had never had sex on the boat. I think she wants to have sex with me on your boat. It'll be the first time."

"No, it won't. Over the years, I have made love with Terry and Vicky and Miyo on the boat." My last tryst with Miyo came unbidden to my mind; I pushed it aside. "How many dates have you two had?"

"Three."

"*Hmm*. That would be the fourth date. If you two were in your twenties, I'd say it's time, even overdue. As for teenagers, I have no clue."

Clint stirred his iced tea. "What should I do?"

"Are you asking for permission? Use the *Gator Raider* whenever you want. You know where we keep the keys. As for the sex, you're an adult. You don't need my permission, and I happen to believe sex is great with someone you love or at least care for. Just make sure there are no... unintended consequences."

"You mean like a baby. Don't worry. I always carry a condom in case I get lucky.

I smirked. "Remember to change the sheets afterward. Oh, wait... Madison isn't eighteen, is she? Are you afraid her parents will find out and charge you with statutory rape?"

Clint stood and paced around the kitchen. "That's not it, bro." He stopped and cleared his throat. "It will be my first time. Period."

Awkward silence. "Oh," I said. "There's a first time for everybody. It's no disgrace."

"I know. It's just... I'm pretty sure Madison isn't a virgin. She said she never had sex *on a boat*, but she didn't say she had never had sex *period*. I don't want to be embarrassed."

"Oh. That's different." I took another bite of hamburger while I ruminated. I knew what I should do, but it was embarrassing. I decided to make the sacrifice.

"Clint, old buddy, I have my own embarrassing history which I never told anyone."

"I can hardly wait."

"Promise you will never share this with another living soul."

Clint raised his hand. "I swear."

"Did I tell you about Liz Johannes, my first love?"

"Nope."

"Liz and I met when we were sophomores at Theodore Roosevelt High

School. I made the football team and played a pretty good second-string tight end. Liz was in my homeroom and flirted with me all through football season, but I was terrified of girls."

"You? Afraid of girls? You're not afraid of anything."

"You better believe it, bro. Not only was I afraid of girls in high school, I still am. Here's the first humiliating secret: I've never asked a girl for a date—not the first date anyway. Every woman I have ever dated asked me first."

Clint's eyes narrowed. "Really?"

I raised my right hand. "Hand to God. I never asked any woman for a first date. I can converse with any adult, man or woman, on regular social topics: weather, sports, the economy. Even religion and politics. But girls terrified me. The spring semester of our sophomore year, Liz cornered me after a school assembly as we walked back to class. She grabbed my hand, pulled me into a janitor's closet, and kissed me so hard I thought she would suck my tongue out of my head. Startled the heck out of me."

"No kidding?"

"No kidding."

"That was your first French kiss?"

I nodded. "Next excruciating secret: I said the most stupid thing I could say."

"What was that?"

"I said, 'What did you do that for?'"

Clint smirked. "You didn't."

I raised my hand again. "Hand to God. And Liz answered, 'Because I want you to be my boyfriend.' I said okay, and she said I should learn to kiss better. She promised to teach me after school, because we shouldn't be late to class."

"That's incredible. Now I don't feel so bad."

"There's more. After school, she took me back to the janitor's closet and gave me kissing lessons." I grinned. "She was a good, enthusiastic teacher."

"Did, uh... did you... have sex with her?"

"Not then. A few days later, we were making out in the janitor's closet, and she said, 'Now that we're boyfriend and girlfriend, I want us to have sex, but not here. Our first time, we should do it in a bed. After that, it's okay to sneak around, but our first time should be special.' Two weeks later, her parents went to the movies, Liz called me to come over, and we made love in her bedroom. It was my first time, but not hers."

Clint asked, "How'd it go?"

"Sloppy, awkward, embarrassing. And wonderful. Like that old joke: The worst sex I ever had was magnificent. Again, Liz was a good, enthusiastic teacher. To tell the truth, I believe part of my attraction for Liz was she figured me for a virgin, and she wanted to be my first."

"You think Madison sees me as another notch on her gun? Or maybe her bedpost?"

"I have no experience of such things other than Liz Johannes. Maybe Madison likes you."

THIRTY

Pete Martinez came back from L.A. on Wednesday and brought a McDonald's sack into my conference room. He dumped a half-dozen Egg McMuffins on the coffee table. "I drove straight from the airport. I haven't had breakfast."

"If you came straight here, where did you buy the Egg McMuffins?"

"Okay, smart ass, I came *almost* straight from the airport. I stopped at a McDonald's drive-thru. You hungry?"

"I'm always hungry." I pulled two Egg McMuffins toward me.

"I know it's eleven a.m. for you, but it's eight a.m. in L.A., and I caught the red-eye from LAX. I avoid airline food. Consider this my late breakfast and your early lunch. I got four hours sleep, but I flew business class. It wasn't so bad."

"You avoid airline food, but you bought breakfast at McDonald's."

"Don't be such a snob; it's actually quite healthful."

"Hey, I love McDonald's too, but I also eat airline food. I never met a meal I didn't like."

The receptionist walked in with two coffees.

"Thanks, Betty."

She closed the door behind her.

I unwrapped my first Egg McMuffin. "What did you learn in L.A.?"

Pete washed down a bite of sandwich before he replied. "It's not Carmelo Sarducci nor Georgy Pops that killed the girl. I have a friend who has a friend in the FBI. He introduced me to this guy in the Los Angeles field office. They have surveilled Carmelo and Georgy Pops for the last six weeks. Wiretaps, surveillance, a regular full court press. Sarducci and Pops did shady stuff, but none of it had to do with a hit in Port City or Nashville, not even in Chicago."

That's all I needed—another dead end with the first Orlando concert in two days.

Terry Kovacs sauntered into Jerry's Gym as I was banging out quad extensions on the leg machine.

She cast an eye over the noisy room until her gaze caught mine. She smiled and glided across the floor like a debutante enters a ballroom. She moved so gracefully that I stopped pumping iron to watch. She wore stretch jeans and a red tank top over a pink sports bra. Two braided hoop earrings hung from each ear with a matching gold necklace. Her makeup and hair looked as good as I had ever seen it.

"We need to talk, Chuck. How long before you finish?"

"Hello to you too. Did you come to work out?"

"I worked out this morning." If she had dolled up for me, it was working.

"If you worked out today, why did you come back?"

She scanned the area to see if anyone could overhear us. "You're sharper than this, Sherlock. I worked out three times in the last two weeks while you were here. Each time I made sure you noticed me."

I had noticed Terry. Boy, how I had noticed her.

It had been ten months since two gangsters invaded my home and almost killed my fiancée, Miyoki Takashi, by mistake. I still felt responsible.

Miyo's parents had opposed our engagement and had disapproved of me personally. As soon as Miyo had gotten out of the ICU and improved enough to travel, her parents flew her to California for her physical rehab.

158

A few months later, I learned she had returned to Port City, but she never answered my messages or texts. After a couple of weeks of being ghosted, I got the message: Miyo never wanted to see me again.

Each night for ten months, I had stared at the ceiling and contemplated the damage I might cause to another woman if I fell in love again.

Two years before, I had been falling in love with Terry before she dumped me. Now here she was. If I let myself, I could fall in love with her again. Doing that would put her at the same risk as Miyo. Not to mention my personal pain if another girlfriend broke my heart or, God forbid, got killed because of me.

Then, two weeks ago, Terry had shown up at Jerry's Gym looking as good as she had two years before.

She clapped her hands and waved in front of my face. "Earth to McCrary… Do you read me? Come in, McCrary… Where did you go?"

"Sorry. I was thinking of something else. You were saying…?"

"I've worked out here for the last two weeks, and I made sure you saw me each time. As you often say: Do the math. I put three strikes across the plate and you didn't swing at a single pitch."

Terry stopped and waited for me to say something.

Of course, I had spotted every pitch. I didn't swing at one because I knew I might hit a home run, and I wasn't ready to get in the game. Silence was working for me, so I stuck with it.

Terry leaned closer. "I figured it was time to take direct action. After my shift, I drove by and recognized your car in the lot. And, no, I wasn't dressed this way at work; I went home to change. I hope you appreciate the effort." She put her lips to my ear and whispered, "I'll wait at Java Jenny's while you clean up."

Her scent filled my nostrils and stirred feelings that had lain dormant since Miyo's near-fatal injury. Her whisper in my ear stirred other things. I remembered the same light-headed feeling the first time we met, so many centuries before. Or was it yesterday?

"I'll be there."

Terry Kovacs

Terry wanted the window table where she and Chuck sat on their first *almost-date*, as she had called it. Another couple sat there, dawdling over their empty cups.

Terry bought two coffees and two chocolate chip cookies and put them on a tray. She stood near the window table holding the tray, hoping the couple would take the hint and leave before Chuck arrived.

The man eyed Terry and resumed his conversation with the woman. Five minutes later, Terry cleared her throat and stepped closer. "Excuse me, but can I ask you all a small favor?"

The couple glanced up.

"My boyfriend is meeting me here. It's the third anniversary of our first date, and we sat at this exact table three years ago. I hoped he and I could sit here, if it's no trouble." It wasn't their third anniversary, but she didn't feel bad telling the white lie. Chuck wasn't her boyfriend anymore either, but she had hopes.

The man frowned, but his date stood and smiled at Terry. "That's so romantic." She smiled at the man and gestured him up. "Of course, you can have this table. We were killing time. We can do it elsewhere."

"Thanks so much."

The woman slipped her hand through her date's arm as they walked away. "Happy anniversary."

Terry arranged the coffee and cookies with a sigh of relief and waited for Chuck to show.

Twenty minutes later, she watched Chuck dodge traffic through the light sprinkle as he crossed the street.

He saw her through the window and waved.

She waved back and remembered their first, almost-date three years earlier...

Terry was a take-charge person from the first time she spoke to Chuck. She had worked out at Jerry's Gym for two weeks, eyeing the tall, handsome, well-built stranger whenever she could. She smiled at him every time, but he didn't notice. She wondered if he was gay, but Kennedy Carlson, the gym owner, assured her he was straight and unattached.

She wore tight shorts and bikini underwear that a blind man would notice. She smiled at the mysterious hunk each time he passed. For a week, he remained oblivious.

One day the hunk smiled back.

She widened her smile and nodded a greeting as she glided to the stair-climber. By God, if he didn't ogle her first-class ass and bikini underwear, he was dead inside.

After she finished the stair-climber, she peered over her shoulder and the guy was pumping leg presses with a faraway look that said his mind wasn't on her.

She walked to the leg extension machine near the entrance to the men's locker room. He had to pass there to reach the showers. She vowed to pump leg extensions until the hunk passed by or she collapsed from exhaustion, whichever came first.

It hadn't taken long. The stranger walked her way and she smiled wider this time. He stopped and watched her from a short distance. After a minute or so, he resumed his walk toward the locker room.

Okay, she had thought, *time for Plan B.*

Terry paused to catch her breath. "I joined the gym."

The man stopped dead—a deer-in-the-headlights look on his face.

Omigod, is he shy? A hunk like him? Ken didn't mention that.

Terry continued. "Ken said you've been a member of the gym for a long time?" She made it a question, giving the hunk a great opportunity.

He nodded.

Geez, talk about a man of few words. Didn't his momma ever give him flirting lessons? How do I get this guy to talk?

She raised an eyebrow and waited.

He spoke. "I joined three years ago. It's convenient to my office and townhouse."

"I take it Ken owns the place?"

He nodded again.

Looks like I need to carry this conversation. Perhaps I should ask a question he can't answer with a nod. "Why does Ken call it Jerry's Gym?"

"Ken bought it from a guy named Jerry. Ken jokes he was too cheap to buy a new sign."

She pumped the leg machine once more, then stood. "Makes sense. If it ain't broke... You said your office is nearby. What do you do for a living?"

"I'm a private investigator."

Now we're making progress. "What a coincidence; I'm a cop." She wiped her hand on a towel and stuck it out. "Teresa Kovacs."

After showering, he met her twenty-five minutes later at Java Jenny's. But after two hours of getting-to-know-you, she had to coach him on how to ask her to dinner.

After the dinner date, she invited him into her apartment and asked him to stay the night.

Months later, after Chuck got serious about the relationship, she had dumped him with a text message. She felt terrible then, and she felt guilty now. She was no alcoholic, but she knew how to make amends. That's why she was here now, waiting for Chuck...

And there he was, crossing the street.

Chuck pushed open the glass door, sat across from her, and unwrapped a cookie. "Thanks for the cookie and the coffee."

He bit off a chunk of cookie, sipped his coffee, and waited.

That was so like Chuck. She had approached him, and he was clueless how to handle her. He was letting her make the next move.

Terry set her cup down. "I don't know how to say this."

"Try it in English, Spanish, or Pashto. Those are the only languages I understand. Well, that and Pig Latin."

"I'm serious, big guy."

"You know me. I'm seldom serious. One of my numerous character flaws."

Terry felt her eyes fill with tears. She clasped his hand and remembered the speech she had prepared. "I treated you badly when you didn't deserve it. I bailed out on you at the first sign of trouble, and I made a dark time even darker." Good. She had remembered her speech. Grace under pressure.

Chuck didn't squeeze her hand back, but he didn't pull loose either. "You'll get no argument from me."

She used her other hand and dabbed her eyes with a napkin. "Now that I have you cornered, you may have noticed I'm holding your hand so you can't escape."

"I didn't come here to escape. I came to discuss whatever is on your agenda. How could I say no to someone who plies me with cookies and coffee?"

He smiled and her pain lifted a little.

She released his hand and blew her nose in the napkin. "I'm sorry. I'm..." She stuck the napkin in her purse. "Sorry."

She held his gaze. "I came to apologize."

"It's not necessary."

"It may not be necessary for you, but it is for me. I memorized this speech."

Chuck smirked. "By all means then..."

She cleared her throat. "I've felt guilty for two years. I'm sorry for leaving you the way I did. I'm sorry for running out on you when you needed friends. And I'm sorry for not accepting Clint as part of your life."

Terry had resented Chuck letting Clint into their cozy relationship. To her regret, it had been one more thing that tipped her scales and caused her to dump Chuck.

She smiled. "I also apologize for other things that I can't even remember."

"Okay." Chuck squeezed her hands and released them. "If that's what bothered you, be bothered no more. I forgave you a long time ago for everything you assume you did."

"Just like that?"

"God, no. That doesn't mean that forgiving you was easy. It took time and, truth be told, a few tears." Chuck broke off another cookie chunk. "Like your apology, forgiveness wasn't something I did for you. I did it for me."

"I know what you mean." She copied his move with her own cookie. She read somewhere that mirroring another person's behavior builds rapport. She wondered if it were true.

Chuck chewed before he spoke. "I felt bitter for a long time. My anger ate at me. Eventually, I decided those negative emotions hurt me, regardless of how they affected you, or even if you knew about them."

"I felt the bad vibes, believe me."

Chuck washed his cookie down with a slug of coffee.

Terry did the same. *Whether it builds rapport or not, it can't hurt.*

They watched out the window as the afternoon rain began to fall in earnest.

"I could never have loved Miyo the way I did if I hadn't forgiven you," Chuck said. "If it makes you feel better, I never regretted one second you and I spent together."

"That does make me feel better."

"You dumping me was largely my fault. I put pressure on you—the exclusive relationship, taking Clint into my home, and all that. Our relationship wasn't ready for that much upheaval, but I pressed the issue. My mistake."

"*Girls just want to have fun,* right?" She smiled without humor.

"You told me that was your theme song."

"It was. *Was*, in past tense."

"You don't feel that way any longer?"

This was where she had been leading the conversation all along. "A lot of water has flowed under the bridge since we..." She moved her chin sideways and back, a shrug without moving her shoulders. "...since we parted. I'll admit I jumped in a couple more beds. Casual sex was fun for a long time. Today, sex seems trivial without an emotional connection." She spread her hands. "I've grown up, and I'm ready for a relationship based on more than good times and good sex."

"I changed too, Terry. After Miyo was almost killed..." Chuck stopped. His eyes were red. He swallowed. "I have taken the better part of a year to reflect on what happened and why. Miyo's father called me a vigilante and said I have an affinity for savagery. He claimed that I placed everyone I care for in danger."

Chuck twirled his cup in his hands. "Maybe he was right. If Miyo had never met me, she'd be happier today."

164

He drained his cup. "My profession is incompatible with a family or even a serious relationship."

"What about Vicky Ramirez?" Terry bit her lip. Too late to call the words back. "Sorry. I should not have said that. It's petty."

Terry knew about Chuck's relationship with Vicky. Sometimes it seemed as if everybody on the planet knew.

"Vicky and I are more buddies than lovers," Chuck said. "Our relationship can never get serious because she doesn't want a family. I respect her boundaries."

"I hope so. Even if she changed her priorities, she's beyond prime child-bearing years." Terry bit her lip again.

Damn, every time I open my mouth, I say the wrong thing.

Chuck stood. "I'm not ready for this, Terry." He left without a backward glance.

THIRTY-ONE

Carlos McCrary

Orlando's Friday night concert sold out. Nothing keeps you on your toes like watching 10,000 suspects.

After the bomb scare in Tampa, the Orlando police assigned extra officers and gave me a police radio to communicate with them. I hoped I wouldn't need it.

Since the last Tampa concert, Cleo had received no more emails from Weirdo. Five days of silence didn't mean the threat was gone; he had skipped days between emails in the past.

LeMarvis received his threatening email the Monday after the Tampa concert. It was now Friday.

This swine hasn't faded away like a bad dream. He's somewhere in the arena, watching. Whether he'll do anything tonight is a whole 'nother question.

My security team and I had watched several rehearsals and four actual concerts. Knowing the order of the music made it easier to focus on the crowd and watch for unusual behavior. We weren't surprised or distracted by the indoor fireworks, theatrical smoke, or costume changes. We knew the routine.

I hoped this made us better at the job instead of complacent.

The opening act finished. The stage lights dimmed, and the band gathered their instruments before leaving the stage.

It was fifteen minutes before Cleo and her band came on. Some patrons headed to the restrooms, concessions, and souvenir stands.

From the press box, I scanned the scrum of fans through my binoculars as they milled at the exits. Many fans sported Cleo's Summer Fun Concert Tour tee-shirts.

Automatic gunfire shattered the murmuring crowd noise.

People dived for the floor; others stampeded toward the exits. In the grandstands, fans heard the bangs, saw the flashes, and dived behind the seats.

My cellphone flashed to life and played *Reveille*. Adding to the chaos, the Orlando police radio squawked at me.

I lowered the binoculars to widen my field of vision and scanned the area for muzzle flashes. In two seconds, I found them.

Some idiot had brought a string of firecrackers left over from the 4th of July and lit them on the arena floor.

I answered my cellphone with my left hand and the police radio with my right. "It's a string of firecrackers. Center aisle, back section. It might be a diversion. Keep your eyes peeled for action."

Four cops converged on the center aisle and grabbed a man in a black cowboy hat with a feather in the braided leather band. They frog-marched him off the floor to the cheers of the crowd.

Crowd voices rose. "Did you see that? What an idiot… I thought we were dead… I damned near wet my pants…"

I texted my security team:

Snoop is in charge. I'm headed to the police HQ to talk to the pyromaniac."

For their control center, the police had selected a medium-sized conference room on the concourse behind the stage. That's where they would take the suspect.

A twenty-something girl in western clothes stood outside the door talking to a uniformed cop. She held two plastic beer cups. She dressed like a country singer herself. "What's the big deal? It was a practical joke, for

God's sake. Chet didn't mean anything by it. Nobody got hurt. Can't you let him go?"

Stopping six feet away, I didn't want to invade her space. "Are you with the guy who set off the fireworks?"

"Who wants to know?" she asked.

"I'm head of security. I'll see what I can do for your friend."

The guy was handcuffed, sitting at a six-foot catering table against the back wall. An Orlando cop set the suspect's cowboy hat on the table and removed the handcuffs. "You want coffee?"

The suspect's eyes were wide and his face flushed. After the cops manhandled him out, I doubted he expected them to offer coffee. "No, thanks. I left my beer with my girlfriend."

"She's outside waiting for you," I said from the doorway.

"Oh, geez." He tucked his long-sleeved, khaki western work shirt back inside his faded boot-cut blue jeans. He sported a tooled leather belt with a silver buckle the size of a license plate and shiny black cowboy boots with a walking heel. Late twenties, three-day beard, neatly trimmed. He dressed like a Wrangler ad.

Orlando Police Sergeant Jack Wilson saw me and nodded me over. "You want in on this, Chuck?"

"I would. Thanks, Jack."

Wilson was Hollywood's archetype Good Cop. Steel-gray hair, close cropped. Angular chin, hawkish nose. Ice blue eyes. Near retirement, but with a don't-mess-with-me build, all angles and planes. Grabbing a folding chair, I sat across from the hapless urban cowboy.

Wilson settled in his chair. "I'm Sergeant Jack Wilson. What's your name, son?" Yep, he was gonna be Good Cop. I could play Bad Cop if needed, but the guy was already scared.

"Chet Stroud."

Wilson wrote that down. "Tell us what happened, Chet."

Another uniformed cop walked over with a fingerprint scanner. "Put your right thumb on this, please."

Chet gaped at the scanner. "Where do I put it?"

"Place it on this screen... Good." The uniform punched buttons. "Now your left... Thanks." He faced Wilson. "That should be enough to identify him, Sarge."

Wilson nodded his thanks and refocused on Chet. "What happened, Chet?"

"How much trouble am I in?"

Wilson spread his hands. "If you cooperate with us, a misdemeanor. It's your choice. You've been read your rights. You want to discuss it?"

"This guy came up to me at the beer stand and asked if I had a sense of humor."

Wilson's eyes cut to me. "What guy?"

"Some guy. He asked me if I had a sense of humor, and I said of course I did. Then he showed me these firecrackers he had under his jacket and offered me two hundred bucks to light them during intermission."

"How much you had to drink, son?"

"A couple of beers is all."

"Describe this guy."

"He was taller than me."

"Did he wear boots?"

Chet's eyes widened. "Oh, shit. I didn't notice. That makes a difference, doesn't it?" He regarded his own boots. "Maybe two inches."

"And how tall are you?"

"Six-two."

Wilson waved a hand. "What color hair?"

"Regular hair. Brown but kinda long."

Wilson eyed me again. I had briefed him on the wig we found in Tampa.

"What color were his eyes?"

"Didn't notice. He was white, though, if that helps." His eyes shot wide open. "Blue eyes. I remember because he reminded me of Keith Urban, what with the hair over his ears.

"How old was he?"

"Mid-thirties maybe? I didn't pay attention. I was scoping out the girls in the lobby." His eyes widened. "For God's sakes, don't tell my girlfriend. She held our seats while I bought the beer."

He gazed back at Wilson. "He was just a guy you talk to in the beer line, y'know?"

"What was he wearing?"

"A blue jean jacket."

"Pants?"

"Didn't notice. Sorry."

Wilson glanced my way. "Any questions?"

"Yes." Shaking hands with Chet, I said, "Chuck McCrary. I run security for Cleo and her band."

"You mean you work for Cleo?"

"That's right. Did you know there was a shooting at her concert in Port City?"

Chet nodded. "My girlfriend said something about a mob hit at a concert. Was that Cleo's concert?"

"Right again, and did you know about the bomb scare in Tampa last week?"

"Bomb? There was a bomb?"

"No. It was a bomb *scare*, not a real bomb. It wasn't armed, and we found it during a routine security check before the concert." That was true-ish. No point in freaking out our best witness. "But you can see why my security team is concerned for Cleo's safety more than at a regular concert. Do you still have the two 100s?"

"If was four 50s. I used one of them to buy the beer." Chet started to reach in his pocket and I put a hand on his arm.

"Don't touch the money. It's evidence in a murder case, and Sergeant Wilson wants it. It may have the suspect's fingerprints. Put on these gloves before you take your money out so you don't get more prints on it." I handed him a pair of crime scene gloves. "Don't worry. I'll give you different bills to replace the evidence."

Chet tugged a wad of bills from his pocket and laid them on the table.

Wilson put on gloves and peeled three 50s from the outside of the roll. The remaining bills were twenties or smaller. "These the ones?"

"Yes, sir."

I handed Chet two 100s. "Keep the change. Thanks for your

cooperation. Please show us the beer stand where the guy gave you the money."

The cop who took Chet's prints approached the table. "He's clean, Sarge. No record."

Wilson stood. "Chet, after you show us the beer stand, I'm gonna let you go. Please don't do anything like this again, okay? You might cause a stampede and people could get trampled. Maybe even you and your girlfriend."

As the three of us exited the room, the girlfriend jumped up from the bench she was on. "I brought your beer."

The four of us walked down the corridor, and the opening chords of Cleo's entrance echoed from the arena.

"Is Cleo as tall in person as she looks on YouTube?" Chet asked.

"She's six-foot-four, but you can see for yourself. After you show us which beer stand, you're free to go."

The rest of the concert proceeded without incident. After Cleo left the stage, I returned to the police HQ.

Sergeant Wilson cued the security videos from the beer stand. "Got a good picture of the suspect, not that it does any good."

"Why not?"

"You'll see." He played the video.

Chet Stroud was eight people back in the beer line. His black hat with the feather in the band made him easy to spot. Our suspect walked up from an angle which kept his back to the camera. Straight brown hair reached to the collar of his blue jean jacket. He wore a generic beige cowboy hat with a plain black band.

"He never faces the camera," Wilson said.

"Did you find him coming through security?"

"Yeah. I'll punch it up." He fiddled with the keyboard and another video played. "That's him in the sunglasses. Between the shades and the hat and the wig, we don't know what he looks like, just that he's over six-feet-four-inches." Wilson leaned back from the controls. "At least we know he has blue eyes."

I shook my head. "This guy is smart. He wore a rubber skull cap beneath his wig in Tampa and vinyl gloves. We've never found a fingerprint. Easy enough to obtain blue contact lenses."

I didn't know, and I didn't know what I didn't know. I felt helpless, as if an elevator had dropped too fast. When and where would I hit bottom?

THIRTY-TWO

It was midnight when I walked across the parking lot. My Dodge Grand Caravan squatted on the tire rims. I walked around the crouching vehicle. Someone had slashed all four tires. *Guess who?* My stomach turned a backflip as I realized Weirdo knew who I was and what I drove.

I wasn't anonymous, but he was. I didn't care for those odds.

I dropped to a crouch and scanned the nearly empty lot. The distinctive red laser light of a gunsight flashed a warning.

I dove to one side. The muzzle flash confirmed the shooter's location. An eyeblink later, my van fender thrummed as a bullet punched a hole in the metal as the bark of a gunshot reached me.

Cascading metal chips pelted me as I rolled behind the van and drew my pistol.

Another shot punched through the van and exited the window I had ducked behind.

I rapid-fired four rounds toward the muzzle flash.

My ears rang from my own shots, but I heard a big engine start. Far across the lot, a dark-colored pickup truck with no headlights roared to life and sped away on screeching tires.

I squeezed off four more rounds, but at that distance I had less chance of hitting it than I did of shooting a basket from the far end of a basketball court. Perhaps it would discourage the bastard, but I doubted it.

The lot had no security cameras; I wouldn't find the pickup unless I had gotten lucky and punched a bullet hole in it. Even then, if it were drivable, the shooter could patch the holes with Bondo and touch-up paint.

I knew he drove a dark-colored pickup. *Whoopee!* There were gazillions of dark pickups. Weirdo knew I had spotted him; he would change vehicles.

I was still nowhere.

I holstered my pistol and examined my hands. My dive and roll across the pavement had left the knuckles on my left hand and the heel of my right hand scraped and bloody. The knees on my khaki pants were shredded.

The pain from the scrapes on my hands wasn't what kept me awake that night. What the hell did this guy have planned for tomorrow night's concert?

The cop who took my report eyeballed the antiseptic ointment on my hands and asked about it.

"I took a dive the instant I saw the laser light. Shredded the knees on my pants too."

He regarded my pants, nodded, and took some notes. "Let me see your sidearm."

I handed it over, butt first, and he smelled the barrel. "How many shots did you fire?"

"Eight, I think. Let me check the magazine."

"I'll do it." He ejected the magazine. "Eleven left. Yeah, you shot eight times." He handed the Glock to me.

"It's the same guy I mentioned." I described where the shots came from. "You should find two spent 5.56-millimeter NATO cartridges there."

"We did."

"If it's like his first attack, the cartridges have fingerprints from a man named Jeffrey Wister." I explained the prints the Port City cops found.

"The prints aren't from Jeffrey Wister."

That was a shock. "Who are they from?"

"They aren't in IAFIS, so we don't know yet."

"It's gotta be the same guy who shot Fortunata Torelli."

"You know anybody else that wants you dead besides your Port City shooter?"

"I've got enemies, yeah."

"Could be one of them, or it could be the Port City shooter collected brass from a different patsy who was shooting at the Everglades Gun Range or even a different range. No way to tell. You gonna cancel tonight's concert?"

My watch said it was 3:30 a.m. Now it was Saturday, July 15. "I'll recommend that, but it will be up to my clients."

"If they hold the concert, I'll increase our uniformed presence." He smiled. "I have a hunch you're right; it is the same guy."

I returned his smile. "Always glad for assistance from our uniformed friends."

Cleo and LeMarvis took the news of the attack on me in stride. Maybe there had been so many dangerous episodes that they were used to explaining them away.

Or maybe having stars in their eyes made it hard to see the real world.

"There's no need to cancel the concerts, Chuck," LeMarvis said. "Attendance has exceeded our expectations. The next few concerts will sell out. Cleo is on her way to stardom." He smiled at her. "That's what Cleo wants—to be a country music superstar, and that's what I want for her."

"I hate to talk myself out of a job, folks, but I think it was the same weirdo. He will attack again, and he could kill again. You should cancel the concert tour until the cops can put this nut behind bars."

"I disagree," LeMarvis said. "Maybe some vandal shot out your windows, and you were in the way. Or maybe it was one of *your* old enemies. *Our* weirdo paid the guy to set off fireworks. There was no real danger; it was a prank. The shots at you were after the concert. I don't think that had anything to do with Cleo."

From my viewpoint, Cleo and LeMarvis had fallen waist-deep into a cesspool of wishful thinking.

If it served their egos to view the world through rose-colored glasses, nothing I could say would change their mind. I hoped their gullibility didn't get another innocent person killed.

Or me.

By that evening, the skin on the heel of my right hand and the knuckles of my left felt stiff from new scabs, but they didn't restrict my movements. I had left the scrapes unbandaged to avoid calling attention to them.

Saturday night's concert went so well I was afraid the ceiling might fall or lightning might strike. I waited for the other shoe to drop.

It appeared that Cleo and LeMarvis's optimism was justified.

I convened our usual after-action debrief with the security team. I gestured at the smaller table in the corner. "There's more coffee."

The door flew open and an Orlando cop barged in. "There's been a shooting in the parking lot."

THIRTY-THREE

A body sprawled on the pavement like a doll dropped by a careless child. His sightless eyes gaped at the midnight sky. He wore an orange golf shirt, blue jeans, and leather sandals that I recognized from earlier in the day. A gym bag lay nearby. A nimbus of blood spread a halo around his head. A pea-sized hole marred the victim's forehead. It was smaller than a 9-millimeter slug. Judging from the brain matter sprayed across the asphalt, the exit wound in the back of his head was the size of a golf ball, not a softball.

Three uniformed cops with their arms extended barred the small crowd from the area where brains and blood stained the asphalt. Another cop laid down yellow evidence markers to delineate the crime scene.

The stench of blood, urine, and feces hung in the humid, windless air. From Afghanistan to Iraq to Port City, I had witnessed too many scenes like this. My stomach clenched as I swallowed my gorge.

"Anybody recognize him?" a police sergeant asked.

"It's Andy Stanley," I said, "the drummer."

A thirty-something blonde in a dark blue pantsuit stood as I walked into the precinct interview room. "I'm Detective Ella Meyer."

I heard the capital D in Detective. Ella Meyer was a successful woman in what had once been a man's world, and she was proud of it.

We shook hands. "I'm Chuck McCrary."

"I appreciate you coming down on a Sunday, Mr. McCrary. What can you tell me about the drummer?"

"I'll tell you everything I know, but it's not about the drummer. The murderer intended to terrorize Cleo Hennessey. And please, call me Chuck." I filled her in on the events of the last few weeks.

Detective Meyer sipped her tea and made notes in a small, neat hand while I talked. She didn't interrupt me often. When she did, her questions were insightful. She was interested in how the fingerprints of Jeffrey Wister were found on the shells from the first shooting. She was polite and in control of the interview. After dealing with Bubble-Gum Beltran, I enjoyed the chance to work with a professional.

Thirty minutes into our interview, she peered at her empty cup and consulted her watch. "I could use another cup and a bagel. Can we move this interview to the break room?"

"I second the motion."

Ella Meyer sat across from me in the break room and spread crème cheese on a bagel.

I stirred half-and-half into my coffee. "We never had crème cheese when I was on the job. We ate donuts and *pastelitos* back in the day."

She slid the cheese container across the table to me. "It's not like we have a crème cheese budget. We take turns bringing it from home."

There was a large glass jar with dollar bills and quarters inside on the service counter. "Is that the coffee kitty?"

She peered over her shoulder. "Yeah."

After stuffing a fiver in the jar, I returned to the table.

"You didn't need to do that, Chuck. You are a guest of the department."

"My ole grandpappy says that his philosophy is to always leave the woodpile higher than he found it."

"In that case, help yourself to a bagel."

I smeared a dollop across a raisin bagel. "Thanks."

She chewed on her bagel, swallowed and wiped her mouth with a paper napkin. "You said the killing is about Cleopatra Hennessey instead of the drummer. You might reconsider."

My mouth was full, so I motioned her to go on.

"Andy Stanley's rap sheet came back from Port City, along with a phone call from a buddy in the Port City Organized Crime Division."

"I've read Stanley's rap sheet, Ella. He was a junkie. According to one cast member I interviewed, half the band does drugs."

"Stanley didn't just take drugs, Chuck; he *dealt* drugs. OCD never arrested him for dealing, so it's not on his record. After I requested the rap sheet from Port City, my buddy saw my name and called me with a heads-up. He told me that Stanley was a dealer and a user, and he heard rumors that Stanley stiffed a supplier. He called to warn me that Stanley was involved with a gang."

That surprised me; Snoop said Stanley wasn't the type. "What gang?"

She nodded. "The Garcias."

That put a whole new light on the killing. A cold chill ran down my spine as I recalled meeting the *jefe*—chief—of the South Florida drug cartel. "I crossed swords with the Garcias last year when I investigated a different gang, also involved in sex-trafficking." In that undercover role, I played a would-be supplier and risked my life every time I was with the *jefe*, an inhuman predator with eyes that showed as much life as two ball bearings.

She lifted her tea cup. "The Garcias have a reputation as ruthless, predatory killers with long memories."

"That's true, Ella. No one with two brain cells to rub together double-crosses the Garcia gang."

"The two shell casings from the guy who shot your car Friday night had unidentified fingerprints on them. The reporting officer's notes said that you think it's the stalker who killed the girl singer."

"Gotta be. What about the guy who shot Andy Stanley? Find any brass?"

"Yeah. Two .22-long-rifle casings with no prints."

"Different gun. If my weirdo wanted to terrorize Cleo Hennessey, he might use the same gun. It's a different shooter, unless he's wants me to

179

think it's a different shooter, throwing me off track. He's devilishly smart."

Ella nodded. "I gotta start somewhere. The Garcias often use .22-long-rifle slugs. I intend to investigate the Stanley murder as a gang killing."

Despite the different bullets, the murder didn't smell like a Garcia hit. Ruthless, yes, but the Garcias made bad examples of dealers who didn't pay. They would have tortured Andy Stanley before killing him. Snoop described Stanley as an easy-going country boy. Stanley hadn't struck me as either brave enough or stupid enough to cross the Garcias.

There was no point in arguing with Ella Meyer. Perhaps she was right, but I would make my own investigation regardless.

Lester

Lester read the Monday Orlando newspaper and laughed out loud. His ruse worked. The Orlando cops thought the assassination was drug-related.

Another stroke of luck. The Demons of Revenge looked up from hell and smiled on me. Even I couldn't anticipate that the idiot drummer was involved with the Garcia gang.

He was glad he had switched tactics on his terror campaign. Let the bitch think he'd gone away. Then... Wham!

But I need McCrary out of the way. How the hell did he dodge that bullet?

THIRTY-FOUR

Carlos McCrary

Monday morning, I arrived at Jerry's Gym while our local Mexican free-tail bats hunted insects in the pre-dawn twilight. After I had busted my butt in Orlando for four days, I needed a workout and a sweat to clear my pores and my head.

I had worked my way to the lat pull-downs when Terry emerged from the women's locker room. She scanned the room, smiled as she spotted me, and headed my way like a heat-seeking missile.

That put an end to clearing my head. After our coffee date at Java Jenny's, I had left for Orlando and we hadn't talked since. That was fine with me. I hadn't given our relationship—or lack thereof—any thought.

Again, Terry was pressing the issue.

"In case you wonder how I knew you were here," Terry said, "I asked Ken to text me when you got back."

"Ken is a big fan of romance." I toweled my face and hands. I didn't expect a hug or a cheek kiss. We never did that when we were sweating in the gym. "I'm glad to see you. I was insensitive last week."

"I deserved it," Terry replied. "I acted like a jealous bitch even though I have no claim on you. Mentioning Vicky was off base."

"Let's finish our workouts and meet across the street. I'll buy this time."

Might as well get it over.

Someone was sitting at our favorite window table. Another table was available in the back, and I bought two coffees and two chocolate bagels. I finished my first bagel and bought another before Terry showed.

As I stood to greet her, she kissed my cheek. Her familiar fragrance made my head swim. Again. This would be a difficult conversation, but I owed it to her.

She lifted her coffee. "You smell good, Chuck. What's that fragrance?"

"Soap."

"Well, whatever it is, I miss that."

"That's what I want to discuss. To explain why I'm not fit for a serious relationship."

Terry's eyebrows rose. She must not have expected that.

"Have one." I shoved a bagel across the table. "There are more if you want."

She unwrapped it. "You're not *fit* for a relationship? What does that mean? Do you think you're undeserving?"

"You heard about the murder at Cleo Hennessey's concert at the Falcon's Nest three weeks ago?"

"Yes. A girl singer was shot. Were you involved in that?"

"Yes. I'm in charge of security for Cleo's concert tour. The guy who did the shooting is a nutcase, but he's a smart nutcase." I related the events of the previous three weeks and included the attempt on my life after the Orlando concert.

"This guy is smart. He's rich enough to throw around money, buy illegal explosives, travel to Cleo's concerts, and then abandon expensive weapons. To top it off, he's crazy. That's a bad combination. Anybody who is connected to this—to me—is in danger."

"Why doesn't Cleo cancel the concert tour?"

"She convinced herself—I think her agent helped convince her—that the singer's death in Port City was a professional hit hired by a Southern California *mafioso*. The dead girl was involved with some L.A. drug scene seven years ago. The Orlando police detective figures the Garcia gang killed the dead drummer because the shooter used .22 long-rifle bullets and they found no prints. The shots fired at me bore unknown fingerprints, so we can't tie them to anyone. Three different guns maybe, but I believe it was the same shooter."

Terry absorbed that before replying.

"So, your client or her agent rationalized that the danger is over," she said.

"Or never existed in the first place. Cleo and her boyfriend LeMarvis Jones have stars in their eyes; they refuse to see any evidence that she is in danger, but they're wrong. The guy is after me too. That means anyone I'm close to is a target."

"Chuck, let me tell you about my week. The day after I button-holed you at the gym, I investigated a drug dealer we had put a full-court press on. I worked a part of Uptown the yuppies haven't gentrified yet. A meth-head assaulted me with a seven-inch knife. He was so cranked that I hit him twice with a taser before he dropped. Last Saturday, I attended the funeral of a patrol cop killed as he and his partner responded to a domestic violence case. His partner is in the hospital, but she'll make a full recovery."

She squeezed my hand. "I'm in a dangerous profession myself. Cops, firefighters, hell, even EMTs get ambushed. You and I live in dangerous worlds. It comes with the job, and that won't change whether you and I get together or not."

She held my hand while she talked, and I drank my coffee with the other hand and considered how to explain my state of mind.

"After Miyo…" I choked and tried again. "After Miyo… I'm not sure I could take that again." I pulled my hand loose. "I won't take the chance. I'm sorry."

THIRTY-FIVE

Weirdo's emails stayed quiet. He hadn't sent any more *Defender of White America* emails to LeMarvis either, assuming he was the same nut. My desperate shots at a fleeing pickup truck wouldn't scare him off. He was out there, waiting for the Jacksonville concerts to make his next move.

Once again, I asked Cleo to cancel the tour. No luck. She and LeMarvis were so giddy that the concerts had sold out, I was lucky they didn't cancel my security contract.

I felt like the cowboy in the movie cliché who stands guard in Indian territory. The first cowboy says, "It's quiet out there," and the other cowboy says, "Yeah. *Too* quiet."

My security team did our usual prep work in Jacksonville. We searched and sealed the hiding places we could find. We tested the security cameras that recorded every vehicle entering the parking lot and adjacent garage. We would send the record of every license plate to a security software company who would compare the license plates of all vehicles that entered all three nights. If Weirdo hadn't changed vehicles, we might get a vehicle description and a license plate.

The hall was smaller than the one in Orlando. Cleo would perform three sold-out shows. Seven thousand suspects to watch at once. Whoopee.

My observation post was a metal platform near the ceiling at the rear of the hall, far from the stage and its flashing lights. Two spotlights and their operators occupied each end of the same platform. I took the middle space which was designed for a TV camera. The platform provided me and the two spotlight jockeys a view of everyone in the hall.

We had ten minutes before the doors opened, and we chatted a while. The jockey on my left was a Jacksonville native, a sophomore at a local university studying theater and drama. The jockey on my right described himself as a West Virginia hillbilly who loved country music.

A proscenium arch filled with video screens soared from one side of the sixty-foot stage to the other. Above it, a navy-blue curtain hung from the seventy-foot ceiling to the top of the arch. As the fans entered, the video screens flashed a rainbow of colors, painting the arch with bands of red, orange, yellow, green, blue, indigo, and violet. Outside the video screens, two dozen automated, movable spotlights flashed and twirled with an infinite number of colors. A dozen more spotlights with operators ringed the mezzanine seats.

The previous three venues lacked a proscenium arch, let alone one equipped with wall-to-wall video screens.

It was enough to give a guy a migraine.

Snoop and Gunner were posted to my left and right, respectively. Pete Martinez and two other operatives guarded the backstage area.

Mentally crossing my fingers, I waited for the opening act to finish.

No fireworks between acts this time. No bomb scares. No sniper attacks. When I returned to my van after the show, the tires were intact.

Friday's concert had passed without incident.

All was quiet—too quiet.

But we were still in Indian territory.

Lester

Lester reached the catwalk, opened the compartment door, and noted that the hand-lettered sign he had left two weeks before was undisturbed.

$50,000 reward!!! You have won the Hidden Treasure Hunt. Call this number to collect your prize!

No one had called the burner phone he purchased for this test.

No one had been here. He wouldn't be disturbed.

He lifted a folded quilt from his duffel bag and spread it on the compartment's steel floor. Thirteen hours until the concert. Lester smiled. *I literally have thirteen hours to kill.* The pun pleased him.

Carlos McCrary

I nodded at the two spotlight jockeys as I took my position between their high-tech lights. The fans began to arrive for Saturday night's concert as I scanned the floor and watched. My phone signaled a text from the woman monitoring license plates.

I called her back. "I'm new at this, what does the text mean?"

Rebecca Toussaint, the security software supervisor said, "It's a license plate and description of a vehicle that attended last night's concert."

"I recognized that it's a license plate." I pulled out a notepad. "What's the vehicle description?"

"It's a silver Chevrolet Malibu. The numbers in the text mean the model year was in that range."

"It says 2004-2008. Which year?"

"Sometime between the 2004 and 2008 model years. Those years look so similar that our algorithm can't tell the difference."

"Did you check it against the employee license plates?"

"Yes, sir. It's not on the list you gave me."

"Where is it parked?"

"The interior cameras aren't connected to our license plate algorithm, only the ones at the entrance and exit ramps. Sorry."

"No problem, Rebecca. This is good information. Good job."

I called Pete Martinez.

"Pete, our shooter may be here. Rebecca Toussaint alerted me that a silver Chevrolet Malibu 2004 to 2008 model entered the garage, and it was here last night. Who's guarding backstage?"

"Robby and Morris." Morris Martinez, also a cop, was Pete's cousin.

"Take Angelina Curtis. Start at the top floor of the garage. Angie can start at the bottom. Find that car and post a guard on it. I'll text you the license number."

"I'm on it, boss." He disconnected.

I forwarded the text to Pete and Angelina.

My phone rang again: Rebecca Toussaint. "We got another alert. Wait... two more alerts."

"Two more cars that came last night?"

"Yes, sir. That's unusual so I decided to call instead of text." She read me the vehicle information.

"Think with me, Rebecca. How could that be?"

"Perhaps they enjoyed last night's concert so much they wanted to see it again."

"All three concerts sold out several days ago."

"You don't know much about concerts, do you, sir?"

"I don't get out often. What did I miss?"

"Scalpers and ticket-resellers. It's easy to get seats to a sold-out concert. All it takes is money."

This wasn't the first time I had felt stupid, and it wouldn't be the last.

"Thanks for telling me, Rebecca. Anything else you think I should know?"

"Yeah, another car came in that was here last night. This one's from Georgia."

By the time the opening act finished, I had received twenty-three alerts for license plates that entered the lot or garage the previous night.

I called off Pete and Angelina's car search and told them to return to their posts.

The idea had looked good on paper. Sometimes reality sucks.

Lester

The opening act music woke Lester from a sound sleep. *I must be exhausted to sleep through the musicians' tune-ups. I'll need the energy soon.*

He listened to the music as he fastened the climbing harness and laced his boots. He tidied the nest and arranged things for the Crime Scene Unit to find later. The adrenaline pulsed through his veins, purging the last of his sleep. He loved the high from anticipating the action.

Lester pulled the carbine parts from the duffel bag and assembled them, humming the tune to *Dry Bones* in his head. *The butt stock's connected to the [click] lower receiver. The lower receiver's connected to the [click] upper receiver. The upper receiver's connected to the [click] magazine. Now hear the word of the Lord.*

He smiled at his cleverness. Doing the work of the Lord.

He lifted the gunsight from its case and clicked it into position. He smoothed the quilt, stretched out, and placed his left hand under the carbine's foregrip.

He edged the gunsight's ocular lens to his eye and twisted the side focus adjustment...

Carlos McCrary

The intermission after the opening act ended, and the lights dimmed again.

Cleo's entrance was risky. Before Friday night's concert, I had objected to it, but she overruled me. "These folks paid good money to come see and hear me. Their seats are so far from the stage that they deserve a chance to get closer. If he's even here, he won't try anything with all them other people around."

Last night's entrance had gone well. Hopefully, I was worried for nothing.

Someone in the crowd chanted, "Cleo... Cleo... Cleo..." Others joined in. Soon the hall rocked to the chant and clapping hands.

The Kentucky Hillbillies struck the first notes of their opening song, amplifiers cranked up to *jet-engine* volume.

Cleo made her entrance through a set of double doors below my post. She stood on the back of an open-topped, red, white, and blue golf car—lights flashing. My agent drove the car down one of the aisles that separated the ground-floor seats into three sections. Another agent rode in the passenger seat, his head on a swivel.

Cleo held a rail mounted on the platform behind the driver where the golf clubs would be. She waved to the crowd and high-fived the fans as the car inched its way toward the stage through the pandemonium.

My agents on the golf car studied every person who extended their hands to touch Cleo's outstretched fingers. Cameras mounted in their sunglasses videoed every person.

The flashing spotlights around the proscenium blinded me again with an almost physical stab whenever the beams passed across my binoculars. Lowering the binoculars, I scanned the crowd with naked eyes.

The platform I shared with the spotlight jockeys vibrated with ear-splitting music.

The A/C vents rippled the curtains above the proscenium. Left of center in the curtain wall, the air currents opened a small gap, and a laser's red dot flashed.

Impossible. It had to be a video screen malfunction. Two spiral staircases climbed to the catwalks above. One of my agents was at the bottom of each. The shooter couldn't be there.

The laser's red dot flashed again.

No way. How could...? The attack I had dreaded and prepared for was happening. My stomach clenched like a fist.

Where was the son-of-a-bitch? Scanning the arena frantically, I hit the radio to alert my driver to grab Cleo and hide her. An eye-blink later I realized the red light had not been targeting Cleo.

The red laser scope was targeting me.

I dove off the platform, plunging seven feet to the sidewalk behind the mezzanine. The crash when I landed on my left elbow knocked the radio from my hand as I rolled to one side. On my back, I stared up at the platform I had jumped from. The two spotlight jockeys were still exposed.

One operator saw me jump. She gawked at me with concern on her face. I shouted at her to duck, but she couldn't hear me for the music. I waved at her as a bullet punched her chest and slammed her against the wall. The other jockey was so intent on swinging his light across the crowd that he was oblivious to my dive off the platform and the other operator's fate.

A fistful of bullets sprayed the spotlights, the wall, and the other operator. Chunks of insulation showered me and nearby fans. Both spotlights shattered in a hail of bullets, metal, and glass shards.

I found the radio and punched the *all-call* button. "Take Cleo down," I shouted. "The shooter is on the catwalk above the proscenium arch, behind the blue curtain. Send men to the catwalks above the stage. *Go, go, go.*"

Through it all, the Kentucky Hillbillies played on, not noticing my men had spirited Cleo back the way she had entered.

Bolting through the exit, I dashed for the stairs, knowing the action would be over before I arrived.

My agents had the shooter trapped on the catwalk. As I ran, I knew they would advance up both staircases. They would capture or kill the shooter before I could reach the backstage. Nevertheless, I sprinted at top speed.

I hit the ground floor and was halfway to the stage when the music stopped. My agents on the golf car had hustled Cleo to safety, and Pete's instructions were to clear the stage. Rule Three: *First things first, hide the women and children.*

Cleo was on her way to her dressing room surrounded by my people. Now I focused on nailing the bastard who shot the spotlight jockeys and tried to kill me.

A few ticket holders filtered from the exit into the corridor. Ignoring their shouted questions, I dodged around them, slowing just enough to open the door without crashing into it.

Backstage was chaos. Angelina Curtis corralled the band members and herded them toward their dressing rooms.

"Angelina," I called, "who went up?"

"Pete, Morris, and Robby."

In two jumps, I took the steps to the stage and leapt over the band instruments scattered on the floor. Stopping at center stage, gun drawn, I rubbernecked up.

The steel catwalks thirty feet overhead rang with my agents' steps. Pete stood on the center catwalk, Morris and Robby at either end.

"Pete," I hollered, "where is he?"

"Gone," Pete called back.

"He can't be. I'm coming up." I ran up the stairs.

Pete waited for me in the center of the proscenium. "There's an equipment room here that you can't see from the stage. He left another M4 carbine, a folded quilt, and a canvas equipment bag. He must have run after he fired the shots, but there's no way down from here. He had less than sixty seconds before we arrived. He disappeared like Houdini. Did he hit anybody?"

I felt as if someone had gut-punched me. Feeling sorry for the victims could wait. It was too late to help them, but I might catch the guy who shot them. If he had only a sixty-second head start…

THIRTY-SIX

ete indicated a small door in the rear of the proscenium. "That compartment is large enough to hide a man. He fired over the arch, then ran. I snapped photos, which I already texted to you. From what I see without climbing inside, the shooter took the scope with him and left the rifle the same as he did at the Falcon's Nest. That pile of fabric in the corner looks like a duffel bag. I didn't touch anything. How the hell did he get down those spiral stairs without us seeing him?"

"There must be another way out. He can't have gone far." I spun away from to the shooter's nest; the crime scene wasn't going anywhere. Where did the shooter go? Smart as he was, he planned an escape route. What had we missed? No, what had *I* missed?

You have seconds to catch this guy. Think fast, dummy.

Two spiral staircases. The one I ran up ended at the catwalk. The other one twirled still higher. I hadn't noticed that when we made our security survey. I assumed there was nothing above us but the girders that support the roof. Why did the stairs continue? What was at the top?

I ran to the opposite stair, my shoes clattering on the metal catwalk, and scrambled up. Two more turns on the spiral and I reached a metal platform at the top. It was squeezed under the domed roof where it slanted down. A roof-access door two feet wide by three feet tall opened off the platform, inset into the slope of the roof.

It was unlocked.

After drawing my Glock, I wedged the door past its watertight weatherstripping as I slammed the steel door open to stand on the roof, catching my breath. The night wind chilled my head, my hair wet with sweat. A skid-proof walkway painted the same color as the roof slanted down to the edge. I dashed down the walk to the metal safety rail that circled the entire roof. Lights from the ten-story parking garage next door cast a dim illumination across the scene.

A rope was knotted around the safety rail. It trailed down eighty-five feet to a grassy lawn. The sight gave me that queasy feeling I get whenever I imagine falling.

A tangle of equipment lay on the grass near the bottom of the doubled rope. Was that a climbing harness? Did the shooter rappel down the wall?

Fifty yards away, a figure in black carried a five-gallon paint can across the grass to the sidewalk. Why was a maintenance man there at this hour? He continued toward the garage, dodging concert patrons who were still arriving.

Nobody on the ground saw me.

Whipping out my phone, I snapped a picture. Bad light, bad angle, and no time to zoom in or focus. Still, even a bad picture was better than no picture.

The maintenance man, if that's what he was, disappeared around the corner of the garage.

As I trudged back to the roof access door, I felt like I was walking the last mile to my execution.

I had failed again.

Before he left the arena that night, LeMarvis pulled me aside and asked me to meet him in his and Cleo's hotel suite at eleven the next morning.

He must have wanted to fire me face-to-face.

The Summer Fun Concert Tour was toast. Weirdo killed Fortunata

Torelli and Andy Stanley. He sent the two spotlight jockeys to intensive care or worse. No way LeMarvis or Cleo would expose the cast or the music fans to this mad murderer again.

Yet Weirdo was out there. Unless Cleo became a hermit in LeMarvis's multi-million-dollar cave, she was still at risk. I assigned Snoop and Gunner to escort them to the hotel.

I met with Sergeant Daniel Griffin from the Jacksonville Sheriff's Office Homicide Unit until two a.m.

I tossed and twisted all night. I woke before the alarm, knowing I had failed. Again.

THIRTY-SEVEN

The next morning, I checked with Pete at the hospital before I met with LeMarvis. The woman spotlight operator died en route to the hospital, the other made it to the hospital alive. His life was touch-and-go. Pete told me it didn't look good.

Cleo and LeMarvis's suite was crowded with people.

LeMarvis slumped at the head of the dining room table. He seemed smaller than the last time I saw him. His eyes were red and droopy, like he hadn't slept either.

Cleo and Avery Harper flanked him on either side. Cleo's eyes were downcast, and Harper's shoulders slumped.

Cleo and LeMarvis no longer had stars in their eyes. Reality had body-slammed them both to the mat and broken their rose-colored glasses. They had ignored my warnings of the danger, and I had been right. They would feel guilty and blame me even more for what happened. That was all right; I blamed myself anyway.

A brunch buffet stretched along one wall. It looked like no one had touched it. Perhaps I was the only one with an appetite. Whenever I'm sad or upset, I get hungry. Whenever I'm happy or hopeful, I also get hungry. Getting hungry is pretty much how I respond to every emotion.

Might as well eat while I waited to find out what the future had in store. After filling a plate, I sat opposite LeMarvis.

Tank Tyler sat on my right. Hound Dog Hannigan had again wrangled a seat at the table.

Hound Dog beheld the sad faces around the table. "What is this, a goldarned wake?"

Cleo's shoulders twitched, but she didn't look up.

LeMarvis glared at him. "The shooter has killed three people and put one in the hospital in critical condition. Sounds like a wake to me, Hound Dog."

LeMarvis appeared more upset than he had been from the first shooting. I ate faster.

LeMarvis gestured with his coffee cup. "Tank, you're the money man. Why don't you tell everyone what we decided last night?"

Tank set his cup down. "The tour is canceled. Hound Dog, please contact the cast and express our deep regrets. I arranged late checkouts for everyone. My office will mail their checks this week."

Tank referred to his notes. "Avery, inform the arena management that we have cancelled the concert. Call a news conference. Tell them Cleo is distraught over the loss of life, and she doesn't want to endanger anyone else, etc. You know what to say."

Hound Dog started to speak, and Tank interrupted. "Hound Dog, the subject is not open to debate. We will pay everyone in accordance with their contracts. Do what I ask and contact everybody, please."

Hound Dog stood. "I was gonna say that I understand, y'all, and the cast understands, and it's been a pleasure to work with y'all..." His face turned red. "Except for the goldarned murders, of course. I mean..." He scanned the table. "Y'all know what I mean."

He left the room.

Tank cleared his throat. "Avery, please contact the Atlanta venue on Monday and cancel. My office will see to the ticket refunds."

He rotated in my direction with an expressionless face, but he didn't quite look at me. "McCrary Investigations' security contract is cancelled. Send me your final bill."

I braced my hands on either side of my plate. "LeMarvis, I understand you canceling the security contract, but remember, somebody wants to kill Cleo. That nutcase killer is out there. We can catch this guy."

LeMarvis sprang to his feet. Cleo flinched when his chair fell over and banged the wall behind him, but she didn't look.

"The way you protected the cast and crew members? No way. Three dead and one in critical condition? Your contract is terminated."

"LeMarvis, Cleo is in danger. You might be also. There are certain things the cops won't do, but I will. Let me catch this guy."

"McCrary, I tried to be diplomatic and use Tank to terminate your contract, but you don't get the message. This guy is smarter than you. He's killed at least three people—four, if the other spotlight operator dies, and you don't have a clue who did it or how to stop him."

Cleo's left eyelid fluttered. Her lips moved, but she said nothing.

LeMarvis peeked at Cleo, then back at me. "We've lost confidence in you. You're fired. Our relationship is over. Get out." He eyed Tank, maybe for support.

Tank focused somewhere between LeMarvis and me. His lips moved, but he didn't speak.

Cleo gazed at the table. She had twitched and flinched but hadn't spoken since I arrived. Something weighed on her mind, but she kept quiet.

What did she know that she wasn't telling?

In the hall outside the suite, I texted Gunner and Snoop to meet me in my hotel room.

Snoop called. "I'm with Detective Griffin. You want me to cut it short?"

"No, finish with him. Don't tell Griffin, but we were fired. Tell him I'll see him tomorrow. Meet me in my hotel room."

"Give me twenty-five minutes."

Down the hall, Hound Dog Hannigan was waiting for the elevator. He gazed my way.

"Don't feel bad, Hound Dog. Your music was a success. I'm the one who blew it."

"The operation was a success but the goldarned patient died?"

"Something like that. At least everyone enjoyed the music."

The elevator doors slid open. I punched the button for my floor.

Hound Dog shook my hand. "Don't blame yourself for this. Whoever he is, the guy's a goldarned madman. No one can predict what a madman will do."

"Thanks, Hound Dog. Take care."

Calling the front desk from my room, I closed my room account for billing to Tank. Then I opened a new room account in my name. I was staying.

Gunner sat in the desk chair and I took the recliner. "Just because the client fired us doesn't mean I'm quitting. You, Pete, and Snoop are on the payroll today. I still intend to catch this guy."

Gunner said, "Nobody's paying you, boss."

"Forget the money. I screwed up the building security survey when I missed that roof access door and the compartment in the arch. That's on me. It's my responsibility to nail this bastard."

"How did he get onto the roof?"

"That part is easy. Four external fire escapes run from the roof to the ground, spaced equidistant around the arena. He used one not visible from the street. Climbed it sometime after we locked up after Friday night's concert and before dawn Saturday."

There was a knock on my door. Snoop and the coffee arrived together. Snoop poured a cup and sat on the bed.

Gunner acknowledged Snoop. "Chuck and I were discussing how the shooter got into the building."

"Apparently from the roof, through the access door," I said. "He must have explored the arena a week or more before the concert, before we established security on the building. At the time, I noted that arena security is weak to non-existent if there are no events scheduled. He discovered that compartment above the proscenium and left the roof access door unlocked. It's seldom used. No one would notice it."

Gunner scowled. "You think the killer carried a duffel bag with his gun and climbing gear into the arena before dawn on Saturday? From the roof? That's pretty audacious."

"So is killing four people."

Snoop said, "He must have hidden there fourteen or fifteen hours."

"He would need a bathroom break," Gunner said. "Even if he took no food and water, that's too long to hold it."

A BFO—blinding flash of the obvious—smacked me upside the head. "The SOB carried a camp toilet. Here, look at this fuzzy picture I snapped of the man in black. It looks like a five-gallon paint can, but it was a camp toilet. A duffel bag that size would hold the disassembled rifle, camp toilet, climbing gear, plus food and water. Anything with DNA—saliva on water bottles and food wrappers—he stashes in the camp toilet. He takes it with him in one convenient carry-all. If I were the shooter, I would park a few blocks away in an apartment complex. That's a good place to leave a car unnoticed for that long. After the shooting, he walks back, no hurry, carrying the camp toilet. He drives away."

I almost admired Weirdo's guts and intelligence. Almost considered him an evil genius. Almost.

"Any chance the CSU will find DNA on the stuff he left?" Snoop asked.

"He's never left any before. He must wear vinyl gloves since he doesn't leave fingerprints either."

"What do we do now?" Gunner asked.

"You, Snoop, and Pete are on the payroll for today. Gunner, you return to the arena. Look at the sniper's nest again with fresh eyes, assuming he hid there all day. We found similar hidey-holes in Afghanistan. See what the CSU missed. Find the fire escape he used. Maybe he left a scrap of clothing snagged on a metal splinter. Perhaps he dropped something as he ran across the roof. Maybe he left a drop of sweat on the quilt he laid on."

"The CSU took the quilt for evidence."

"Whatever. Recheck everything. Weirdo is smart, but nobody's perfect. That nest above the stage was the most complex crime scene he has left so far. He touched lots of items. Eventually, he will make a mistake. Let's hope it was last night.

"Snoop, send Flamer the list of license plates that showed at both concerts. Liaise with him to check out the owners of those vehicles."

"You said the shooter was in his hidey-hole hours before the concert started," Gunner said.

"Rule Thirteen: *Sometimes you're wrong.* What if Weirdo was in one of those vehicles at Friday's concert? Those license plates meant something. That's twenty-three rocks we gotta turn over."

To be precise, it was twenty-three rocks for Flamer to turn over and Snoop to look under.

"What are you gonna do, bud?" asked Snoop.

"Go to the hospital. One of the spotlight jockeys is in the ICU, a nice kid from West Virginia."

On my way to the hospital, I grabbed a sandwich from a drive-thru. I sent Pete to the arena to help Gunner until the end of his shift. After that, he was off duty and off the payroll.

I sat with the West Virginia hillbilly's fiancée and her parents while the four of us waited for news. She was four months pregnant. They planned to marry next month. The young man's parents were flying in from West Virginia. They arrived at six p.m.

At seven, the young West Virginian died. The six of us joined hands, prayed for his soul, and cried together. Both sets of parents thanked God that the fiancée would have a grandchild for them.

I dragged back to my hotel room to meet Snoop.

I ordered room service dinners for us both while Snoop reported on his afternoon.

After lunch, he had sent Flamer the twenty-three license plate numbers of the fans who attended both concerts.

In eight hours, Flamer traced the vehicle owners and ran criminal background checks. Snoop said they were a cross-section of country music fans from the region. Most hailed from greater Jacksonville. One came from Tallahassee, three from southeastern Georgia. Among the criminal records, Snoop found a typical array: DUIs, drug users, one arrest for assault with a deadly weapon on an ex-girlfriend's new boyfriend. None came from the Port City area, and none smelled like our shooter. If Snoop said none of them was our shooter, then none of them was our shooter.

Lying in bed, I felt bluer than the ocean. No matter how sorry I felt, there were two families from Jacksonville and West Virginia who felt worse. At least they would have a child and grandchild to carry on. What would my family have if something happened to me? At least I wasn't an only child.

Staring at the ceiling in the dark for an hour, I knew something wasn't kosher, but I couldn't put my finger on it. As I fell asleep, it hit me.

I had been so focused on Weirdo's obsession with Cleo that I had overlooked one fact: Cleo was never the target for the Jacksonville concert; I was.

Weirdo wasn't just looking to frighten Cleo; he wanted to kill me.

THIRTY-EIGHT

Monday morning, Sergeant Daniel Griffin poured me a coffee. "Creamer and sugar over there. The bagels look nice."

On the way to the sheriff's office, I had bought a dozen assorted bagels. "We always appreciated a bagel or donut at the station when I was a cop."

"The raisin ones are my favorite." Griffin selected a bagel. "By the way, it's a double murder. The other spotlight operator died last night."

"I know. I was with his fiancée and his parents last night. If I hadn't missed the compartment above the arch..." I shook my head. "That's one reason I want to help your investigation. If I did my job better, you wouldn't have to do this job."

Griffin grunted. "You have anything to add to our interview from Saturday night?"

I selected a plain bagel. "Yesterday afternoon, I sent two agents back to the arena to re-examine the sniper's nest, roof, and fire escapes."

Griffin broke his raisin bagel in half. "You think my guys missed something?" He raised an eyebrow. No cop likes to be second-guessed.

"*Nah.* Yesterday morning, I met with my guys to discuss the case. We figure the shooter hid in that cubbyhole all day without a bathroom break, and I remembered I saw a man in black with a five-gallon paint can after the shooting. You remember I mentioned that?"

202

"It's in my notes somewhere. What about it?"

I showed him my phone picture of the man in black. "That paint can had to be a camp toilet. The shooter hid in the arch all day."

"Why didn't you show me that picture Saturday night?"

"I forgot I took it until yesterday. I'll text it to you."

In a few seconds, Griffin's phone signaled he had received the photo. "Perhaps our IT guys can do their magic and enhance it. Couldn't hurt. Did you find anything else?"

"My guys found fresh scuff marks on the rear fire escape. We believe that's how he accessed the roof."

"What scuff marks?"

I showed him a picture on my phone. "Might be from the boots he used to rappel off the roof."

Griffin studied the picture. "When you rappel, you push off the wall with your feet, don't you? I saw that in a movie."

"Yeah, it's called 'bounding' and it leaves scuff marks. Could your guys take samples of the marks on the fire escape and look for marks on the exterior wall?"

"Okay, I'll send my CSU to sample the fire escape marks and look for rappelling marks. Perhaps we'll match the rubber from the boots to a boot brand. If we find the guy's boots, we might prove they were consistent with the boots used on the arena wall."

I spread crème cheese on a plain bagel. "The shooter could have explored the arena a couple of weeks ago, found the cubbyhole, and unlocked the roof door from the inside. On D-Day, he climbs to the roof before dawn with the duffel bag. He attaches the rope to the railing and leaves it coiled between the lip of the roof and the walkway. No one would see it, and it saves seconds when he escapes. He enters through the roof door and hides in the arch. After he shoots, he drops the rope off the rail and rappels down, carrying his waste in the camp toilet. A minute later, I arrive at the top of the rope and see him walk away. Does that fit with your evidence?"

"Let's take these to my desk." Griffin started walking. "I didn't connect the paint can to a camp toilet. *Hmm*. He could stay hidden all day if he had the toilet." He gestured me into an extra chair and cleared a desk corner for our bagels and cups. "We figured he stayed in the hidey-hole a couple of hours."

I set my coffee next to his. "My team sealed the doors to the arena at one a.m. Saturday after the Friday concert. We unsealed them Saturday morning at ten a.m. We watched everyone who came and went. We checked souvenir vendors, concessionaires, and arena employees. No one brought in a duffel bag. He didn't climb the stairs to the catwalk. He was already there. Had to be."

Griffin chewed his bagel and nodded, not that he agreed, but as if he was reflecting. "What if the shooter climbed to the roof late that afternoon, before the concert? It's a big roof and nobody looks up anyway. Even if somebody noticed him on the roof, it wouldn't raise eyebrows."

"That's possible, but this guy is smart and careful. He wouldn't take the chance someone would see him on the roof ahead of time. And one of my people might hear him walk across the catwalk. The metal walkway rings loud as a bell when you're up there. If we assume he hid above the arch all day, would that change how you examine the evidence?"

"The longer he hid, the more chance he left DNA on the quilt. Maybe he sweated or drooled or spilled something as he used the camp toilet. Yeah, we'll check the quilt thoroughly." He nodded again. "Couldn't hurt."

The radio was off as I drove home on I-95. A smorgasbord of speculations danced through my mind at the edge of conscious thought.

Cleo Hennessey was hiding something. In hindsight, I now realized she had lied when I asked who wanted to harm her. Her body language told me she lied about her childhood and family in Tennessee. She had rejected her family, their name, their culture, and her native state. Why?

In the hotel suite when LeMarvis said I didn't have a clue to the killer's identity, her eyelid fluttered. She had done that before—always when I suspected she wasn't telling the truth. Or at least not the whole truth. What did she know that I didn't?

And why did Weirdo shift his focus to me? Was it vanity to assume he was afraid to attack Cleo so long as I protected her? Did my well-developed sense of self-esteem color my opinion? I'm known for that, also for my modesty. Was I thinking too highly of myself?

I had driven halfway home when Clint called. "Where are you?"

"Just south of Titusville."

"Can I borrow the *Raider* this afternoon and tonight?"

"Sure. You make a date with Madison?"

Clint laughed. "How did you guess?"

"I'm the world's greatest private investigator. Are you carrying?"

"Without fail."

"One piece of advice: You may feel like hurrying, but don't. This was her idea, and she's not going to change her mind. And don't expect to execute everything flawlessly. If it were me, I would tell Madison that it's my first time. Lower her expectations. Sex is like riding a bicycle; no one does it well at first. Practice, practice, practice."

"That's three pieces of advice, bro. Four, if you count the practice, practice, practice."

"Check the fuel level. Don't run out of gas in the middle of Seeti Bay. Use my credit card in case you need to fill it."

When I reached the condo garage late that afternoon, Clint's car was there. Hadn't he left to pick up Madison? Then I remembered that she lived in a waterfront house. He picked her up with the boat. Now that's *romance*.

Tuesday morning, Clint was asleep when I left for the office. I skipped breakfast so my kitchen noise wouldn't wake him.

At the office, I was sipping my first cup of fresh coffee as I clicked *Send/Receive*. I deleted a few spams, then saw the next subject line: *McCrary, Cleo Hennessey and LeMarvis Jones must die before they mongrelize the Black race.*

The email was jammed with racist boasts, ominous threats, and derisive taunts from a black power group. Outside the window that looked onto Bayfront Boulevard, traffic must have passed. It passed, but I didn't see it. By the time I finished deliberating the problem, my coffee was cold.

I called Tank, then Snoop. "You free for lunch?"

"You buying?" Snoop asked.

"Of course."

"I'm free. Fat Tummy again?"

"If you insist." Fat Tummy was a local greasy spoon. Snoop regards the four basic food groups as fat, salt, ketchup, and beer. You get all four at Fat Tummy and not much else.

"I insist."

———

Halfway through lunch, Snoop set his beer down and wiped his mouth. "I've never seen you this way, bud. You haven't complained about my eating habits. You didn't kid around with the server. You didn't order your ridiculous vegetarian pizza. You haven't made any bad jokes. In fact, you haven't spoken six words since we sat down. If you have nothing to say, why did you call me?"

"It's the Cleo Hennessey case. I received an email about her and LeMarvis this morning, and I'm not sure what to do about it." I handed the printout to Snoop.

He read it. "Holy shit."

"I'm lost for ideas. I made an appointment with Tank. He'll be a go-between with LeMarvis, if necessary. They should see this."

"Yeah, that's the first thing to do," Snoop said. "They ought to see this, one way or other."

"What about the cops? Do I tell Bubble-Gum Beltran?"

"Don't tell him before you discuss it with Tank and hopefully with Cleo and LeMarvis too."

"I'll nail Weirdo whether LeMarvis hires me back or not. Sergeant Griffin's CSU may find something I can use."

Snoop scoffed. "And the Tooth Fairy will grant you three wishes."

"You mixed two different myths."

"Whatever. Don't count on Griffin's CSU. Even if he finds something useful and shares it with you, you're fired, bud. First thing, Tank needs to get you back on the case officially. Right now, you're no fun to be around."

When I arrived home, Clint and the boat were both gone. He had left a note on the kitchen table saying he had another date with Madison.

I felt a bit jealous. Okay, more than a bit. Clint had found someone to warm his heart while my heart was still an iceberg.

THIRTY-NINE

By Wednesday, I caught up with the mail, both paper and electronic, that had accumulated while I was in Jacksonville. I didn't have another interesting case to work, just three routine divorce and insurance investigations, and I put Robby Gorski on them.

Gazing out my window at Bayfront Boulevard, I obsessed over the danger to Cleo and the fact that she had lied to me. I was treading water with her stalker. Worse, I was off the case and forced to wait for Tank to intervene on my behalf. My emotional state was spiraling toward a crash. I grasped at Tank's influence with LeMarvis like a homeless beggar might buy a lottery ticket. Fortunately, Tank had good odds of paying off.

At 10:30 I took the new email to Tank's office.

He gazed at it. "Tell you what: I've searched for a reason to put you back on this case. This email is a good excuse. I'll arrange another meeting with LeMarvis. Cleo wasn't happy that he fired you. Hard to tell with her because she often defers to LeMarvis. He's had three days to cool off. Perhaps he's had second thoughts."

My phone signaled a text from Griffin:

Please call Sergeant Daniel Griffin in Jacksonville ASAP.

I called. "Daniel, Chuck McCrary, what you got?"

"Good news for a change. My CSU found two drops of sweat and a spot of saliva on the quilt."

"I'm in Tank Tyler's office. He is an advisor to LeMarvis Jones and Cleopatra Hennessey. He needs to hear this. Can I put you on speaker?"

"Sure."

I set my phone on Tank's desk. "Go ahead, Sergeant."

"My Crime Scene Unit found sweat on the quilt. Saliva too. I think the shooter took a nap and drooled while he slept. And my IT guys analyzed Chuck's photo of the shooter. They say he's six-foot-five."

Tank mouthed "photo?" at me.

I lifted a figure to signal I would tell him in a minute. "Did you analyze the scuff marks from his boots?"

"No joy there, Chuck. They're Vibram rubber soles. Half the hiking boots in the universe are made from that rubber. Good catch finding the marks, though."

"The scuff marks and the photo I snapped are the first mistakes he's made."

"Yep. Those and the DNA. My CSU takes four or five days to process and run DNA against the CODIS database."

"If he's in CODIS." The FBI runs the Combined DNA Index System (CODIS).

"Don't rain on your own parade, Chuck. Think happy thoughts. I'll send the DNA report to Detective Beltran."

Griffin was right. I was looking at the hole and not the donut. Weirdo had made his first mistakes. Three of them, in fact. His height was consistent with what Chet Stroud told us in Orlando.

Tank looked at my blurry photo of Weirdo.

"See that paint can?" I said. "It's not a paint can." I explained what we found.

"I'll call LeMarvis," he said.

LeMarvis invited us for breakfast the next day.

Cleo met me at the front door. "They're in the breakfast room.

LeMarvis is over the funk he had in Jacksonville. I'm real glad, because that crazy person, he's still out there."

As Cleo and I entered the kitchen, LeMarvis grinned like a schoolboy at a carnival. The breakfast area was larger than my dining room and had a wall of glass overlooking Seeti Bay. "My cook makes this crazy omelet with some fancy cheese I can't spell. Helga, tell Chuck and Tank."

Helga stood between the kitchen island and the breakfast area with a large silver tray. She was a middle-aged, chunky woman with smiling brown eyes and dark brown hair she wore in a tight bun. Her apron said *When I cook, I wear my cape backwards*. "It's made with Kashkaval cheese, Hungarian wax peppers, and onions. I call it a Macedonian Omelet. I learned the recipe during a vacation I took at Lake Ohrid in North Macedonia. Cleo and LeMarvis love it. I hope you and Mr. Tyler will like it too."

The warm welcome surprised me. LeMarvis was ebullient, effervescent, and enthusiastic.

As Helga served out plates, LeMarvis grinned so wide I thought his cheeks might split. "Cleo and I set a wedding date—September first. It's a Friday. You're both invited."

That's what made LeMarvis excited.

Tank shot me a look.

For a second, I considered my own wedding that never happened. The happy couple didn't know about my personal break-up. I returned Tank's look and nodded. Suppressing my own disappointment, I joined in the congratulations.

We enjoyed the breakfast and discussed wedding plans and potential honeymoon sites until Helga cleared the table and left a tray of homemade sticky buns and a fresh pot of coffee.

"Helga," LeMarvis said, "leave the dishes until later. Tank and I need to discuss things. You can do the grocery shopping now."

He watched her leave the room before he spoke. "Tank said you received an email that Cleo and I should see."

I handed the email printout to LeMarvis.

"Tank, have you read this?" he asked.

"I peeked at it. I knew you'd want to see it. Might be good for a laugh."

Good for a laugh? At a hate email? What does Tank mean?

LeMarvis frowned, then smiled, and he laughed. He grabbed a sticky bun from the tray, still laughing.

"What's so funny?" I asked.

"Tank saw it right away. It's a hoax."

"A hoax? How so?"

"The guy claims to represent a black power group that's opposed to mixed-race marriages, but he's not black." He handed the email to Cleo. "If you do an internet search for his so-called organization, I bet you won't find it." He slid the tray of sticky buns to Tank. "You're all skin and bones, bro. Eat a bun."

Tank weighed somewhere north of 300 pounds, and it was all muscle. Nevertheless, he selected a bun and attacked it with gusto. He pushed the tray back to me. "Good sticky buns, bro. Have one." He wiped his fingers on a linen napkin.

Cleo dropped the email on the table. "This thing ain't funny, y'all. It's awful and hateful."

LeMarvis laid a giant hand lightly on her arm. "Honey, the guy who sent that isn't even black. He may not be white, but he sure as hell isn't an American black."

"How can you tell?" she asked.

LeMarvis grinned. "It's a black thing." He and Tank burst out laughing.

"I don't get it," I said. "When I read this, I broke out in a cold sweat that there's another crazy killer on the loose. You two clowns read it and break out laughing." I munched a bite of bun. It was delicious.

LeMarvis lifted his cup. "There are several clues that it's a fake, some of them subtle. The guy writes his insults to white people—meaning you and Cleo—and to black people—meaning me—with words a white person might imagine a black radical would use. It's a caricature of black slang. Same thing with his threats of what they intend to do to Cleo and to me. The euphemisms for copulation, castration, and assassination—they're not credible. No black activist phrases things that way. Maybe I should be the detective instead of you."

He smiled at Cleo. "Besides, if it were real, you know what Cleo and I think of people who want to keep us apart." He grabbed her hand and smiled.

"Screw 'em," they said.

I swallowed another bite of sticky bun. "Come to think of it, he didn't say anything about the Jacksonville shooting that wasn't public knowledge. He didn't show inside knowledge of the killings. Might be, he's a random kook. He might not be our same weirdo."

"I didn't say he wasn't the shooter; just that he's not black," Tank said. "If he is the shooter, he's trying to throw you and the cops off the trail."

FORTY

F riday morning, Bernie Beltran called. "The DNA report on the Jacksonville sniper came in, Mac."

Don't call me Mac, I thought automatically.

"It's worthless. It doesn't match anything in CODIS. The killer doesn't have a record."

Bubble-Gum Brain was wrong as usual.

CODIS starts with state and local DNA index systems. The FBI adds its DNA profiles of federal criminals and arrestees. Each state maintains its own DNA database, and each state sets its standards for uploading to CODIS. Some states are less strict than the national level, and many DNA profiles in state databases are not in the national database.

Weirdo's DNA might be in a state database somewhere. I asked Beltran to send a DNA request to the Florida Department of Law Enforcement and the Tennessee Bureau of Investigation.

"Why Tennessee?" Bubble-Gum asked.

"The shooter may be from Tennessee."

"You know something I don't?"

I resisted the temptation to answer his question truthfully. "I can't tell you. Not yet. Just do it, okay?"

When I arrived home from the office, Clint was watching a baseball game on television.

"Date with Madison tonight, bro?"

"*Nah*. I'm taking a break to clear my head. I'm considering breaking up."

"You want to discuss it?"

Clint paused the game. "How did you break up with Liz Johannes?"

"That's a long, painful story. Let me get a drink."

Clint followed me to the kitchen.

After opening a beer, I sat at the kitchen table. "Help yourself."

"Don't mind if I do." He got one from the refrigerator. "So, tell me about your breakup."

I tipped my beer and took a swallow. That first swallow of the day tastes best. "I didn't break up; she did."

Clint twisted open his bottle. "How long were y'all together?"

"Over two years. By the time we were in the spring semester of our senior year, I was in love. I planned to propose at our Senior All-Night Party."

"You're kidding. You intended to propose, yet you had never dated another girl?"

"It sounds improbable, but I was as romantic as any teenaged girl. I confused sex with love. I was making love, but Liz was having sex, if you see the distinction."

"How did you discover she didn't love you?"

"The night of the Senior All-Night Party, she said she had been accepted at Northwestern University and intended to start summer school in Chicago after graduation. We had never discussed our plans after high school. She never asked my plans before she made hers. In hindsight, I realized that my plans were irrelevant to her decision."

Clint took a swig and belched. "Sorry. Why didn't you go to Northwestern to be with her?"

"She never encouraged me, not even a little bit. Having had more girlfriends since, today I realize that I was a high school romance to Liz. I was her training wheels for real love." I tipped my bottle again. The second swallow tasted nearly as good as the first.

"How did it end?"

"After graduation, we had one last date. She screwed my brains out in the hayloft of our barn one last time. After she rolled off, she said she was driving to Chicago the next morning."

"Bummer. Did it hurt?"

"No. The worst sex I ever had was magnificent." I grinned and drained half the bottle.

"Very funny, smart guy. You know what I meant. Did it hurt emotionally when she left?"

"Naturally, it hurt, but I survived. I always survive. It helped that Dad told me three different girls broke his heart before he met Mom. I told myself, 'That's heartbreak number one,' and joined the Army the next week."

I swallowed more beer. "Why would you dump Madison? You couldn't possibly know each other that well yet."

Clint held the bottle to the light and studied the label. "I feel like her trophy."

"You mean she bagged you like a deer or a pheasant?"

"That's a pretty good analogy." He drank a long pull and set the bottle on a coaster. "I'm her pet nigger."

That surprised me. "I don't understand."

"Madison doesn't see me for who I *am*; she sees me as what I *represent*. She never asks my opinion on anything meaningful or intellectual. She behaves as if she already knows my opinions about politics, global warming, the Middle East situation, about *everything* because I'm black, and all blacks think alike. We haven't engaged in a meaningful conversation about life. We talk about superficial stuff—music and movies and celebrity gossip."

"She screws your brains out mainly because you're black?"

He smiled. "She sees a poor but deserving member of an oppressed race whom she, as a politically sensitive modern person, wants to help get along in life."

"By screwing your balls off on my boat?"

215

"You're not taking this seriously."

"No, I'm not. Your heart may be broken several times before you meet the right woman. You will know the right one when she comes along—which she will. You think you're a pity fuck?"

"She displays me to her friends as a symbol of how progressive and open-minded she is. Like she's saying, 'I date a black man. See how enlightened I am?'" He drank again.

"I met her just the one time, so I don't have an informed opinion, but I doubt she sees you in racial terms. I don't get that vibe from her. Before you dump her, give her a chance. See if you can engage her in a discussion of politics, or religion, or global warming. Discuss something that's not superficial. She may have depths you have yet to explore."

Saturday morning was Clint's turn to cook breakfast. He chose a Western omelet.

"I made a lunch date with Madison." He pulled down a ten-inch stainless steel bowl, a cutting board, and three measuring cups. A typical rookie mistake.

"Why three measuring cups?" I asked.

"I'm new at Western omelets." He pointed at his laptop on the island. "The online recipe calls for a half cup of diced onions, a half cup of diced bell peppers, and a half cup of diced ham."

"Yeah, but you'll put the onions and peppers into the skillet together, right?"

"Yeah. So?"

"Chop the onions and put them in the measuring cup, then put the peppers on top in the same cup. One less dish to wash."

"That makes sense. Any other advice, O kitchen guru?"

"You'll put the ham in the skillet later. You can measure it in the same cup after you dump the onion and peppers into the skillet. Two less dishes to wash."

"Brilliant, bro. The guy on YouTube had all three ingredients on his kitchen counter, already chopped."

"That's television. TV isn't real life. I'll bet he doesn't wash his own dishes either."

Clint put two measuring cups back in the cabinet and splashed some milk into the bowl.

"Where you intend to take her?" I asked.

"That's where I need your advice." He pulled an egg carton and three slices of ham from the refrigerator. "We need to have a significant conversation to find out if she sees me a person or her pet nigger."

"Please don't say that word, bro. It sets my teeth on edge."

"Sorry. I used it for shock value." He cracked six eggs into the bowl and whisked the mixture.

"It worked; you shocked me."

"Can I call myself her token black boyfriend?" He grinned as he chopped the onion and bell pepper and scraped them into the measuring cup.

"Token is a good word. I was a token Mexican-American once or twice myself. The sex was still good."

"Okay. Where do we go for an authentic, non-superficial discussion?" He diced the ham and left it on the cutting board. "Is that half a cup?"

"This ain't rocket science, bro. It's close enough," I answered. "Take her to Java Jenny's."

"Why Java Jenny's?" He cut a chunk of butter into a skillet and placed it on a low-heat burner. It melted in seconds.

"Some of the most significant conversations I've had were at Java Jenny's. That's where Terry and I went on our first date."

He dumped the onions and bell pepper into the skillet and stirred as he consulted the laptop. "What does it mean to stir until translucent?"

"They mean the onions. Peppers don't get translucent."

"Ah." He stirred. "Yeah, I see that."

He referred to his laptop and scraped the diced ham into the measuring cup. He grinned. "Close enough for government work." He dumped the ham into the skillet and set a timer for one minute. "Tell me more." He kept stirring.

"My first date with Terry lasted two hours and we communicated: life, career, family history, the works. There's something about coffee, as compared with alcohol, which promotes discussion."

"Whereas alcohol…" He let that taper off to silence.

"Alcohol is when you want giggles. Alcohol talk is romance, laughter, and sex. Good subjects, but not for consequential conversation. That first two hours with Terry, I learned eighty percent of what I needed to know to start a relationship."

The timer dinged and Clint grabbed the mixing bowl.

"You gonna add salt and pepper?" I asked.

"I'll do that after it's cooked."

"It tastes better if you add it while it cooks. The seasoning permeates the omelet. Trust me."

"How much, bro?"

"Season to taste. With those aluminum shakers, I use two shakes of salt and three of pepper."

Clint shook the salt and pepper over the eggs and stirred it in. "How do you learn the other twenty percent?"

"Ten percent comes from experience. Spend time together and pay attention to what she says, what she does, and what she likes and doesn't like."

"And the other ten percent?"

"That comes from sex. Lots of sex."

He poured the beaten egg mixture into the skillet and swirled it around. "The YouTube video I watched looked better than this."

"I'll bet it wasn't the guy's first time to make a Western omelet."

He grinned. "Guess not. Practice, practice, practice."

"I'd put the lid on the skillet for a minute if I were doing this."

Clint set the lid on the skillet and punched the timer again.

"Back home in Texas, we add grated cheese and salsa on top after it's on the plate. I'll grate some cheese."

"Thanks, bro. I'll get the salsa. Java Jenny's, huh? I go there for coffee, but I never considered eating lunch there."

"They make good sandwiches and a soup of the day. Sometimes it's broccoli and cheese soup. That's my favorite."

"What do we talk about?"

"There's one sure way to start a deep discussion with Madison."

"What is it?"

I smirked. "Ask her opinion of Donald Trump."

Clint came back from his lunch date late that afternoon.

I muted the baseball game on television. "How did lunch with Madison go?"

"Surprisingly well. I learned I am not her token black boyfriend."

"Does that mean you're not dumping her?"

"Not for a while," Clint answered.

"*Hmm*. Interesting reply. Care to elaborate?"

"I know why Madison never discusses current events like you and I discuss. The good news is, she doesn't see me as a racial stereotype. She sees me as a real person."

"If she sees you as you, why wouldn't she talk about current events?"

"Because she never *thinks* about politics or religion or current events. Madison never had an adult brainwave in her life, other than about sex. Talking with her is like talking to *Cosmopolitan* magazine. The reason she discusses sex and movies and music is that's all she thinks about."

"And that's good news?"

"Yeah, but as the joke says: There's also bad news."

"I'll bite again. What's the bad news?"

"One you look below the surface, there's nothing there. Intellectually, she's still a child and, except for sex, she's boring and shallow."

"Hang on a second, Aristotle. You blame her because she's a high school girl. Consider your life experience compared to Madison's. You had to grow up fast to survive on the streets with no adult supervision. The first time I met you, you were a hardened, distrustful cynic. Madison still believes in the Easter Bunny."

Clint nodded. "I see what you mean. She leads a sheltered life. She never worries where her next meal will come from or where she'll sleep tonight. She has a normal childhood."

"Not quite normal, bro. She has a *privileged* childhood. An *ivory* tower childhood. That's different. In some ways, she's still a child despite her physical maturity; she has one more year in high school. Give her a chance to grow intellectually. She may adopt a more adult view of life once she registers to vote, and certainly after she starts college. A person that age can change a lot in one or two years. I know I did."

FORTY-ONE

It was Monday before the Florida Department of Law Enforcement and the Tennessee Bureau of Investigation replied. They did not find a DNA match.

I dropped in on Port City Police Lieutenant Jorge Castellano, an old friend. When I was a rookie cop, Jorge took a bullet that a gangbanger intended for me. Years later, Jorge was framed for murder and I found the real killer. We owed each other enough favors to last two lifetimes.

"What's in the box, *pastelitos*?" he asked.

"Bagels."

"Great. Crème cheese, *amigo*? Let's hit the break room."

After we spread our crème cheese, mixed two iced coffees, and took our first bites and first sips, Jorge leaned back in his chair and smiled. "This can't be a social call," he said in Spanish, "since we ate lunch last week. To come back this soon, you need a favor. Bernie Beltran giving you trouble?"

I responded in Spanish. "The guy is dumber than a tree stump. The Jacksonville Sheriff CSU sent him my shooter's DNA. He runs it through CODIS, doesn't find a match, and proclaims the sample worthless. It didn't occur to Bubble-Gum Beltran to search the FDLE database. I had to suggest it to him. How did this imbecile get promoted to detective?"

"It doesn't matter," Jorge said. "He made it, and he's Civil Service, here to stay until hell freezes over. How can I help?"

"Access my shooter's DNA sample and run a familial DNA search. I believe the shooter is related to my client, Cleopatra Hennessey. Maybe a cousin."

"Has she been convicted of anything? Would she be in the database?"

"No, but she comes from a long line of Tennessee moonshiners. Look for one of her extended family convicted for moonshining."

"If they were convicted since 1994, they're in the database. Was it that recent?"

"Run it and let's see what we find. Can you do it?"

"Do fish swim? Let's head to my computer."

Twenty minutes later, Jorge swung his monitor toward me. "Your shooter is a close relative of Chester Walter Lynch, convicted moonshiner, bootlegger, and attempted murderer of a federal revenue agent. Chester was paroled from Lee Prison in Pennington Gap, Virginia in February of this year after he served twenty years."

As I heard the name *Lynch,* My ears perked up. "How close is the DNA match?"

"It's a twenty-five percent match. Your shooter is a grandparent or grandchild, an uncle or nephew, or a half-brother. Since Chester Lynch is... fifty-seven years old, if your shooter was a grandson, he would be a teenager or younger. Therefore, he's gotta be a nephew or half-brother. Does this help?"

My intercom chirped. "Ms. Hennessey and Mr. Jones are here, Chuck."

I had asked Cleo to come alone because of the disturbing news I had learned from the DNA analysis. I preferred to discuss the DNA results in private. The discussion would be hard enough without LeMarvis's presence complicating the personal dynamics. Too bad, but there was nothing I could do about it now.

Cleo and LeMarvis rose to their feet as I entered the reception area. This time, she didn't give me a toothpaste-ad smile, and she didn't seem as tall as when we first met. Was it only six weeks before? It felt like six months. She acted as if she faced the sentencing phase of a trial where the jury had already found her guilty.

LeMarvis shook my hand. "You asked Cleo to come alone, but she insisted I come with her."

"Let's wait to talk until we're in my conference room."

He glanced around. "Oh, yeah, sorry."

"Is Betty getting you something to drink?"

Cleo nodded and grabbed LeMarvis's hand.

"Great. Let's go to my office." I gave Betty a smile. "A coffee for me please, Betty, and hold my calls."

We entered my conference room, and I remembered my mental note to buy a wider love seat. Too late.

Cleo clung to LeMarvis's hand like a life preserver in a stormy sea.

The incidents of the last six weeks had worn her down. Too bad that I had to knock her down more, but she hired me to discover who was behind the emails. I was about to uncover the man who wanted to kill her, and she already knew his identity. She just hadn't admitted it to herself.

Cleo spoke first. "Chuck, you asked me to come alone because we're gonna discuss my family, and LeMarvis don't know anything about them. I know what you're gonna say, and I can't marry LeMarvis if he don't know my entire story—warts and all." She focused on LeMarvis. "He deserves to know, so he can run for the hills if he wants."

LeMarvis raised his eyebrows and opened his mouth, then closed it.

"Okay, Cleo," I said. "You're the boss."

I explained how the shooter hid above the arch in Jacksonville and how he got into the arena. "The Jacksonville Sheriff's Office Crime Scene Unit found the shooter's DNA on that quilt. This is the first time he's left DNA. You with me? You know how DNA works?"

She nodded. "You use it to tell who he is."

"Yes, if he was arrested and there is a sample of his DNA in the national DNA database. In this case, the shooter has never been arrested."

"You didn't find a match?" LeMarvis asked.

"Not a direct match," I responded. "I had the police run a familial search to see if any of the shooter's family had DNA in the system. We found a match—Chester Lynch. He's related to the shooter. Chester Lynch was released from prison last February after serving twenty years for attempted murder of a federal agent."

Cleo's jaw dropped. "Cousin Chester? It can't be; he died before I was born. He—"

A knock on the door sounded. Betty carried in a tray with our drinks on it.

After I thanked her, she left, closing the door behind her.

"LeMarvis, honey, I told you Cleopatra Jane Hennessey is my stage name, and you said you didn't need to know my real name. Now I gotta tell you it's Katie Boone Lynch. I changed my name when I was seventeen and ran away from Thornburg, Tennessee, where I was born. I never lived in Pine Hollow, Kentucky. That was a bunch of lies."

I drank my coffee and watched the scene unfold.

LeMarvis patted her hand. "Babe, I told you our lives began when we met. I meant that. I don't care what you were, or who you were, or what you did before I knew you. As far as I'm concerned, it's ancient history."

"Except it ain't ancient history, honey. These old lies are sprouting like weeds in a garden. There's more."

She faced me. "Tell us the rest, Chuck. How can Cousin Chester be alive?"

"He's not. Your Cousin Chester's full name was Chester *David* Lynch. This new Chester is Chester *Walter* Lynch. He's Chester *David* Lynch's grandson."

Cleo's eyes widened. "I forgot young Chester Lynch. I remember hearing that a cousin was serving time. I never met him and he never come to no family reunions, or weddings, or funerals, him being in prison and all."

"Let me tell you about your DNA, Cleo. You and the shooter share 4.87 percent of your DNA. That means the shooter is somewhere between your second cousin and your first cousin once removed. Do you know what 'once removed' means?"

"Sure. We Lynches been marrying cousins off and on for two hundred years. Once removed means my great-grandfather was his grandfather. His daddy or momma is my first cousin, right?"

"Yes."

LeMarvis raised a hand. "Whoa there, Chuck. Cleo never gave you a DNA sample. At least, if she did, she didn't tell me."

"She didn't know I had the sample. I always collect DNA samples from clients when I can. In your and Cleo's case, it was from glasses you two used when you visited my office the second time. In case you're curious: Yes, I got your fingerprints too."

LeMarvis squinted at me with one eye. "I don't know whether to be impressed with your thoroughness or pissed off that you did it without our knowledge."

"I learned the hard way from another case where a client tried to kill me. Always get the client's DNA. Rule Six: *You never know what you'll need to know.*"

"Rule Six?"

"My private investigator rules. If I hadn't needed the DNA samples, I would have destroyed them after I finished your case. The DNA results told me where to find the shooter. And I found him."

Cleo's face turned whiter. "LeMarvis, honey, the man who killed Faye, I mean Fortunata, and Andy, and them two spotlight operators, he's gotta be my cousin Lester Lynch."

She faced me. "It's Lester, ain't it?"

"Yes. Lester Riley Lynch is Chester Walter Lynch's nephew. What I haven't figured out is why he wants to kill you."

"Lester don't want to kill me." Cleo looked at her fiancé. "He wants to kill LeMarvis."

Bam. That revelation crashed like a brick in the middle of a dinner table.

I wondered if LeMarvis felt as gobsmacked as I did. Then the pieces clicked into place, and the whole weird case made sense in a twisted, screwball way.

"Me?" LeMarvis said. "Why would he want to kill me, babe?"

Cleo's voice broke and she cried. "Because Lester wants to marry me."

Cleo covered her face with her hands and bent over sobbing. "Now that Lester's found me, he'll spoil everything."

LeMarvis patted her on the shoulder, then touched her back. "It's okay, babe. Everything will be all right. Chuck will find this nut and the cops will lock him up."

LeMarvis and I watched Cleo for a minute while she brought herself under control.

Their drinks were untouched. I sipped my coffee and waited.

Cleo sniffed.

I handed her tissues. Maybe I should buy them by the case.

LeMarvis wrapped his mile-long arm around her shoulders and hugged her to his chest. "We'll be all right, babe. You'll see."

"You don't know Lester, honey. He intends to kill you at our wedding."

LeMarvis faced me. "You *will* find him before the wedding, right?"

"You bet your ass I will." I wished I felt as confident as I sounded.

Cleo blew her nose. "Oh, God, I hope so. If he's still out there..."

I held out a waste basket for the used tissues, then set the tissue box in front of her.

"Babe, why would this... this... *lunatic* believe you might marry him if he killed me? That makes no sense."

Cleo cried again and grabbed another tissue. "It's what we do in the Lynch family. Men fight over the women. That's why I ran away—because I wouldn't marry Lester."

She looked at me. "I didn't think of Lester when we first hired you because I figured after all these years he had forgotten about me."

LeMarvis's eyes narrowed.

"It's a family tradition," I said, "marrying cousins."

"Lester started courting me when he was seventeen and I was thirteen. I'd already reached six feet and was filling out pretty good. Most Lynches marry young."

"But at thirteen?" LeMarvis asked.

"No, no. Not that early. Lester, he began to court me. We wouldn't get married for years, maybe after I was sixteen, but he kept sniffing around like he expected me to go into heat."

LeMarvis seemed like he couldn't believe what he heard. If I hadn't done the research on the Lynch family, I would not have believed it either.

"Another family tradition," I said. "Teenage marriages."

"Regardless of what Momma and Daddy said," Cleo continued, "I wasn't going to marry young and have babies and not have no music career, and I for sure wouldn't marry Lester. He was... I don't know how to put it... He was *creepy*."

"That's okay, babe. Take your time. What happened?"

"Lester, he was real smart and he did real good in school. He had a thing for guns. He wanted to be a cop so he could shoot people. See what I mean about being creepy? After he graduated high school, he joined the army. He said in the army he could shoot people for real, plus the army hitch made it easier to get a job as a cop. He wrote me real letters on paper every week and sent me these weird emails with pictures of targets he shot at the army gun range. He said when his hitch was up, he'd come home, be a cop, and marry me."

She grabbed LeMarvis's forearm. "He was real insistent. Then he emailed he was getting out in two weeks, and I ran away."

I had not told LeMarvis the final family tradition: Murder your romantic rival. Several family feud murders had been over intra-family romantic rivalries.

My deadline to find Lester Lynch was September first. Otherwise, Lynch would attend Cleo and LeMarvis's wedding, and it wouldn't be to throw rice.

FORTY-TWO

Tank shut his office door behind us and dropped into a leather-upholstered chair in his informal conference room. The room was more living room than office.

He peeked out the window. "It's five o'clock somewhere. Drink with me or people will think I'm a lush."

"I thought you'd never ask."

We fixed drinks and put our feet on the coffee table.

"How did it go with Cleo and LeMarvis?" he asked.

"Better than I expected when LeMarvis showed up. He took the news in stride. He wants to marry Cleo and they still plan to on September first. They even picked the wedding party."

"Anybody I know?"

"Cleo chose Godiva Simpson to be her maid of honor. Her bridesmaids are two of her friends from Thornburg High School. LeMarvis asked Jamir Lawry, a fellow Peregrine, to be best man. His groomsmen are two teammates from Duke that he's remained close to."

Tank sipped his Scotch. "What if Lester Lynch is still at large?"

"I have thirty days to find him."

"No, bro. We have thirty days to find him. LeMarvis and Cleo are my clients too."

There is no good way to get to Thornburg, Tennessee. Tank and I flew to Knoxville and rented a car to drive sixty-five miles through the Appalachian Mountains. The scenery was beautiful. I might have enjoyed the drive more if we weren't looking for a serial killer. A killer who qualified as Expert Marksman as a U.S. Army Ranger.

I wouldn't admit it to Tank, but I was glad he wanted in. From what I knew about the Lynches, they didn't take kindly to strangers who poked around the mountains near their moonshine stills. The idea of a six-foot-seven, three-hundred-pound giant in my corner appealed to me since I knew the Lynches tended toward giant-economy-size also.

We drove to the Sheriff's Office in Chesterfield, the Goswell County seat. The one-story red brick building sat on the corner of Dixie Highway and Court Street, across from the Goswell County courthouse.

The gold-lettered sign on the glass door said *Sheriff Jeremiah Hickenlooper.* You gotta love a town with a glass front door on the local law enforcement office. They must have a low risk of burglary in Goswell County.

An old woman in a police uniform sat at an oak rolltop desk that predated the Spanish-American War, perhaps even the Civil War. She wasn't as old as the desk, though she was close. Perhaps she was the sheriff's grandmother. She gawked at Tank. "Damn, but you're big. You ever play football?"

"Yes, ma'am."

"Figures."

She noticed me. "Can I help you, sir?"

"We would like to speak with the sheriff, please."

"He ain't here. I'll call him. Take a seat." She gestured at a row of green molded-plastic chairs against the wall. She grabbed a handheld microphone. "Sheriff, this is Central. Two men here to see you."

A wall-mounted speaker above the desk asked, "What do they want?"

"Stand by. You heard the man. What's this about?"

"We're looking for a man from Thornburg, Lester Riley Lynch. He's a person of interest in four murders in Florida. We wanted to pay the sheriff a courtesy call and see if he could tell us where to find him."

She keyed the microphone. "They're looking for one of them Lynch boys. He killed four people down in Florida."

"Tell them I'll be there in five minutes, Blanche. Make a fresh pot of coffee, will you?"

"Central, out." She set the microphone down with a *clunk*. "You boys want coffee?"

Sheriff Jeremiah Hickenlooper was a size XXXL man in a size XL uniform. His shirt buttons strained to hold his forest green uniform shirt together, and his black duty belt struggled to support both his gut and his sidearm. If this were a movie instead of real life, John Goodman would play Sheriff Hickenlooper. His ruddy face cracked a broad smile as he pushed open the glass door and saw Tank and me rise from our chairs. I knew from the internet that Hickenlooper was in his fourth term as sheriff. A born campaigner, he offered his hand. "Sheriff Jeremiah Hickenlooper at your service. Did Blanche get y'all coffee?"

"She's brewing a fresh pot."

We introduced ourselves. His eyes twinkled when he heard Tank's name.

He squinted one eye and considered Tank. "You're Tank Tyler? Hall of Fame defensive end for the Port City Pelicans? That Tank Tyler? Of course, you are; look at the size of you, for goodness sakes."

Tank smiled. "Yes, sir. Pleased to meet you."

Hickenlooper grabbed Tank's giant hand in his and pumped it like a jack handle. "I've never met a Hall of Famer in person. I'll never forget that playoff game against the Titans. You and Bigs Bigelow sacked the Titan quarterback five times. Mind you, I'm a Titans fan, but I picked the Pelicans to beat the spread. You made me a pot full of money that day, yes you did. It's an honor to meet you." He handed his cellphone to me. "Could you take a picture of me and Tank?"

Photography session completed, he rolled his beefy neck in Blanche's direction. "Bring three cups and the fixings into my office soon as they's ready. Okay, Blanche?"

He led us into an office right out of Mayberry, North Carolina. I expected Deputy Barney Fife and Aunt Bea to come in. Sheriff Hickenlooper's chair complained when he sat in it. "Make yourself at home, gents." He gestured at two oak side chairs.

After we sat, he leaned back and laced his hands across his considerable stomach. "Blanche said something about the Lynch boys?"

"Yes, sir. Tank and I are looking for Lester Riley Lynch. He's somewhere in Port City, Florida, and we want to interview his family and ask them to help locate him." I handed Hickenlooper a photo I obtained from the Defense Department.

"Are you two law officers?"

"I'm a private investigator and Tank is a private citizen." I showed the sheriff my PI license and concealed weapon permit.

Hickenlooper studied the photo, then set it on his desk. "I known Lester since he was a pup. He's wearing a Ranger tab in this here photo. I knew he joined the U.S. Army, but I hadn't heard he was a Ranger."

"He's not anymore. He was discharged for the good of the service."

"What did he do?"

"He beat up another soldier and put him in the base hospital fighting over a poker game. He served thirty days in the stockade, then asked for an OTH discharge."

I saw Hickenlooper's confusion and added. "OTH means *other than honorable*. His commanding officer was glad to see him go. Said Lynch didn't take orders well and was too enthusiastic about shooting and guns."

"Them Lynch boys, they's, uh, different. If they stay in Thornburg, we leave 'em alone. I never want to tangle with them, especially now I know Lester was a Ranger. Them Rangers are bad dudes. Lester was plenty dangerous in high school. No telling what he's up to today."

He leaned forward, his gut bulging across the desk. "To tell you the truth, the Lynches scare the pee-waddle out of me."

Blanche pushed the door open and carried in a school cafeteria tray with three cups of coffee, a sugar bowl, a cream pitcher, and a stack of sugar-substitute packets. She set the tray on the sheriff's desk. "Anything else I can do for y'all?"

"Thanks, Blanche. We're good." He grabbed a cup and slurped coffee. "Y'all help yourself."

I told Hickenlooper what Lynch did at the Florida concerts.

"Lester was strange, even in high school. The violence hid beneath the surface all the time. He played center on the Thornburg basketball team. Thornburg played Chesterfield High and my sister's boy Dennis was on the Chesterfield team. Lester threw an elbow at Dennis that broke his nose and knocked him plumb unconscious on the gym floor." He shook his head. "Dennis didn't come around for near on ten minutes. I threw him in my patrol car and ran him to the hospital. That concussion kept him dizzy for weeks."

"Did you press assault charges against Lester?"

Hickenlooper's eyebrows rose. "Are you nuts? In the first place, the Lynches would claim that accidents can happen in a hard-fought basketball game, and they'd be right. No jury in Goswell County would convict. In the second place, Lester's Uncle Chester Lynch would back-shoot me. I don't mess with them Lynches if I can avoid it. It wouldn't be good for my health."

"Tank and I plan to visit Lester's family in Thornburg and see if they've heard from him. Perhaps they know where he's staying."

Hickenlooper laughed. "Y'all are nuts. In the first place, them damn Lynches stick together. They won't tell you doodly-squat. In the second place, they might shoot you dead and bury you in some holler where nobody would ever find your body."

"The woman Lester is terrorizing is his cousin. She's a Lynch herself. Wouldn't that make a difference?"

"Everybody knows them damn Lynches is always marrying cousins, and everybody knows half the killings in the Lynch feud are because of who marries who. You want my advice, stay away from Thornburg."

He winked at Tank. "They's one more thing: Folks in Thornburg, they live in the last century when it comes to race relations. They don't cotton to black people. Hell, we have a handful of black folks in Chesterfield and they's none in Thornburg. Tank, if I was you, I wouldn't go there on a bet. I know you're big and you're tough, but them Lynches, they're pretty big too, and they got y'all outnumbered. Thornburg is full of Lynches."

"I appreciate your concern, sheriff. We'll be careful."

I finished my coffee. "Sheriff, would you consider coming with us to keep them under control and enforce the law while we interview them?"

Hickenlooper guffawed. "Go with you. Go with you. That's a damn good one." He laughed again. "Not enough gold in Fort Knox."

FORTY-THREE

Lester Lynch's parents were dead and his Uncle Chester was next of kin. If anyone in Tennessee knew where Lester was, it should be Chester. His parole officer gave his registered address as 417 Berry Street in Thornburg.

My GPS sent us past the town square.

"What's that building?" Tank asked.

"The old courthouse. Thornburg was the original county seat. After the Civil War the railroad bypassed Thornburg, and they moved the county seat to Chesterfield."

"And I suppose you know that because you studied Tennessee history in high school in Adams Creek, Texas?" Tank asked.

"Internet search last night. That nineteenth-century courthouse is a museum and office for the Goswell County Historical and Genealogical Society, open Monday, Wednesday, and Friday from ten a.m. to two p.m. and by appointment."

"What's that statue between the Tennessee flag and the Confederate flag?"

I stopped at the corner. "It's on your side. Read the inscription."

"*To Our Honored Dead.* I recognize the statue. It's a generic Confederate soldier. The United Daughters of the Confederacy erected these all over the Old South early in the twentieth century. We used to have them in every town square in Alabama."

"I'm surprised it hasn't been moved somewhere else," I said. "Check out the Confederate battle flag on county property."

"The sheriff was right about Goswell County. In the last U.S. Census, Goswell County was 97.78 percent Caucasian, bro. All the African-Americans must live in Chesterfield."

"And I suppose you know that because you studied Tennessee history in high school in Alabama?"

Tank grinned. "Wikipedia last night."

"I guess no one's objected to the statue."

"Or the flag. Not enough blacks willing to come from Chesterfield to make a decent protest. The past dies slowly in small towns."

Slipping the car back in gear, I followed the GPS directions.

The Berry Street house was like a double-wide made of brick. I circled the block. Half the lots were vacant, so I saw all four sides of the house. An A-frame single-car garage with peeled paint sat behind the house, its doors falling off the hinges. An ancient Ford Econoline sat on flat tires in the gravel driveway. Tall grass grew around it.

"No one's home," Tank said. "You hungry? We could eat, then come back."

"Tennessee makes great barbecue."

I had the GPS find the nearest barbecue joint. Big Al's Barbecue Barn was a block off the square.

The front door tinkled a bell as we walked in. A dozen or more customers, 97.78 percent Caucasian, were eating at a half-dozen picnic tables inside. They stared at us. Must not have been much going on in Thornburg if two strangers could bring the place to a dead stop. Then again, maybe the locals noticed the bulges under our jackets. Or Tank's coffee-colored skin.

As Tank and I crossed to the counter in the back under the *Order Here* sign, our footsteps were the only sound other than the wall air-conditioning unit.

An oversized man in a black apron with *Big Al's Barbecue Barn* embroidered in red script stood at a cutting board. "Afternoon," he said, looking at me. "Welcome to Big Al's. I'm Al. What can I get you?"

There was a big menu on the wall behind Al. "I'll have a pulled-pork platter with coleslaw and beans. Unsweet tea."

"I'll have the same," Tank added, "but with potato salad and beans."

"Pulled-pork platter with coleslaw and beans." Al grabbed a plate and filled it with pulled pork. "You want spicy or mild sauce?"

"Spicy," Tank and I said together.

"You from around here?"

"We're new in town," I answered.

He set the plate on a tray. "Passing through?"

"We came to see Chester Lynch."

If possible, the room grew even quieter.

Al spooned coleslaw into a serving dish. "Are you friends of his?" The spoon clanked on the steel pot, noisy in the sudden silence.

"We've never met." My voice carried throughout the restaurant.

Several chairs scooted back from the tables behind me.

Stepping to my left, I leaned my hip against the counter and twisted where I could watch the tables. Tank mirrored my move. He tucked his jacket behind the grip on his sidearm and moved his hand near the pistol.

Four men who had been seated behind us now stood between us and the door. Four tall men. Three had bulges under their jackets which I should have noticed as we walked in. Stupid lapse of judgment. I hoped it wouldn't get us killed.

The unarmed fourth man was Chester Lynch. As a paroled felon, he would go back to prison if he was caught with a firearm. I didn't recognize him earlier because he had grown a beard after his release from prison.

My stomach knotted when several other customers abandoned their food and moved toward the exit. Another Western cliché: The saloon patrons dodge for cover when the gunmen face off. Big Al probably kept a weapon behind the counter also. That made it four against two, and they had us in a crossfire if the balloon went up.

Al spooned baked beans into a dish. "Mind if I ask what business you have with Chester?" Al gave me a crocodile smile and dished my coleslaw.

"Do you know Chester?"

"I know everybody." Al stood upright with my food tray. He was as big as Tank, but his bulk was fat and Tank's was muscle. Was Big Al a Lynch?

He set the tray on the counter and added a plastic glass. "Iced tea, utensils, and napkins at that table over there."

"You haven't filled my friend's order."

Al didn't move. He had not peeked in Tank's direction the whole time we stood at the counter, nor did he acknowledge anything Tank said.

Nobody moved. The room could have been a tableau in a wax museum.

I held his gaze. "My friend will have a pulled-pork platter with potato salad and beans and unsweet tea."

Al's eyes cut to Tank, then back to me. "Sorry, we're out of food."

Tank kept his focus on the four men.

I moved my jacket to free my Glock 19. "Al, I am a peaceful man who avoids trouble whenever possible. I will pretend I didn't hear that, and I will pretend you didn't hear what I said. In the interest of giving you an opportunity to reconsider, I'll repeat myself one time: My friend wants a pulled-pork platter with potato salad and beans." I emphasized each word.

Al pointed at a sign on the wall behind him. *We reserve the right to refuse service to anyone.* "Read the sign, mister."

While Tank watched the four men, I walked behind the counter and shouldered Al aside. "You won't have to serve him; I will."

A Smith & Wesson revolver waited in a cubbyhole beneath the counter, ready to grab. I stuck it in my jacket pocket. That improved the odds.

Grabbing a plate from the stack, I piled it high with pulled pork. "Oh, looky here. There is some food you overlooked, Al." Setting the plate and two small bowls on a tray, I dished servings of potato salad and beans. I moved the tray to the counter and placed a plastic glass on it. "We'll help ourselves to iced tea, utensils, and napkins at that table over there."

I walked around the counter, collected both trays, and carried them to an empty picnic table.

Tank and I sat with our backs to the wall. We began to eat, and the four men sat and continued their meals and conversation as if nothing had happened.

Halfway through our meal, Chester Lynch walked over. He stopped three steps away. "What business do you have with Chester Lynch?"

"Cut the bullshit, Chester. Is your whiskey as good as they say?"

Chester cracked a smile. "You folks in the market for 'shine?"

I smiled too. "If we were, I wouldn't say so in public."

Chester jerked out a chair and sat across from us. He focused on Tank. "Forgive Cousin Al. We figured you fellows was Feds."

"What made you decide we weren't?"

"No Fed would pull that trick with Al behind the counter, dishing his own food. And Al, he put on a show for the locals. If the money's good, I do business with anybody. I'm an equal-opportunity moonshiner." He grinned, but the grin didn't reach his eyes.

I extended my hand. "Fred Remington, from Atlanta, and this is Tiny." He shook hands with us both. "Let's visit a spell."

After lunch Chester invited us to his house to sample his moonshine and get to know each other.

An hour after that, Tank and I sat at a chipped Formica kitchen table in Chester's brick mobile home.

I sipped a glass of his White Lightning while we negotiated a supplier contract with my Atlanta organized crime gang. I told Chester that Tank had liver trouble and couldn't drink. That way, Tank could drive after we finished our informal interrogation.

Getting a witness drunk is an interrogation technique I did not learn as a police detective. I discovered the tool early in my PI career when my own client drank three cocktails at a lunch meeting in a local restaurant. She had hired me to catch her husband cheating. She got sloshed and made a pass at me, confessing that she cheated on her wealthy husband whenever she could. She promised me a memorable "afternoon delight." I demurred, but added *get-the-witness-drunk* to my toolkit of PI techniques.

Then I added Rule Twelve-A to McCrary's Rules. Rule Twelve was *People lie.* Rule Twelve-A was *In vino, veritas. In wine, truth.*

After Chester had gotten himself sozzled, I asked him to confirm a rumor I had heard that the hot, new Kentucky country music star Cleo Hennessey was secretly a Lynch from Thornburg, Tennessee.

After a second glass of White Lightning, Chester had trouble sitting upright in his chair. "Yeah, the bitch turned her back on her family. She was borned Katie Boone Lynch, but, no, that weren't good enough for her. Her daddy and me, we fixed her up to marry my boy Lester soon as he got out of the army. They was betrothed. We made that deal when they was teenagers. But she run away. She went against her daddy's wishes, and her own momma and daddy won't have nothing to do with her." Chester laid his head on his arm on the kitchen table. "She ain't no Lynch no more," he mumbled. He began to snore.

"Did he pass out?" Tank whispered.

My own head swam, even though I drank a fraction of what Chester consumed. "Our new hooch supplier won't remember our conversation tomorrow, but his kinfolks from Big Al's know we came to buy whiskey. Let's stay in character and take the two quarts of firewater we bought for a sample."

As I stood, I grabbed Tank's chair to steady myself. "Geez, that mountain dew packs a punch. I can hardly walk. You carry the bottles. Take the car keys."

Tank wedged the moonshine behind the rental car's spare tire and punched the Knoxville airport into our GPS.

After the Thornburg city limits sign showed in my side mirror, my gut unknotted. Drawing a full breath for the first time in three hours, I belched and tasted spicy barbecue sauce mixed with moonshine. *Ugh.* That was enough to make me a little nauseous.

"Whew," Tank said, "your breath could peel paint off a wall."

"Stop in the next town that sells coffee."

"And mouthwash. Tell me, bro, was this trip as wasted as I think?"

"We had to try, big guy. We learned that the whole Lynch family knows who Cleo is. She doesn't need to worry they'll find out; that ship has sailed. We learned that her own parents don't consider her family anymore, so she can save the postage on their wedding invitations."

Tank punched the car up to forty-five, fast enough for the winding two-lane road. "Did you notice how poor Chester Lynch was?"

"Yeah. He lives in a sixty-year-old house that's as small as a mobile home with a junk car in the back."

239

"The other Lynches we met in Big Al's, did they look like they had two extra nickels to rub together?"

"Now that you mention it, no. What's your point?"

"Lester abandoned an M4 worth over $1,000 in Port City and another one in Jacksonville. You commented that he spends money to travel to concerts, money to buy disguises, money to obtain illegal explosives and construct a bomb, and money to buy an expensive gunsight and top-of-the-line climbing equipment."

"Yeah, he's well-financed. So?"

Tank slowed the car as we caught up to a heavily-laden lumber truck. "Where did he get the money?"

"Good question. Let's ask Cleo after we get home."

Tank pulled into a convenience store in the next town. We bought coffee, and I bought mouthwash and aspirin. In the restroom, I gargled with the mouthwash. After coffee and swallowing three aspirin, I would feel almost human as the aspirin kicked in.

Before we got underway again, I poured the moonshine on the ground beside the C-store and tossed the bottles in the recycle bin.

"Look on the bright side, Tank: We were outnumbered behind enemy lines and escaped with our lives. We enjoyed authentic Appalachian barbecue. All for the price of two barbecue plates and two quarts of moonshine to take back for our criminal gang in Atlanta."

"Yeah, Fred Remington, indeed. That was fast thinking."

"Chester served time for attempted murder of an ATF Agent. His whole family has made moonshine for generations. He's been out of prison six months. It was a good bet he was back in business."

"What would you have done if your bluff hadn't worked?"

I gave him a palms-up. "We would have died in a hail of bullets. What else?"

FORTY-FOUR

Lester Lynch knew who I was and at least one vehicle I drove—the Caravan he had slashed the tires on. He was smart enough to find my office location on the internet. It was dangerous to meet Cleo or LeMarvis there anymore.

Even though Magnolia Island had a guarded gatehouse, I made sure no one followed me as I drove to LeMarvis and Cleo's home.

"Cleo, Tank pointed out that Lester is spending a lot of money on this… uh… project. Do you have any idea where he gets the money?"

"Lester's real smart, and he's good at math. In high school, he used to brag that he made spending money beating his buddies at poker. He said he was so smart that he didn't have to cheat to win. Could he be playing poker?"

"I'll send my agents to canvass the poker rooms in South Florida with Lester's picture. Perhaps a dealer or employee at the casinos has seen him."

"He'll be easy enough to remember," Cleo said, "He's six-five."

"That's true," I said, "but don't expect a quick answer, even if that's what he's doing. Most poker rooms operate eighteen hours a day weekdays and twenty-four/seven on weekends and holidays, and there are over a dozen poker rooms in Miami-Dade, Atlantic, and Broward counties. That's a bunch of dealers to track down." To LeMarvis: "That takes manpower. It will be expensive."

LeMarvis reached for his checkbook. "How much you need?"

When I told him, his eyebrows rose a fraction of an inch. "I keep telling myself it's just little green pieces of paper." He filled out the check and handed it to me with a sigh.

"That's not all, LeMarvis. We have to assume Lynch knows where you live."

"I own the house in an anonymous trust. It doesn't show under my name anywhere on the internet." He frowned. "Oops. I almost forgot the news media."

"That's right," I said. "You've hosted several newsworthy parties and charity fundraisers at your home over the years. The *Port City Press-Journal* printed several up-close-and-personal stories covering you and your famous house in the sports and local sections. The *Pee-Jay's* back issues are online. Lester can follow digital footprints to Magnolia Island."

"What about our guardhouse? He couldn't get onto the island."

I shook my head. "I had a similar problem with Tank and his house on Pink Coral Island on another case. There are ways to get on the island that the guardhouse won't stop. Plus, look out your window. Imagine there is a boat out there."

They both stared at Seeti Bay.

"Lynch is an expert marksman. He can shoot from a boat and hit you from 500 yards, and those windows won't stop a bullet. If you stay here, you're both targets."

Cleo clutched her fiancé's hand. "What should we do? Leave town? Hide in a cave until you catch Lester?"

"You two should stay with Tank until we catch him. Tank's house is generations older than yours. It's a whole different architecture without floor-to-ceiling windows and wide-open bay views. There's a jungle in his back garden. Lynch would have a difficult time finding a clear shot, even if he knew you were there. Tank thinks it's a good idea."

LeMarvis eyed Cleo. Cleo eyed LeMarvis and nodded.

After I exited LeMarvis's electric gate, I watched in my mirror to make sure it closed.

Clint called. I pulled to the curb and took it as a video call. "Hey, Clint."

"You'll never guess who called your landline."

"The Foreign Minister of Belarus," I said with a straight face.

"What? No. It—where the heck did that Belarus thing come from? Have you even been there?"

"I'm pulling your chain, bro. I'm not even sure where Belarus is. Who called?"

Clint smirked. "Terry Kovacs."

"That's a surprise. Why didn't she call my cell?"

"She called to apologize."

"She did that the other day. I told you."

"No, bro. Terry called to apologize to *me*, not you. She didn't have my cellphone number, so she called the landline hoping to speak to me."

"Why did she apologize to you?"

"She said she treated me unfairly two years ago after I moved in with you. She was jealous because she wanted you all to herself and resented me for moving in."

"That's true. I had forgotten."

"Terry felt guilty and told me it was okay with her that I lived with you. And get this, bro: She said straight up, she wants you back, and she hopes I approve and will put in a good word with you. Me, the pesky kid brother you see in a sitcom cliché."

Clint pointed at his face. "This is me, putting in a good word for Terry. I know you and Vicky get along great. Heck, I like Vicky, but you haven't been yourself since Miyo. Maybe Terry can break you out of your funk. Give her a chance."

"Perhaps I will. She says she's grown some and is ready for a real, long-term relationship. After this wedding is over, I'll give her a call."

"By the way, bro, speaking of growing up, tomorrow is Madison's eighteenth birthday. I'm taking her to register to vote."

Cleo Hennessey

Cleo shook Vicky Ramirez's hand. "Pleased to meet you, Ms. Ramirez. Tank Tyler and Chuck McCrary, they both speak highly of you and your daddy. They said you was the person to do a prenuptial agreement for me and LeMarvis."

"Please, call me Vicky." Vicky Ramirez wore a tan pantsuit with white pinstripes, accented with a heavy gold necklace and coordinated hoop earrings. Even in four-inch heels, she was shorter than Cleo in her flat sandals. "I've worked with Tank and Chuck and their clients many times. I think highly of them also. Come. Let's go to my office. You want something to drink?"

"Bourbon and branch would be nice."

Vicky's eyebrows rose a fraction of an inch. "Why don't we save that for after our conference. Perhaps coffee or tea? A soft drink?"

"Hot tea with lemon would be good."

Vicky gave drink instructions to her secretary and led Cleo to her office.

Cleo peered out the window at Seeti Bay sparkling below.

Chuck said Vicky and her father, Don, ran a thriving boutique law firm which specialized in family law. Cleo gawked at the diplomas, certificates, and bar association memberships on Vicky's office wall and remembered Chuck's ego wall and smiled. Any legal process unsettled her. She told herself that was silly. Goodness knows, Vicky was as friendly as could be and gave her a warm, welcoming smile.

Vicky smiled again. "How did you and LeMarvis meet?"

Cleo told how LeMarvis protected her from a group of drunken urban cowboys in the bar fight. "Afterwards, LeMarvis drove me home, and he acted a perfect gentleman. He said he loved my music and asked if he could call on me. He didn't make a pass at me or nothing like that." Cleo lowered her voice. "Actually, I was kinda disappointed, him being so polite and handsome and all. He was my knight in shining armor, and I would have lifted my skirts if he had asked." She felt her face flush.

Vicky's secretary knocked and brought in their drinks. After she left, Vicky turned back to Cleo. "You were telling me about LeMarvis."

Cleo sipped her tea and blotted her lips with a napkin. "LeMarvis, he called the next day for a proper date. After that, he gave me a ticket to a Peregrines game. I watched him play, and that's what got me interested. Have you seen LeMarvis play?"

"I don't follow basketball."

Cleo flashed a smile. "LeMarvis is an artist on the court. The basketball is an extension of his fingers. He handles a basketball as easily as I play a piano. I loved his artistry first, then as I knew him better, I admired his heart. He's a truly good, good man."

Vicky set her cup down. "Thanks for that wonderful story. I wish you all the happiness in the world."

"Can I ask you a personal question, Miss Vicky? About Chuck."

Vicky made a face. "Chuck is my client, and we have a confidential relationship which covers some of what I know. Anything else, I'll be glad to answer."

"You and Chuck… Are you and him… together? Like boyfriend and girlfriend?"

"What did Chuck tell you?"

"He says you send him clients and you and him have dinner occasionally. It's the way he speaks of you and the way Tank talks about you and Chuck. It seemed there was more to it than that."

Vicky twirled her coffee cup in both hands. "Chuck and I are more than friends, but it's complicated."

"Most relationships are."

Vicky lifted her cup and held it to her lips without drinking.

Cleo figured Vicky didn't want to discuss it. "I'm sorry, Miss Vicky. Everybody tells me I'm nosy. It's not my business. Forget I asked."

"My younger brother, Hidalgo—everybody calls him Hank—he was Chuck's commanding officer in Afghanistan. They were both wounded in Afghanistan and treated at an army base in Germany. They flew back to the U.S. on the same plane, and I met Hank at Dover Air Force base to bring him home. That's how I met Chuck. We chatted a couple of minutes until he left for another army facility for rehab. I flew home to Port City with Hank."

"I saw Chuck's Bronze Star medal in his office."

"That's from when they were wounded. Chuck was wounded worse than Hank." Vicky smiled. "Hank said he got just a scratch. I know it was more than that, but he and Chuck are both modest. It's a guy thing."

They laughed.

"I remember one game when LeMarvis got knocked to the floor and played hurt the rest of the game. He was bruised and sore the next day, but he never complained. I think a lot of men act like that. I asked Chuck about his Bronze Star, but he won't talk about it."

"He never mentioned it to me either, but Hank did. Chuck was wounded more than once and one soldier was killed."

Cleo deliberated for a moment. "That don't sound complicated to me."

"It wasn't complicated at first. After their Army service, Hank came home to Port City and became a cop, and Chuck attended the University of Florida. For the next four years, Chuck stayed with Hank when the Gators played football or basketball against the UAC Falcons or the Miami Hurricanes. Hank and Chuck ate dinner with my parents any time Chuck was in town. My parents always invited me."

"Still don't sound complicated."

Vicky laughed. "Chuck graduated and became a Port City cop. He and Hank were best friends, so I saw him more often."

"That's when he asked you for a date?"

"Not then. Chuck had lived here for three years. Every time I saw him, I sent him signals. He was oblivious; the man ignored every hint. Maybe it was because I'm a decade older than he is. Whatever the reason, he never did ask me for a date."

"Okay, that sounds complicated. You had the hots for him and he ignored you?"

"Pretty much."

"So how did you and him get together? Assuming you did get together."

"I threw myself at him, that's how. I invited him to my place, wore a sexy see-through blouse, plied him with liquor, and asked why he never made a pass at me. That did the trick."

"So, you and him are boyfriend and girlfriend? He doesn't talk like that either."

"That's when it got complicated."

They laughed together.

"Chuck and I want different things. I love my career. I don't want a husband, or children, or a picket fence. Chuck wants a wife and kids and a picket fence."

"LeMarvis wants a whole basketball team of kids."

"Not me. I could never give Chuck a family. That's why we're friends with benefits. You understand?"

"Sure, you like each other as friends, and you sleep together, but you're not in love." Cleo thought that was sad, but she didn't say it. "Okay. I understand. We can do the prenuptial stuff now."

Vicky pulled over a legal pad. "What assets do you have to protect?"

Cleo seemed surprised. "Oh, I don't have nothing yet. All the money I make with my music, I plow it back into costumes, instruments, music, marketing, and such. Tank, he says the money will come if I keep doing this well, but I don't have nothing now. It's LeMarvis who needs protecting."

"I don't understand."

"Miss Vicky, some people believe I'm a gold digger. People look at me and see a tall, good-looking blonde who talks like a hick and comes from a poor family. People think I love LeMarvis because he's rich. Admit it, didn't the thought cross your mind a teensy bit?"

Vicky smiled. "Some people might consider LeMarvis's money part of his attraction."

"That's true. It's *part* of his attraction, I won't deny. It don't hurt none that LeMarvis is rich. When we first met, I was taken with him because he was rich and famous and, well, because he was black." She blushed again. "You know what they say about black men. I wanted to find out if it was true, 'cause I never dated no black man before." Cleo winked. "Between us, honey, it is true."

Vicky laughed with her.

"After I got to know LeMarvis, his money didn't matter no more. He is a good, good man who wants a family and to make the world a better place to raise them. I don't want nobody to think I married LeMarvis for money. That's why I want a prenuptial agreement."

Vicky pulled the legal pad closer. "I understand. Let's focus on your career plans."

"You know, Miss Vicky, I never finished high school, but I'm smart. My grammar ain't so good, and I'm a hillbilly, but I ain't no dumb blonde, no matter how I look and sound."

FORTY-FIVE

Carlos McCrary

A fter three days of interviews at area poker rooms, Angelina Curtis called me. "Lynch was at the Lucky Seven Casino in Humbolt Springs. Lynch was a regular there for a week last month. He won big. The casino security chief gave me a better photo from their security videos."

"Did he stay at the hotel?"

"He registered under the name K. T. Boone, but he checked out two weeks ago and hasn't been back since."

"Nice work, Angie. FYI, Cleo Hennessey's real name is Katie Boone Lynch. Lynch picked Cleo's birth name for his alias. He must feel an emotional attachment to it, so he might keep using it. Send your info and the new photo to Bernie Beltran with copies to Snoop and me. Hell, send copies to Gunner and Pete and Robby also. I promised to keep Bernie Beltran in the loop. Perhaps he can do something with it. Tell Snoop to use the new photo."

"Will do."

"Maybe Lester a/k/a K. T. wore out his welcome with the other players at the Lucky Seven and shifted to a different casino to search for fresh meat. You and Snoop keep searching. Cover every casino and every poker dealer in South Florida."

"Got it," Angelina said. "What kind of weirdo picks his ex-girlfriend's name for an alias?"

"We don't need to understand a pathological killer's pathology to find him. Keep on keeping on. Rule Eight: *Sometimes there is no substitute for shoe leather.* If you find him, remember he's killed four people and trained as a U.S. Army Ranger. He's dangerous as hell."

Angelina laughed into the phone. "So am I, Chuck. So am I."

I called Bubble-Gum Beltran the next day. "Bernie, did you get the lead my agent Angelina Curtis sent you?"

"Yeah, but I don't see how it does any good. She says the suspect checked out two weeks ago."

"Can you do something with the fact that he used the name K. T. Boone? Cleo's real name is Katie Boone Lynch. Lester Lynch may keep using it. My people are checking all the poker rooms and related hotels in South Florida. You could have your guys check the non-casino hotels for a guest registered as K. T. Boone."

"You know how many hotels there are in Port City proper, Mac? And there's the suburbs, not to mention Miami-Dade and Broward counties. It's a needle in a haystack. Think how much manpower it would take."

Don't call me Mac. "Instead of conserving manpower, remember the four people Lester Lynch murdered and the other two people who he's looking to kill next. Your picture could be on the front page of the *Pee-Jay* with a headline about the police detective who caught a serial killer. You might get promoted."

The line was silent a while.

"Serve and protect, right?" Bubble-Gum said. "I'll put guys on it. What are you gonna do? Let's don't step on each other's toes."

"Like I said: My people will check the casinos and casino hotels in the Tri-County area. I'll check as many internet private short-term rentals as I can. You have the perp's picture from the Lucky Seven security video?"

"Yeah. It's better than the Army Ranger portrait you sent me. It doesn't seem right to show his picture in uniform with a U.S. flag in the background. Doesn't respect either the uniform or the flag, him being a multiple murder suspect."

Perhaps Bernie wasn't as bad as I thought.

The internet listed dozens of websites with short-term vacation rentals. Each website featured hundreds of private homes, condos, and non-traditional hotels in Port City alone. And he might be staying in Miami or Fort Lauderdale or Palm Beach or...

This was worse than a needle in a haystack. This was a needle in a field of haystacks.

Rule Sixteen: *Sometimes you have to do something, even if it's wrong. At least you'll know you tried.*

I gritted my teeth and hired more agents to make phone calls.

One thing made it easier: Lynch was six-foot-five. Another was that he might use the name K. T. Boone.

On each call, my agents introduced themselves, explained that they were working with the Port City police, and asked if a man fitting Lynch's description stayed at their property. Now and again, someone recalled a tenant like that. My agent would email the landlord Lynch's picture, and the landlord would reply that it was not him.

Then we would call some more.

The local television news programs interviewed Bernie Beltran and broadcast Lynch's picture from the Lucky Seven Casino security camera with a "Have you seen him?" notice. Beltran told me dozens of people thought they had seen Lynch, but none of the leads panned out.

Meanwhile, Cleo and LeMarvis's wedding date drew closer.

The most frustrating part was I didn't know if I was approaching the Lester Lynch problem the right way. Finding Lynch was like trying to grab a fistful of water.

My team called larger properties first, on the assumption that Lynch would prefer the relative anonymity of hiding in a large pool of guests where he might stand out less. My fear was he had rented a private home. If so, and he rented the house from Craigslist or a similar website, I was screwed. If he rented from my internet list, we had hundreds, if not thousands, of phone calls to make, and some properties rented to tenants without the owner meeting them in person. That prospect was hopeless.

Cleo choked back the tears when she told me none of her Thornburg family would come. All the Lynches had rejected her. "At least, Grandpa and Grandma Boone are coming from Kentucky. Grandpa will walk me down the aisle."

"That's wonderful, Cleo."

Then someone leaked to the news media that Cleo and LeMarvis were engaged and had set the date for September first.

The internet blew up with speculation on where the wedding would be.

FORTY-SIX

M y intercom chirped. "Chuck, Renate Crowell is here to see you."
"I'll be right out."

Before the internet and the 24-hour news cycle, Renate Crowell began as a first-string crime reporter for the *Press-Journal*. Now the *Pee-Jay* struggled with fewer reporters, and she earned her keep writing local news, human interest, society gossip, and, for all I knew, an occasional sports story. Renate survived the newspaper cost cuts by being as cynical as a politician, as persistent as a glacier, and as smart as a rocket scientist.

She was also as hot as a South Florida sidewalk at high noon in August.

Renate appeared at odd intervals to snoop into my newsworthy cases when I least wanted to see her. I nicknamed her the *Princess of the Pee-Jay*.

She kissed me on the cheek and gave me a hug. "Hello, hot shot. Long time, no talk to. How's it hanging?"

"Hello, Renate. Let's stop by the break room for coffee and go to my conference room."

"That's the best offer I've had all day."

We got coffee and sat in my conference room.

"How are you, Princess?"

"Surviving, handsome, I'm surviving. The latest rumor is that the *Pee-*

Jay is cutting staff again. Pretty soon, they'll have me emptying the waste baskets every night."

"If the *Pee-Jay* succumbs to internet and television news, you'll be there to lower the flag and lock the door. Then you'll find another way to survive."

"*Hmph.* You know how hard it is to start over at age forty-three?"

"You could pass for thirty-three, Princess."

"How could I explain working for the *Pee-Jay* for twenty years?"

"Good point, but you didn't come here to bitch and moan. What's on your mind?"

"See, handsome, you were never one for small talk, unless it was pillow talk. You still living like a monk? Or would you accept another invitation for a home-cooked meal and a night of unbridled passion?"

Renate and I had fallen into bed together on occasion, but she had been more subtle in the past. Now she was as obvious as a flashing neon sign. The times, they were a-changing indeed.

"Renate, you always have more on your agenda than to seduce me with lasagna and have your way with me for dessert."

"True, but since the subject is on the table, I make a mean lasagna. Want an encore?"

"Not ready for that, Renate. Thanks anyway. What else is on your mind?"

"Cleo Hennessey's wedding to LeMarvis Jones. Can you get me an invite? If not, I could be your plus-one. Girls are pushovers for sex after a wedding, or hadn't you heard?"

As she said it, I mulled over Terry Kovacs. When Terry dated me two years before, she might have freaked out if I invited her to a wedding. Now she claimed she was ready for a serious relationship. I wondered.

"Vicky Ramirez invited me to be her plus-one," I said.

Vicky's was a business invitation, since Cleo hadn't known Vicky before the concert tour. Vicky knew I would work the wedding anyway. Besides, if Vicky were in a relationship, she and I would not be making belly rubs with each other.

Renate interrupted my reverie. "I still need an invitation, handsome.

This wedding is front-page news, and I need a big story to impress the *Pee-Jay* high muckety-mucks."

"I'll see what I can do."

Cleo and LeMarvis's wedding plans continued while I searched for Lester Lynch. You would assume a man six-feet-five-inches tall would be easy to find. Not in a city with four million people. And that didn't include Miami and Fort Lauderdale.

Three weeks remained before the wedding. Cleo had delayed selecting a venue in hopes we could capture Lynch first, but soon logistical issues of flowers, caterers, and so forth would force her to select a site. The good news was that August is off season on Port City Beach and finding a hotel with space available would not be difficult.

Snoop found another poker room near Fort Lauderdale where Lynch played for one week in late June before he had played at the Lucky Seven Casino.

Was Lynch moving from casino to casino?

Then Angelina found a dealer at a third casino who remembered Lynch.

He had a pattern: Lynch stayed at each casino hotel for one week and played each night at their busiest times unless he was out of town at Cleo's concerts. After a week, he switched to another casino hotel. At all three hotels, he registered as K. T. Boone.

Unfortunately, there were thirteen casino hotels in South Florida, and he could change his pattern on a whim. He might move to Palm Beach County or even Okeechobee.

Plan A: Send all the agents I could hire to show Lynch's picture around the other casino poker rooms in the Tri-County area.

Plan B: Set stakeouts at the three Atlantic County casinos where Lynch had not yet played.

With LeMarvis Jones's millions behind me, I had the resources to do both.

Throw enough lines in the water, and Lynch might bite one.

The next week we found another poker room in Broward County where Lynch had played. Same routine—he played for one week, won big, registered at the casino hotel as K. T. Boone, then checked out.

We kept searching. We had to catch him before he killed again.

Morris Martinez's picture flashed on my phone. "Chuck, Lynch is here. I'm calling from the lobby because they don't allow cellphones in the poker room. He's buying chips."

"Are you sure it's him? He often wears a wig and colored contact lens."

"And he is tonight, but it's him. You can bet on it. Get it? You can bet on it?"

"I'm delirious with laughter. Where are you?"

"High Five Casino in Corcoran Heights."

"Got it. Keep an eye on him. I'm on my way."

High Five had a security setup an international airport would envy—including metal detectors and X-ray machines. No way could Morris carry his sidearm inside. However, Lynch would enter from the hotel wing, so I couldn't be sure he was unarmed. Perhaps the entrance from the hotel had different security. Too many unknowns.

"You want me to take him down?" Morris asked.

Despite his often-inappropriate sense of humor, Morris would attack the gates of hell with a bucket of water. "I admire your confidence, but you're five-nine and skinny as a flagpole. Lynch is built like an NFL linebacker, and he's a former Army Ranger. He's dangerous and he's crazy, a bad combination. We don't know what he'll do if cornered. There are innocent people around. Keep an eye on him; I'll be there in an hour."

Before I left my condo garage, I locked my weapons in the built-in gun safe in my Dodge Grand Caravan. I couldn't carry them into the casino, but I wanted them handy if I needed them later.

As I drove to Corcoran Heights, I called Bubble-Gum Beltran to meet us there.

There was little traffic that time of night, and I made it across town in forty-five minutes.

I slipped the parking valet a twenty and told him to keep my van in front where I could get it quickly. He eyed the twenty disdainfully. I handed him another twenty. "Is that better?"

He grinned. "Park over there and keep the keys. How's that for getting your money's worth?"

I parked where he pointed and threw him a two-finger salute. I locked the van.

I texted Morris that I was in the lobby. He would feel his phone vibrate and come out.

Morris joined me in a corner of the lobby. "There are eight tables in the room. Six of them are in use. Lynch is at the high-stakes table in the center. His back is to the entrance, so I'll bet he won't see us as we walk in. Get it? I'll *bet* he won't see us."

I managed not to groan. "Has he been drinking?"

"Soft drinks."

"Is he armed?"

"I watched his jacket as he leaned in to buy chips. He has a knife up his sleeve. I couldn't tell if he wore an ankle holster. He's not wearing a shoulder holster or a belt holster, that I do know. How do you want to handle this?"

"Detectives Beltran and Feldman are on their way. They'll enter the poker room and slip the other customers out. Hopefully, Lynch will be focused on the players at his table so he won't notice the cops emptying the rest of the room. Two uniforms will join the detectives and they'll surround his table for the arrest. You and I are unarmed backup."

Morris grinned. "Sounds like a safe bet. Get it?"

"Yeah, I get it." You couldn't blame the kid for trying.

I sent Morris back inside and leaned against the lobby wall.

The longest ten minutes of my life later, Bubble-Gum and Feldman appeared with two uniforms. "He in the poker room, Mac?"

Don't call me Mac. "Yeah. I stayed here because Lynch knows me by sight. There are thirty-two customers at the other tables and six at Lynch's table. Morris is inside playing at a low-stakes table. He's unarmed. Lynch carries a knife up his sleeve and possibly an ankle holster."

"Morris Martinez? He's a cop."

"He works for me when he's off duty."

Bubble-Gum nodded. "I know Morris. Weird sense of humor, but a good man to have in your corner. Why isn't he armed?"

"He's off duty. He can't carry his weapon into a casino."

"I didn't know that." Bubble-Gum glanced at Feldman. "Let's move the other gamblers out, one at a time. Quietly."

The uniforms took up post at the double doors and prevented other customers from entering. "Sorry, sir, there's a leak from the cooling system, and the air in the poker room has a nasty chemical smell. They expect to have it fixed in an hour. Come back then."

Feldman pushed through the double doors. Beltran followed. Customers straggled out one and two at a time. Three female dealers in low-cut black cocktail dresses exited. The male dealers wore tuxedoes. This was a high-class casino with high-class people to take your high-class money. I read somewhere that gamblers tip female dealers more than they tip male dealers. Maybe if the male dealers wore low-cut dresses? *Nah.*

I counted twenty-two customers and five dealers out through the doors before I slipped in.

From where Lynch sat, he could see two other tables. One was Morris's low-stakes table. Beltran and Feldman had emptied the other tables, with Lynch none the wiser.

I circled my finger at the people at Morris's table and gestured over my shoulder with my thumb: *Get them out, now.*

Morris raked his chips into a jacket pocket and stood. He murmured to the dealer, who closed and locked her bank. She and the other players stood and stared at the high-stakes table. They straggled toward the exit.

Feldman moved to the dealer at the last table and leaned close to her ear.

Her eyebrows climbed, and she nodded. "Folks, it's time for a break. Carry your chips with you for ten minutes. There are free drinks in the lobby." Locking the cover on her bank, she headed toward the exit and glanced my way. I gave her a nod and a thumbs-up.

Lynch held his cards face down while he gazed left and right, craning his neck to see the other tables around him. Realizing they were empty, he leaped to his feet and threw his cards at Beltran and his chair at Feldman.

He jumped around the table faster than I considered possible for a man his size. He grabbed the dealer's long blonde hair and jerked her to her feet.

The remaining players at the table shrieked and stampeded toward the exit, bowling over the two uniforms entering the room.

Lynch slid a stiletto from his left sleeve, wrapped his left arm around the dealer's neck, and dragged her toward the rear of the room to a service door reserved for cocktail servers. He pressed the point of the stiletto to her throat. Her eyes rolled back and she screamed.

Lynch throttled her to silence with the crook of his elbow. "One move and she's dead." He jerked on the dealer's neck. She was more than a foot shorter than Lynch and her feet dangled inches above the carpet. Her high-heeled shoes dropped to the floor and she kicked her legs futilely.

Lynch was surrounded by four cops, Morris, and me. He scanned the room until his defiant stare locked on me. "Well, if it isn't the mighty Carlos McCrary, the Mexican macho man. How do you feel now, spic? Do you still think you're smarter than me?"

He lowered the dealer until her bare feet reached the floor. She tugged on his forearm. Lynch didn't seem to notice.

"The bitch dealer and me, we're leaving. If anybody follows us, I'll slit her throat. Don't anybody do anything stupid."

He backed through the service door, dragging the barefooted dealer as a shield.

Rushing the door, I peeked through the round window.

Lynch punched the woman on the temple, stunning her. He threw her over his shoulder like a sack of potatoes and ran through the service bar. Two female bartenders gawked at him, not knowing what had happened. Lynch slammed through another set of doors into the casino kitchen.

I jammed through the service door and ran after him.

Beltran yelled at the female bartenders, "Don't let him get away."

In your dreams, Bubble-Gum.

The bartenders backed away.

In seconds, I reached the kitchen doors and stared through one of the round windows. The dealer lay on the floor, blocking our way, writhing in pain.

I lunged through the door.

Lynch yelled in the distance. "The nigger is a dead man, McCrary. If I can't have Katie, I'll take both of them to hell with me. And you too."

Lynch left his ceramic knife stuck in the dealer's neck. She was alive as I knelt at her side, but she could bleed out in seconds if I pulled the knife out. Blood bubbled from her wound and ran down the side of her neck, soaking her hair like red paint. Her frightened eyes seemed big as poker chips.

Beltran knelt beside me. "An ambulance is on the way. Should we pull the knife out?"

"It's plugging the wound. Let the EMTs make that decision." Beltran and I both knew she wouldn't last more than seconds.

I held her hands. "Help is on the way, sweetheart. Hang on. Don't leave me, okay? Don't leave me."

She tried to speak, but bloody bubbles were all that came from her lips. They left red streaks down her cheeks. She groaned like a wounded animal, squeezed my hands, and sagged like a deflated balloon. Her eyes stared sightlessly into mine.

She was gone.

FORTY-SEVEN

Lynch went to ground somewhere. We sent his picture and descriptions of his disguises to every casino in Florida: *Watch for a six-feet-five-inch man renting a room.*

Lynch had evaporated like a puff of smoke in a hurricane.

I told Cleo and LeMarvis what Lynch shouted as he ran away. "He'll show at your wedding; I'd bet the ranch on it. You should postpone it until we find him."

"And what if you don't find him… ever?" LeMarvis asked. "Do we never get married? No, we'll elope. Lester can't stop a wedding that's already happened."

"Eloping won't stop him," I said. "Even if you're married, he would kill you. He would still want to have Cleo. With your marriage so widely known, he's got a September first deadline. That makes him easier to catch. We know he'll show at your wedding."

"Another thing, honey," Cleo said, "All my life I've wanted a big wedding. Me and you, we get married once, and, by the Lord God in heaven above, we're gonna do it in style. Long after Lester Lynch is in jail and forgotten, I want a wedding that we'll remember for a hundred years."

She gazed back and forth between LeMarvis and me. "Chuck, if we pick the right hotel and the right spot so you and your people can give us security, we'll be fine. Lester's crazy, but he don't want to die. Nobody wants to die."

In my experience, that wasn't true. I remembered my shootout with a jilted husband whose hatred so consumed him that he didn't care whether he lived or died, so long as he could take her with him. He tried to kill us both and damn near succeeded with me.

Lester Lynch was smart as hell, yes, but had he crossed the bloody murder-suicide line? Was he as loony as a suicide bomber?

Cleo was so excited about her fairytale wedding that she was in no mood to consider that question.

"No, Cleo, we can't hold the wedding here." I pointed to the balconies above us. "Over 400 hotel rooms overlook this stretch of beach. We can't secure 400 hotel rooms. It's an easy shot for a man with Lynch's skills. If you moved the ceremony behind the artificial waterfall, to the nude sunbathing area, you'd be out of sight of the balconies."

"And out of sight of the ocean. No, let's look at another hotel."

"Let's take a break. I need an iced coffee."

We found a table in the poolside snack bar. "Cleo, we're in the rainy season. With your wedding at five p.m., you have a sixty percent chance of rain. Why not hold the wedding in a hotel ballroom? My team can secure an indoor venue better."

Cleo sipped on a Coco Loco, her third of the day. It was good thing I was driving to the hotel visits.

"The Good Lord will send sunshine on my wedding day. We'll keep a ballroom for backup, but I always assume things will turn out right. Get a to-go glass for your coffee and let's check out the next hotel."

Two weeks before the wedding, we found the right hotel.

The Hotel Royal Sands was the winner. One end of the hotel's beachfront had a stand of Sea Grapes and a hedge of Bougainvillea that shielded it from view of the hotel. There was room for a white canopy sunshade for 400 guests, and it was convenient to the Duke and Duchess Room if it rained. I could guard access to the venue with ten agents.

Finally, Cleo and LeMarvis could print the invitations, including one for Renate Crowell, Princess of the *Pee-Jay*.

After I got home, I asked Clint about Madison. "Since she registered to vote, has she become any more interesting?"

Clint wobbled his hand back and forth. "We've had a few more dates. Some for romance and sex and a couple of lunches for so-called adult conversations."

"And...?"

"She's still shallow and boring. I'm going to let her down easy. In a few days, classes start at the University of Florida. I'll be living in Gainesville, and a long-distance relationship won't be practical anyway."

"Good idea. No reason to make her feel bad. Besides, she's still in high school. Who knows how she'll develop intellectually after she gets to college?"

FORTY-EIGHT

Two days before the wedding, Gunner and I surveyed the Hotel Royal Sands with the eye of a killer. Ava Hayes, the catering manager, accompanied us.

Hayes wore a royal blue blazer with the Royal Sands logo on the breast pocket and a short, white pencil skirt that showed off her tan legs. Her eyes lit up as she checked out Gunner. He did a double-take when she shook his hand. Perhaps they each noticed neither one wore a wedding band.

"The wedding rehearsal is tomorrow afternoon at five," I said as she led us into the Atlantic Room, "and the rehearsal dinner is tomorrow evening, directly after. Lynch may not wait until the wedding to attack. Gunner, if you were Lynch, how would you hit the rehearsal dinner here?"

Gunner scanned the room. "I would pose as a waiter and slit LeMarvis's throat when I served the meal. Then I'd grab Cleo the way Lynch took that casino dealer and haul her out with a knife at her throat. If I wanted to kill them both, I could put a bomb under the head table and detonate it by remote control. We know that Lester has the skills to make a bomb. Or I might poison the food and kill the whole wedding party. I could spray the room with automatic weapon fire." He smirked. "Shall I go on?"

Ava Hayes's face blanched as Gunner recited his laundry list of murder and mayhem. "Don't worry, Ava," I said. "That's what we're here to prevent. Gunner is sometimes, uh, melodramatic. Can you show us the kitchen?"

Hayes pushed open the service door. "The ballroom kitchen is at the end of this hall. It serves the meeting rooms on this side of the hotel. Follow me."

She pushed open the kitchen doors and switched on the lights.

I studied the kitchen. "I'll station Pete Martinez at the employee entrance there." I scribbled a note in my small notebook. "He can vet all waiters and kitchen personnel as they show up for work."

Gunner peered out the employee entrance and stepped back inside. "Have Pete stay until dinner is over, and Cleo and LeMarvis leave. Lynch might show up while the kitchen staff serves dessert."

"Good point." I made another note. "Ava, where do you store the dinner tables?"

"Follow me." Hayes led us back to the Atlantic Room.

"These two store rooms hold the tables and chairs." She opened a door and flipped on the lights. "We'll use one eight-foot table for the bride and groom and set these eight-person rounds for the others. Cleo has three bride attendants and LeMarvis has three groom attendants. Is that right?"

"Yes, plus the minister and two dozen family members from out of town. A total of... thirty-plus, including the happy couple. I'd set for forty. Extra family members always turn up. What time do you set the room?"

Hayes referred to her clipboard. "Tomorrow there's a Chamber of Commerce luncheon we'll need to clear. Say, three o'clock?"

"I'll have Angelina Curtis inspect the tables as they're set, and she'll stay on duty in the room until the guests arrive." I wrote that down. "What time does the kitchen staff arrive?"

She flipped a sheet on the clipboard. "Kitchen staff at four o'clock, servers at six p.m."

"Okay. Pete will be here at four."

We continued to the Blue Lagoon Garden and the beachfront where the rental company had erected the white pavilion. The rental company provided carpets to cover the sand. The carpet kept the folding chairs from sinking into the ground and made it easier for women to walk in their high heels. Not *easy*, but *easier*.

An hour later, Gunner and I finished our survey of hiding places, attack angles, paths for entrance and egress, bottlenecks, and checkpoints.

Hayes placed a hand on Gunner's arm. "Let me buy you gentlemen a drink." She squeezed his muscle and smiled.

Gunner blushed.

"We'd love to, Ava," I responded.

After we were seated in the hotel bar and our drinks arrived, I excused myself and let nature take its course. Either Gunner or, more likely Ava, would make a move after I left. Gunner was almost as shy around women as I was.

I had done what I could for Cleo and LeMarvis—and for Ava and Gunner. It was all over but the waiting.

The ball was in Lynch's court. I was playing defense again.

I love weddings, and it's not just for the cake—though that is a big draw. After I hit my thirtieth birthday still single, I felt a little self-pity whenever I attended one. Most of my buddies from high school, college, and the army had married. Even my friend Hank Ramirez, who started late, had two children.

Was I doomed to die a bachelor because I wouldn't let another woman into my risky life? Terry wanted another chance. My frozen heart was an engine that hadn't been cranked for a year. Had my pistons rusted in place in the cylinders of my heart?

My security plan for the wedding included renting the Royal Sands' beachfront suite on the second floor for both days. It had the only balconies low enough to see under the wedding pavilion and watch the ceremony. The suite's bedroom balcony overlooked the Blue Lagoon Garden, and the living room had a wrap-around balcony facing the ocean and garden. It was the best place to ambush the ceremony; therefore, it was the best place to guard the ceremony from said ambush.

In an abundance of caution, I rented the connecting suite for both days. I hung my formal clothes in the closet for the wedding.

My weather app indicated that seasonal thunderstorms had formed over the Everglades and were moving east. My phone chirped and spoke. "Lightning has been detected."

As the wedding party gathered at the rear of the pavilion for instructions from the minister and the wedding planner, I stepped to the corner where I watched the sky. The afternoon sun shone and the sky was partly cloudy with scattered cumulus clouds. This time of year, the weather often changed in a heartbeat. The high-rise hotel tower obscured the western sky.

Thunder rumbled, competing with the surf and the rattle of wind in the palm fronds.

I had stationed Cole Bailey on the living room balcony an hour before the rehearsal. Cole was a good pistol shot and an excellent hand-to-hand combat specialist in case Lynch showed.

I eyed the balcony and called Cole. "How's everything?"

He waved at me. "No sign of Lynch. I'm melting into a puddle of sweat, hoping the rain cools things off. I can imagine how hot it is down there. What kind of nut has an outdoor wedding in the summer in South Florida?"

"A romantic young woman who's wanted a beach wedding since she was a little girl, that's what kind."

"I'm gonna move back inside. I can watch through the sliders, and it's air-conditioned. Tomorrow I wear a tuxedo instead of a guayabera and it's gonna be even hotter."

"What are you, a sissy?"

"Meow," Cole answered and switched off.

I scattered eight other agents around the hotel grounds to guard every beach access and the walkway to the rehearsal dinner. Two more roamed the Blue Lagoon Garden. I called them all in turn. That took too long. On the wedding day, I would assign half the team to Snoop and half to Gunner and let them keep tabs on them.

So far, so good.

The rehearsal ended with the photographer snapping more pictures, always more pictures. The wedding party drifted toward the Atlantic Room.

The thunderstorm reached us as the last wedding party member made it to shelter in the hotel.

I hoped it wasn't an omen.

Where was Lynch? He was out there somewhere.

The rehearsal dinner had gone as planned. Once again, I was the cowboy in Indian country: It was too quiet. And Lester Lynch was still the invisible man.

FORTY-NINE

Lester

Lester sneaked into the hotel through a freight entrance and climbed the fire stairs two steps at a time. The first three floors held public areas, ballrooms, and smaller meeting rooms. Too many people coming and going. There were more surveillance cameras on those floors.

He reached the fourth floor, where the guest rooms started. There wouldn't be many people to see and remember a tall man carrying a duffel bag.

Lester punched the up button and waited for an elevator. The first elevator carried six people. Too many witnesses. He let it pass.

He punched the button again. The next elevator carried an elderly couple. Lester got on. The fourteenth-floor button was lit.

The fourteenth floor looked promising. The fourteenth floor would have a bird's-eye view of the site where he planned to kidnap the woman of his destiny.

Lester followed the couple off the elevator and down the hallway. They stopped at a room on the wrong side of the hall. He kept walking down the corridor and let them live.

Lester returned to the fourth floor to try again.

Third time's the charm.

The next elevator held a honeymooning couple wearing swimsuits and beach covers who carried Grotto Poolside Bar plastic glasses with the remnants of yellow drinks with paper umbrellas sticking out. They giggled and called each other *Mrs. Gannaway* and *Mr. Gannaway*. The fifteenth-floor button was lit.

They might be the ones. They are so disgustingly silly that I hope they are the ones.

Lester followed the oblivious lovebirds as they strolled arm-in-arm down the corridor to their ocean-view suite. They never noticed Lester behind them until it was too late.

As the young man opened the door, Lester pushed them inside. He slit the man's throat before he could turn around. The bride screamed, and Lester knocked her senseless with a single blow to the neck. Both plastic glasses thumped on the floor, spattering yellow liquid and ice across the carpet.

"Sorry, girly," he told his unconscious victim before he stabbed her in the throat, "you have to die."

He hung the *Do-Not-Disturb* sign outside the door and searched Mrs. Gannaway's purse. It held $178 and her Missouri driver's license in her maiden name and one of their wedding invitations. They had been married for two days.

Isn't that just too bad, you stupid people.

He searched the dead man's pockets. The keys to the couple's rental car showed the license number on a tag. The groom carried $456.

The money and car will come in handy when I make my escape—correction—our escape.

Another pocket held their hotel confirmation. They had reserved the suite through the Labor Day weekend.

This was getting better and better. The Demons of Revenge had smiled on Lester again.

He tossed the man's wallet and the woman's purse into the bedroom closet, then dragged the bodies in after them and closed the door.

He hoped that would keep the smell down.

Lester carried his duffel bag to the balcony. Yes, the room had a bird's-

270

eye view. He scrutinized the Blue Lagoon Garden and beach panorama with binoculars. He spotted McCrary's agent on the beachfront suite's balcony, and he knew why McCrary picked that spot.

That's where I'll attack. McCrary will look like a fool after I kill him.

He watched what he could of the rehearsal, but the angle was wrong. Yes, McCrary had chosen the right suite.

Lester studied the Blue Lagoon Garden and memorized its nooks and crannies, its grottoes and trails, its bars and tables. You never knew what you might need to know if push came to shove. He smiled when he saw the entrance to the Grotto Poolside Bar.

The last meals of Mr. and Mrs. Gannaway were some stupid pineapple rum drinks.

By the time Lester thought about bed, the smell from the corpses in the closet had leaked into the bedroom.

I should have stuck them in the living room closet, not the one in here.

He closed the bedroom door and unfolded the hide-a-bed.

He had slept in worse places in the Rangers.

He raided the minibar, ate all the snacks, and drank himself to sleep.

His last thought was that tomorrow, his dream girl would be his, all his, at last.

Or he and many other people would be dead.

Carlos McCrary

The wedding day dawned sunny, hot, and humid. No surprise there.

The wedding pavilion had its sides rolled up to allow the breeze free access. At my request, the rental company had placed temporary walls of potted bamboo around the pavilion to further block outside views of the ceremony.

I wouldn't give Lynch anything to shoot at.

Long narrow white tents crossed the Blue Lagoon Garden linking the hotel to the pavilion, also lined with bamboo planters. If a thunderstorm hit, the walkway tents would shelter the guests on their way to the backup room inside the hotel.

All my agents wore tuxedos tailored to fit over their sidearms, including the three women agents wearing female tuxedos.

My security plan was the same as for the rehearsal dinner, except there would be ten times more guests, kitchen staff, and servers, plus a band.

For the ceremony, the town of Port City Beach sent two uniformed motorcycle officers who roamed the grounds. After the reception, they would provide a police escort to the airport for the bride and groom's limousine.

Snoop, Gunner, and I toured the hotel with Ava Hayes one last time at four p.m. For the last two days, Ava had given Gunner the eye every time we appeared. Their body language told me they had hooked up somewhere, sometime, and planned to do it again after they were off duty. "You look nice in a tux, Gunner."

Gunner blushed. "Thanks."

Everybody could fall in love but me.

As we walked out to the Blue Lagoon Garden, thunder rumbled in the distance. "Lightning has been detected," my weather app warned.

"Ava, you did set up the backup seating?"

"Don't worry, cowboy, this ain't our first rodeo. In ten minutes, my team can move the whole shebang into the Duke and Duchess Room, flowers and all. We set 450 chairs, just in case. Think positive; just because you hear thunder doesn't mean it's gonna rain."

We finished our tour and I set my agents and the two beach cops in position after a final briefing on various scenarios Lynch might try.

I hit the restroom one last time and grabbed a chair in the back corner of the pavilion.

The wind freshened and clouds scudded across the sky. The breeze carried the smell of rain. I checked my watch. Thirty minutes before the guests arrived.

Where was Lynch?

Five minutes before the guests arrived, the sun came out, and the wind died to a gentle, cool breeze. Perhaps Ava's positive attitude had worked.

I hoped the sunshine was an omen.

Renate Crowell arrived first; no surprise there. I had never seen her wear a dress before. She was on the arm of a man in a dark blue suit who looked familiar. The man wore a plain wedding band.

She steered her date over to me. "Chuck, meet Ed Willis. He's the top sports columnist at the *Pee-Jay*."

Willis grinned. "It's easy to be top columnist since there are two of us left and the other one covers high school athletics."

We shook hands. "Nice to see you, Ed. You and I met at the ESPN Super Bowl party a couple of years ago. I read your column regularly. Are you covering the wedding for the sports section?"

"When a superstar like Marvelous LeMarvis Jones gets hitched, that's big news. And when a pretty girl like Renate asks, how could I refuse?"

Renate winked. "Don't worry, handsome, Ed's married. I don't plan to boink him later."

"I didn't think that, Renate. I know you only have eyes for me."

"That's almost true, Chuck. Leave out the 'only,'" She winked again. "BTW, you look great in a tux. Sexy and handsome."

"Thanks. You look beautiful. That green cocktail dress is the perfect shade for your red hair. It almost makes me reconsider your offer of a few days ago."

Renate steered the sports writer to an usher and they took seats toward the front.

After more guests arrived, Vicky Ramirez appeared. She wore a floor-length blue chiffon with lace straps and a pearl necklace which called attention to her cleavage.

For a split-second I wondered what Terry would have worn if I had invited her.

I bowed from the waist. "Wow. You could be a fashion magazine ad."

"Thank you." She gave me an air kiss and a hug.

Her perfume evoked pleasant memories. "That's the perfume you wore last week."

Vicky winked. "Let's hope it has the same effect this time. I've never seen you in a tux. I love it."

She released me and took the chair next to mine. "You're on duty. Do your thing and we'll meet at the reception if you get sidetracked." She patted me on the thigh. "Until later."

Lester

The hotel maid presented no problem. One quick *zip* of Lester's knife and she fell to the floor of the deserted hall, dead in seconds. He used her master keycard to open the bedroom door without a sound.

The door connecting to the living room stood open. The guard would watch the wedding pavilion instead of his back.

As silently as he stalked a deer in the Tennessee mountains, Lester slithered behind the unsuspecting guard. He looped his arm around the man's throat, planning to break his neck.

The guard lurched backwards, grabbed Lester's thumb, and bent it the wrong way.

Lester screamed as his thumb dislocated, then regained his grip and broke the guard's neck. He clenched his teeth and forced his thumb back into its socket.

He hurried back to the hotel hallway. No one in sight. There was no way to hide the blood on the carpet. They were at the end of the hall. Maybe no one would come that far and notice it.

He dragged the maid's body and the housekeeping cart into the living room.

His dislocated thumb hurt like hell. It was harder to assemble his carbine than he expected. This time, there was no need for silence. He sang the *Dry Bones* tune. "The butt stock's connected to the *[click]* lower receiver."

He stopped and rubbed his thumb. "The lower receiver's connected to the *[click]* upper receiver." He gritted his teeth and continued. "The upper receiver's connected to the *[click]* magazine. Now hear the word of the Lord."

Lester stared out the glass sliders. What was this? The scene around the pavilion looked different from the previous day. The stupid hotel people had blocked his view inside the pavilion with more of those damned potted plants.

Was that McCrary's idea? He bet it was. One more reason to hate McCrary.

With the potted plants in the way, I can't get a shot at the nigger, and I can't see McCrary.

Carlos McCrary

Time flew by as the tent filled. Even though a thick carpet covered the sand, walking down the aisle was as bad as a slog through mud for women in high heels. The string quartet played a love song medley as ushers performed to keep women guests from stumbling. The minister arrived with a beaming smile, and the guests fell silent. The surf sounded faintly in the background.

The minister nodded to the ushers, who seated Cleo's grandmother and LeMarvis's parents.

LeMarvis and his groomsmen entered from behind another row of potted bamboo which made a wall at the front of the pavilion.

The smiling minister shook hands with them.

The wedding planner had created a temporary Bride's Room with more potted bamboo between the pavilion and the Blue Lagoon Garden.

Cleo's bridesmaids stepped into view from the Bride's Room and lined up at the rear. The string quartet played Mendelson's *Wedding March*.

I stepped away from the pavilion to call Snoop. "Report."

"Everything's smooth."

Next, I called Gunner. "Report."

"I can't raise Cole. I was about to call you."

Looking at the second-floor balcony, all I saw was the sky reflected in the glass. "When's the last time you checked on him?"

"Fifteen minutes ago."

"Damn! Lynch may have got him. Meet me at the second-floor suite. *Go, go, go.*"

I sent a prearranged group text to the security team and Ava Hayes, the catering manager:

Code White. Storm is coming. Move wedding inside.

I sprinted across the sand to the *Hotel Guests Only* door to the beachfront suites wing.

We had planned for this scenario. Under Code White, Snoop took charge in the wedding pavilion while I hunted Lynch.

Second, my agents would inform the guests that a major thunderstorm was imminent with destructive winds that might collapse the pavilion and that the ceremony would move inside to the Duke and Duchess Room. Fortunately, the weather confirmed the lie.

Third, Ava Hayes's hotel staff would drop the weather curtains on the pavilion and walkway tents. The curtains would conceal the civilians from Lynch's view, no matter where he was. The civilians could walk unobserved to the safety of the Duke and Duchess Room.

Two other agents would take positions in the Blue Lagoon Garden and on the beach to cut off Lynch's escape if he leapt off either balcony.

That was the plan. However, no battle plan survives contact with the enemy, and my plan involved hundreds of wedding guests and hotel employees. Civilians are unpredictable.

I slid my master key into the door slot, jerked it open, and pounded up the fire stairs toward the second floor.

We had made first contact with the enemy.

FIFTY

Snoop Snopolski

S noop read the text, cursed under his breath, and ran to the pavilion.

He stepped in front of Cleo and her grandfather and the bridesmaids. "Radar shows we have five minutes before we get hit by a major thunderstorm with high winds that might collapse the pavilion. We need to move to the backup location inside. Come with me, please."

Not waiting for Cleo to answer, he caught her arm and moved her toward the covered walkway before she had time to object.

Hotel staff unsnapped the weather curtains and dropped them on the sides of the walkway. Other staff dropped the sides on the pavilion.

"What's going on, Snoop?" Cleo asked, but she kept walking, one hand on Snoop's arm as she struggled across the carpeted beach. The other hand clutched her bouquet.

"There's a major, major thunderstorm with gale-force winds on the way. Don't worry, we planned for the weather. The hotel staff will move the flowers inside through the service entrance. Our other agents are behind us, moving your guests to shelter inside. Let's pick up the pace, okay? By the way, you look stunning, Cleo. The most beautiful bride I've seen since my own wedding. It will be a splendid ceremony."

He gave her a reassuring grin and peeked over his shoulder to Cleo's grandfather and the bridesmaids. "Let's move inside, ladies, Mr. Boone. Please follow Cleo and me." He smiled. "Chop-chop. The storm hits in four minutes, and we have to get all the guests inside too."

Behind Snoop, Ava Hayes ducked through the bamboo wall at the front and approached LeMarvis and the groomsmen. She motioned the string quartet to silence and faced the astonished guests. "May I have your attention, please? Weather radar shows a major thunderstorm with gale-force winds will strike in less than five minutes. The good news is: We're moving the entire wedding inside to the Duke and Duchess Room." She grinned at the guests. "Our Royal Sands staff will move these beautiful flower arrangements. It will still be a lovely wedding—but inside."

She smiled at LeMarvis. "If you head up the aisle, everyone will follow your lead."

One groomsman eyed the side of the tent and made a slight move that direction. "No, don't take the outside route; without the carpet, the sand messes up your shoes and gets on your tux pants. Head up the center aisle. We need everyone to follow your example."

She raised her voice. "Please follow the hotel employees' directions. They will guide you to the Duke and Duchess Room, where the ceremony will continue. Don't worry, folks; we at the Royal Sands know how to handle South Florida weather. We'll take good care of you."

Six uniformed hotel employees entered behind her with dollies and began to stack the flowers for movement. Two more staff brought in the string quartet's instrument cases.

Ava stepped to the front of the center aisle and motioned the guests to move out.

A lightning bolt struck a palm tree. An ear-splitting crash of thunder shivered the ground. The tree exploded into flaming chunks of fronds and tree trunk. Some flaming debris landed on the pavilion.

Several wedding guests panicked and bolted. They tripped over chairs, knocked over the potted bamboos, and ran across the sand toward the hotel. The panic was contagious, and more guests spilled uncontrolled into the Blue Lagoon Garden.

Oh, crap! Shoop thought. *It's hit the fan now.*

Carlos McCrary

Reaching the top of the stairs, I listened at the door to the second-floor corridor. Hearing nothing, I opened it a crack and saw a bloody pool on the carpet. I remembered the fate of the poker dealer that Lynch took hostage. Was the blood Cole Bailey's or someone else's?

Then I saw the tracks of a housekeeping cart leading through the blood into the suite's living room. My chest tightened. Lynch had killed the hotel maid to get her master key. That was how he surprised Cole Bailey. Would I find Cole alive when we got inside? It didn't seem likely.

Gunner sprinted around the corner.

"Call 9-1-1," I hollered, "At least two ambulances."

Rain rattled on the window at the end of the corridor. Lightning flashed. Thunder boomed. The fake storm we had invented turned out to be real, and it was a humdinger.

Lester

The bridesmaids gathered at the rear of the pavilion as Lester watched through his telescopic gunsight. They appeared so close he could count their eyelashes. Katie and an old man emerged from behind a row of bamboo. The old man looked familiar, then Lester remembered: Katie's grandfather Boone.

Where is that goddam LeMarvis?

Then hotel people dropped all the weather curtains.

The dead guard's phone rang. Lester considered answering it, but what good would it do? McCrary would know without doubt where he was. Not answering might gain time before McCrary discovered his location.

Yes! I'll let it ring, and I'll get ready for McCrary. At least I'll see that bastard in hell with me.

He dragged the dead guard's body into the bedroom and propped it against the entrance door. He threw the deadbolt and fastened the security chain.

McCrary won't come in that way unless he smashes the door and

279

shoves his man's body aside. I'll hear the door break and I'll spray it with gunfire before he makes it through.

Minutes later, he heard a shout from the hotel corridor. "Call 9-1-1. At least two ambulances."

A huge roll of thunder drowned out all other sound.

Lester moved to the peephole in the bedroom door, leaned across the dead guard's body, and peered out. The pool of blood from the dead maid lay at the bottom of his fisheye view. Another of McCrary's agents stood beside it. That man stared down the hall toward the other door to the suite.

McCrary intends to crash the living room door.

Lester hurried into the living room and switched the carbine to full automatic. He grinned and aimed the M4, now a machine gun, at the height of McCrary's chest.

He pulled the trigger and swung the muzzle from side to side, hosing the door. He emptied the magazine at McCrary. It didn't matter; he carried two more full magazines.

FIFTY-ONE

Carlos McCrary

I lay on the carpet in front of the suite's door, avoiding the bloody cart tracks. I craned my neck to get my ear in position and listened at the door. I didn't expect to hear anything over the noise of the thunderstorm, but maybe I would hear Cole Bailey talk to Lynch, or *vice versa*. It was a faint hope since I assumed Lynch had killed Cole with a silenced bullet or slashed his throat.

A *bra-a-ap* of automatic weapon fire smashed through the door above my head, stitched holes across the door, and showered me with wood splinters. I rolled to one side and watched the bullets punch holes in the wall across the corridor.

I hoped that hotel room was vacant.

The gunfire answered one question: Lynch was in the living room, and it was suicide to open that door.

I crawled out of range before standing beside Gunner. "Lynch wouldn't leave Cole alive behind him. If that door opens, it will be Lynch. The door next to it opens into the suite's bedroom. He might come out that one also. You know his reputation and his Ranger training. He's deadly. If either door opens, shoot first and ask questions later. Stay here. Don't let him out."

"Where are you going?"

"I'll go through the connecting door from my suite."

"Those doors bolt from both sides, boss. When you break in, he'll hear noise in the other room. He'll drop you before you get off a shot."

"Nope. After I changed into my tux this afternoon, I unbolted both connecting doors and left them closed. I can push the door open without a sound. If he's in the living room, he won't know I'm coming."

"Let me go with you. You go high; I go low."

"You cover these doors in case he makes a run for it."

I called Robby Gorski. "Robby, are you in the garden below the suite?"

"Yeah, boss. There was movement in the living room as I heard automatic weapon fire. I can't see much because of the reflections in the window. What happened?"

"Lynch shot through the door where he thought I was standing. I assume he ambushed Cole. I hope he's alive, but I doubt it. Gunner and I are in the hall outside the suite."

"It's a madhouse here, boss. Wind's blowing like a hurricane. It's raining buckets, and I'm sure you heard the palm tree explode like a mortar shell hit it. Panicky wedding guests are stumbling around the garden, trying to find the hotel through the downpour. Whenever I find one, I point them toward the hotel. What a cock-up."

"Can you see anything in the suite?"

"Between the reflections and the lightning flashes, I can't see shit in either room. Should I shoot out the windows?"

"Don't do that. From your angle, your bullets would shoot through the ceiling and hit someone on the next floor. I'll enter through the door connecting from my suite. If I flush Lynch onto the balcony, or if he shoots out the windows and you can get a shot, take him out. Make sure it's him, because I'll be in the room."

I slid the keycard into my door slot. The light blinked green and I pushed the door open. Before I entered, a uniformed Port City Beach cop rounded the corner.

The cop saw Gunner and me and drew his weapon. "Let me see your hands. Get on your knees."

He did a double-take and lowered his weapon. "Oh, it's you. What's up, Chuck? I heard gunfire."

"You better call backup, Sergeant."

"I called after I heard gunfire." He trotted down the corridor toward us.

"Good," I said. "The gunfire was Lester Lynch shooting through the door. He's inside the end suite. See the shattered door? He killed the maid and my agent stationed inside. This is my man Gunner Knutson, in case you haven't met. Now that you're here to keep Lynch from escaping in this corridor, Gunner and I will breach through the door from my suite."

"Wait a second, Chuck. Lynch is trapped. He can't go anywhere. Wait for backup so we don't get more people killed. He might surrender."

Lightning flashed outside the corridor window and the floor vibrated from the thunder's force. It felt like an earthquake.

"Sergeant, Lester Lynch can jump from either of two balconies. It's ten feet down with soft sand or grass or bushes to land on. There are wedding guests wandering the garden that Lynch could take hostage. We have to get him before he figures that out. I need you in this hall so he doesn't escape through either of these doors. Deal?"

The sergeant drew his pistol again and held it at his side. "Deal."

I motioned to Gunner. "It's showtime."

The palms and shrubs of the Blue Lagoon Garden thrashed like living things in the gusty winds. Lightning bolts looked like God taking flash pictures from heaven. Buckets of rain fell so relentlessly that I could hardly see the pavilion as gale-force winds battered it, searching for a vulnerable spot.

Gunner and I positioned ourselves at the connecting door. "We move on the next thunderclap. Watch for the lightning and follow me through."

Adrenaline rushed through my body, vibrating it like a guitar string.

We didn't wait long. Lightning flashed, and I nodded at Gunner and shouldered the door open. Thunder crashed as I leapt into the room and rolled across the floor, searching for Lynch, Gunner behind me.

The bedroom was empty except for Cole Bailey's body blocking the hall door.

I pushed the vision from my mind. I had to find Lynch first; I would mourn Cole Bailey later.

My cellphone vibrated. Robby. I muted the sound and answered as a video. I pointed the phone at my face without speaking. Even with the thunderstorm's racket, Lynch might hear me speak.

Robby's lips moved. He seemed agitated.

I held my index finger across my lips to signal silence and pointed the phone's camera at Cole's body. Now Robby knew where we were and what had happened.

He made a zipped-lip gesture and mouthed the word "text?"

I nodded and disconnected. In seconds, I received his text:

Sliders to both balconies have opened but I don't see anyone. He must be lying on the floor to open them. Definitely in living room to do that.

Those wide-open sliders were Lynch's escape hatch; he planned to make a run for it.

Pistols in firing position, Gunner and I crept toward the open door.

In the High Five Casino, Lynch had moved like a young Muhammad Ali. Lynch was speedy enough to be an NFL wide receiver, while I was barely fast enough to play high school football. If it came to a chase, I was a pickup truck and he was NASCAR. If he got a lead on me, I was toast.

My nerves were tight as a drumhead.

As I approached the door, something moved in the other room. I ducked and another *bra-a-ap* of automatic gunfire punched the wall behind me. I rolled left and rapid-fired at Lynch as he sprinted across the room. My shots traveled wide and shattered the glass sliders.

Lynch's foot skidded sideways on the wet balcony tile. He regained his balance like a circus high-wire walker and leapt over the balcony rail.

Robby fired at him from below.

Gunner and I rushed to the balcony, sliding the last two feet on the wet, slippery tile. Our patent-leather formal shoes had slick leather soles. *Too late to change shoes; I can't go barefooted.*

Lynch disappeared into the jungle. His jungle camouflage would be hard to see in the downpour. I couldn't shoot because there were wedding guests in the garden.

"Cover me," I called to Robby and Gunner.

Lynch had leapt from the balcony without hesitation, but he was running from my bullets. I couldn't risk a sprained ankle or broken leg. Instead, I stepped over the railing and stood in the torrent on a narrow, tiled ledge. Clutching the slippery rail with my left hand, I squatted on my heels to lower my center of gravity. I had planned to ease the ten-foot fall to the grass, but my leather soles failed me again. They skated off the edge of the wet tile and I fell on my butt on the balcony edge, bruising my right hip and elbow. I bounced off and fell into an Ixora bush. Thank God it wasn't a Bougainvillea.

Robby ran to my side as I extricated myself from the Ixora. "Lynch headed toward the volcano."

"Send a team text: Code Roundup. All agents surround the garden. Pen him in and take him down. Don't let Lynch get to the beach and, for God's sake, don't let him into the hotel."

Gunner landed on the grass beside me, graceful as a butterfly.

"Gunner, clear any remaining guests from the garden. Make sure they all made it inside. We can't have innocents on the battleground. Robby, you help him after you send the Code Roundup text."

Canvas ripped as the pavilion lost its fight against the gale. The white fabric crumpled like a paper wad and soared through the rain like a swimming jellyfish. The tent ropes were trailing tentacles as the storm lofted the tent toward the Atlantic.

Snapping a fresh magazine into my pistol, I limped off in the direction Lynch disappeared. I shook my left hand to get feeling back into it.

FIFTY-TWO

Lester

Lester cleared the balcony banister with a foot to spare and tumbled through space to land clumsily on his left side. Stumbling into a roll across the wet St. Augustine grass, he popped up, running like a gazelle across the clearing toward a Gardenia hedge. His extra magazine fell from his belt as he rolled to his feet. He heard several gunshots but needed no urging to hit top speed as he sprinted toward the jungle.

He dodged through foliage, tripping over decorative stonework, until he stopped at the wall of potted bamboo, now tumbled over from the storm, and weather curtains hanging from the tented walkway. He couldn't turn right; he'd hit the hotel. McCrary had agents guarding the hotel. He couldn't turn left; the curtain wall ended at the beach, now a bare patch with the pavilion blown away.

His breath came ragged. Drenching rain made it hard to see.

Lester lifted the weather curtain and ducked under. He stumbled on the carpet laid to protect the lawn but regained his footing. He raised the opposite curtain and ducked into the undergrowth. There was a fake fiberglass volcano and waterslide ahead with a choice of grottoes to hide in.

286

Where is the volcano? I can't see anything in this damned downpour. You memorized this whole garden from the balcony yesterday, genius. You're smarter than all of them. Think, man, think.

He pushed his way through a Croton hedge. The faux volcano and waterslide loomed through the cloudburst. He would shelter in the Grotto Poolside Bar beneath the volcano. He stumbled toward the slope of the manmade mountain.

He leaned against the fiberglass and patted it with his left hand like a faithful old horse. Turning his back to the slope, he slipped behind an Oleander hedge and crabbed sideways until the flowering shrubs concealed him.

Lester struggled to catch his breath. His heartbeat pounded in his ears; it thumped in his chest; it throbbed in his temples. Rain streaked his face and mixed with his tears.

Everything has come apart, everything. He suppressed a sob. *Everything was going so well until McCrary...*

He would never have Katie Boone Lynch, the girl he was literally born and bred for. McCrary had been a thorn in his side from the beginning, and now McCrary was trailing him like a bloodhound, practically on his heels. His money was gone and he'd lost his extra ammunition as he jumped from the balcony. He examined the magazine in his M4 carbine. Twenty rounds left. He promised himself that he would make them count.

Carlos McCrary

Pushing through the Gardenias, I watched for any movement, either a wedding guest or Lynch.

Lynch had the advantage of knowing where he was going; I followed cautiously, alert for any threat. The gardens covered two acres, and he could hide in a dozen places. I might have to search them all.

Lynch left a trail of wet scuffs across the grass. The downpour erased the faint trail as I watched.

The trail stopped at the weather curtain wall. Lynch could lurk on the other side, waiting for me to duck under the curtain, or he could have searched for a hiding place.

Stooping under the curtain, I would be defenseless. God knows where Lynch would be if I took the time to go around; he might even escape entirely. I kicked the tent stakes on one section loose, then yanked them out. The canvas wall sagged between the tents on each side. Moving to the next section, I tugged two more stakes and the wall sagged more. Two more sections, and the wall fell away from me. It collapsed against the lawns, flower beds, and bushes.

Alert for movement, I picked my way across the fallen canvas and tumbled bamboo plants and searched for Lynch's trail. Gone.

Lester

Lester slid between the hedge and the slope, desperate for a place to hide. He slipped into an entrance with a bamboo sign *Grotto Poolside Bar* beside it. It was under the volcano with a bar guests could swim to. The bar was dark and deserted.

Or was it?

In the shadowed interior, a woman in a wet cocktail dress slumped on a bench, sheltered from the storm. Her dark hair fell limply over her shoulders, plastered flat by rainwater, and her makeup ran in dirty streaks on her cheeks. She looked worse than a zombie in a horror movie.

The woman saw Lester loom in the entrance to the bar, rifle hanging from his right hand. Her eyes widened. She inched sideways until she butted against the armrest.

Lester stared at her like a statue. Rainwater in his eyes mixed with tears to blur his vision.

With her eyes riveted on the gun, the woman bent over and felt her feet, removing her stiletto heels by touch.

Lester wiped his eyes with the back of his free hand. His thumb felt better. *What was she doing?*

She rose to her feet, shoes in one hand, and grabbed the sodden material of her skirt with her other hand. She pulled the clinging wet fabric loose from her thighs.

Lester gaped, fascinated without knowing why. What was she doing here and how did she find this place? Had the Demons of Revenge sent her to help him? Just as his hope had run out, the Demons led him to a hostage.

The woman threw her shoes at his face and bolted for the exit.

Lester ducked and the woman scurried across the floor, shrieking loud as a siren. He dodged around empty tables and chairs and lunged after her.

As she reached the pavement's edge, the woman screamed for help and surface-dived into the shallow pool. She stroked strongly toward the frothing fury where the waterfall plunged into the artificial lake. She held her breath and dived out of sight. How long could she hide in four feet of water?

Lester stared after her, uncertain how to proceed. To take her hostage, he had to capture her, but she was in the pool.

Carlos McCrary

A woman screamed, and I sprinted toward the sound.

The volcano appeared to rise from the tropical-themed swimming pool. Instead of lava, an artificial river cascaded down fiberglass flanks and collected in a reservoir above the Grotto Poolside Bar. The reservoir fed a waterslide from one side and the waterfall from the other.

Jolting to a halt at the pool's edge, I peered into the darkened grotto.

Lynch faced the other way, watching a woman who thrashed in the water.

Dashing toward Lynch, I lowered my shoulder and walloped him with a blindside block that would have been illegal when I played tight end for the Theodore Roosevelt High School *Rough Riders*.

Lynch flew face-first into the pool. His carbine splashed a few feet away.

I bounded high in the air for maximum force and crashed like a 225-pound pile of bricks on Lynch's back, landing with both knees on his kidneys.

My dive-bomb aerial attack was intended to knock the wind from Lynch's lungs. My knees hit the yielding hardness of a bulletproof vest under the bastard's camo shirt. The vest distributed the force of my landing harmlessly across his entire back.

Damn! And he might have bought military-grade floating armor while he was at it.

My momentum carried us toward the bottom of the pool. I couldn't shoot him in the torso because of the vest. Throwing my left arm around his throat in a chokehold, I tried to press my Glock to his head.

Lynch grabbed my gun hand in a vise-like clench as he pitched and thrashed like a bronco beneath me. He grabbed my left arm and pulled it away without apparent effort.

What was this guy? Superman?

He gathered his feet under him and pushed upward. He breached like Moby Dick and heaved us to the surface with me as Captain Ahab on his back.

Lynch grunted and moaned without words. A cry of pain, but, as far as I knew, he wasn't wounded. Yet.

I fought, but Lynch pulled my gun to the side. I was draped across his back like a cape but I couldn't choke him. He held me tight with his right fist around my gun hand, and his left hand seized my left wrist like it was encased in cement.

Lynch twisted and rotated our backs to the edge of the pool. He vaulted backward, crushing me between his back and the pool coping, knocking the wind from my lungs. I lost my grip on the Glock, and it fell from my fingers with a splash.

As Lynch pivoted to bear-hug me, he released me, and I dove to the bottom.

Swiping with my hand to feel for my Glock, I accidentally pushed it beyond reach.

Lynch lunged toward me.

I kicked backward underwater while I ripped open my pants leg and drew my Ka-Bar knife from the sheath strapped to my calf.

When I stood, Lynch was ten feet away.

"I'll carve you like a turkey, McCrary." He brandished a ceramic knife.

Panting like a racehorse, I struggled to recover my wind. I grinned at Lynch to stall while I wheezed for air. I flourished my own knife until I could speak. "Catch me first, Weirdo." Still panting, I backed toward the pool's center, where the water deepened.

Lynch waded after me.

As I reached five feet of depth, I kicked off my shoes and swam backward. "What's the matter, loser? Don't know how to swim?"

Lynch chased me as I swam farther from the woman and toward the deep water.

"I'm a U.S. Army Ranger, McCrary. I swim better than you."

"Fat chance. Show me, Weirdo." I backed farther and treaded water.

As he reached deeper water, Lynch's vest lifted his feet off the bottom. He lost traction and bobbed in the pool.

"I'll gut you like a deer, McCrary." He swam my direction with powerful strokes.

Backing across the pool, I lured him farther from the woman. "You don't swim so well, Lynch. Can't even catch me when I swim backward."

We reached the center where the water slide ended. Ten feet deep.

Taking three deep breaths, I exhaled the final one and dropped to the bottom. Lynch could not submerge because of his vest.

I swam under Lynch, my vision blurry underwater. Pushing off the bottom, I jammed my Ka-Bar into his thigh, aiming for the artery. I jerked the blade sideways and out. Blood flowed into the water, but it didn't spurt. He was wounded, but I missed the femoral artery.

Lynch slashed blindly downward and gashed my left shoulder. My tuxedo shoulder pad caught part of the attack, but the injury throbbed.

I kicked to the bottom and watched for another opening. My lungs burned from lack of oxygen. My own blood clouded my vision. I swam sideways for a clearer view.

Lynch swam toward the woman, leaving a bloody red trail.

I kicked after him, leaving a pink trail of my own.

Lynch was right: Even wounded, he swam better than I did.

Surfacing, I grabbed another breath. "Dive to the bottom," I yelled at the woman.

She screamed and ducked beneath the surface.

Lynch paused, debating whether to pursue the woman or engage me.

"I'm coming for you, Lynch." Favoring my wounded left shoulder, I stroked toward him.

He spun toward the woman as I approached.

I grabbed his boot in my left hand. Ignoring the pain, I pulled closer and slashed across his Achilles tendon. More blood colored the water.

Lynch screamed and thrashed toward me, knife flailing. Like Moby Dick, he was wounded but still dangerous.

I dodged aside. I didn't want to end up like Captain Ahab, killed by my own quarry.

Diving to the bottom where he couldn't come, I watched for another opening, then pushed off. I stabbed his thigh again, jerked, and twisted. This time I hit his artery.

A jet of blood spurted with each frenzied heartbeat.

I avoided the frenzied thrusts of his knife while his beating heart finished killing him. It took fewer than ten seconds. He stopped moving and drifted away.

It was good that we were in a swimming pool instead of the Atlantic Ocean. Enough of Lynch's blood filled the water to attract every shark within miles.

FIFTY-THREE

The woman was standing in the shallow water behind the waterfall. My feet scraped the bottom and I stood. "Are you all right, miss?"

Her eyes were wide as she gawked over my shoulder at the billowing patch of red in the pool. Lynch's body floated face down. "That man. He had a gun. Is he...?"

"You're safe, miss. I'm Carlos McCrary, the security chief for the wedding." I kept my distance, giving her space. "Everything's all right, miss."

Taking a path at right angles to the woman, I waded to the side of the pool. "Why don't we find some dry clothes?"

I gazed at the sky. The rain had stopped.

Gunner and Robby stood in the Grotto Poolside Bar, both holding towels.

I climbed the steps, then reached back to help the woman.

Gunner found an electrical panel concealed in a wall and switched on the lights. "Got a text from Snoop. Cleo and LeMarvis's ceremony went off without a hitch in the Duke and Duchess Room. Cleopatra Hennessey is now Mrs. LeMarvis Jones." He grinned. "May they live happily ever after."

Cleo and LeMarvis stood in the receiving line in the King and Queen Ballroom, giving hugs and kisses to the guests as they arrived from the Duke and Duchess Room.

As always, the photographer took more pictures.

I stood at the rear, obscured by more potted bamboos. My appearance might distract from the reception, but I wanted to see the fruits of my labor.

LeMarvis looked handsome in his size oh-my-God tuxedo. Cleo was radiant in a gown that cost as much as the national debt of a small country. I was sure that LeMarvis would consider that it was money well spent. Look up "happy couple" in a dictionary, and you will see their picture.

For the thousandth time, I wondered if I would feel that someday. Not if I wasn't willing to love someone and risk another loss.

Vicky Ramirez appeared. "I've been expecting you. Oh my God, you're dripping wet. Did you get caught in the storm?"

I chuckled. "Something like that. "

She saw my shoulder. "What happened to your tux? Is that blood?" She looked down. "And where are your shoes?"

FIFTY-FOUR

S tanding on the dock, I offered Terry Kovacs my hand as she stepped onto the *Gator Raider Too*. She was agile as a mountain goat, and she didn't need my help; I wanted to hold her hand. It had been a long time.

She grinned at me from beneath her wide-brimmed hat. She wore a translucent black caftan beach cover over her yellow bikini. "Thank you, kind sir. You're taking good care of me."

"Nothing but the best."

Grabbing the picnic basket, I followed her onto the boat.

Twenty minutes later, I dropped anchor in Seeti Bay and unfolded a table in the shade of the hardtop.

Terry slipped out of her caftan and helped me set the table. "Have you heard from Cleo and LeMarvis?"

"They sent me a text and picture from Moorea."

"Let me see your shoulder."

Shrugging out of my guayabera, I twisted so she could see the bandage. "It's much better. The stitches come out in three days."

We finished our sandwiches and a bottle of Pinot Grigio and stretched out on sun lounges on the bow.

Terry unfastened her top and draped it across the lounge. "I'm glad you called me. What changed your mind?"

"Clint had something to do with it."

"You mean my apology to Clint helped my cause?"

"Yes, but there's more. I just wanted you back."

We lazed under the summer sun a few more minutes.

Terry propped herself on one elbow to face me. "I missed this. I love the sun, and the *Gator Raider* is the perfect place." She lay down again.

"I missed it too." I reached over and stroked her arm with my fingertips. "And I missed *you*."

She stroked the front of my swimsuit. "It feels like you're inspired too."

She grabbed my hand. "Let's go below and rock the boat."

And we did.

The End

FOUR YEARS GONE
CARLOS MCCRARY PI, BOOK 8

The pavement two yards from me cratered and dust flew in the air. A split second later, the sound of the gunshot reached my ears. I juked sideways and ran at right angles to the direction of the gunshot. Someone wanted to kill me, and I had to lead them away from the students.

Sound travels a thousand feet per second. A rifle bullet fires between 2,000 and 3,500 feet per second. The instant the bullet hit the pavement I reflexively began counting one-thousand-one. I never finished the first one-thousand. The time between the shot hitting the pavement and the sound reaching me meant the shooter fired from more than two hundred feet. From that distance, he had to be shooting a rifle.

The shot came from the steep hill across the street. Limestone strata stepped like giant shelves twenty feet high as they climbed two hundred feet from the street to the top. Junipers and live oaks covering the hillside concealed the shooter.

Another bullet whizzed close enough to feel the shock wave. I saw a muzzle flash halfway up the slope.

I carried a handgun. Not a chance against a rifle at that distance, even if I spotted the shooter. I had to get closer.

I sprinted across the street, dodging traffic as I ran. One thing was sure:

The shooter was a lousy shot. His first bullet missed by six feet when I was a sitting duck.

Another bullet struck the windshield of a passing car where I had just cut to my left. I assessed where the shot had come from. Juniper ten feet tall shaped like a Christmas tree, live oak with a fork in the trunk seven feet up. One hundred feet vertically from the street. Got it.

I lunged into the shrubbery at the base of the mesa and clambered up the slope. Glancing over my shoulder when I reached the first limestone shelf, I saw the car with the shattered windshield had pulled to the side of the road. Hopefully, the driver had not been hit.

Clawing upward, feet slipping on the stony soil, I grabbed branches to assist my mad rush toward the shooter.

He must have parked at the top, maybe in the city park on the ridge. Then he climbed down to hide close enough to take a good shot at me. Now that I was chasing him, he'd be scrambling back to his car.

My mind raced as I scaled from the limestone slope. How had he known I was at Bonham High School? He must have followed me. But from where? Where had I picked up the tail?

Nelson. Nelson was the source. He'd alerted an accomplice when I left. The accomplice follows me to the school, then—figuring I would be inside for a while—parks at the top of the mesa and climbs down the slope to get closer to me. He shoots at me when I return to the visitor's parking lot.

I needed to cut him off before he could gain the park.

He had a three-minute head start since he was already halfway to the top. Also, he had at least a passing familiarity with the path back to his car. I, on the other hand, made several false starts and turn-backs, snaking my way from shelf to shelf.

Still forty feet below the top of the mesa, I saw the shooter climbing with an M16 rifle slung across his back. He scrambled to the base of the park's limestone retaining wall. His dark green jacket silhouetted against the white stones as he ascended.

I shouted for him to halt, hoping he would look back and I could see his face.

The shooter never looked back as he scaled the limestone.

I held my breath. Easy squeezy, nice and easy. I got off two shots. He topped the wall and disappeared. The first bullet kicked up a limestone cloud. The second bullet hit him in the middle of the back, but he never slowed. Either he was Superman or he wore a Kevlar vest under his jacket.

By the time I made it over the wall, he was gone. The park was deserted.

I called Detective Goodman. While I waited for her, I slid down the mesa and asked the driver of the car with the shattered windshield to wait for the cops.

I must be closing in on the killer. Or he believed I was getting close. But close to whom? Nelson wasn't the shooter, because Snoop and Gunner had surveilled him 24/7 since the day after they arrived.

Either Nelson was not the kidnapper, or he had an accomplice. My money was on an accomplice.

Available in Paperback and eBook from Your Favorite Bookstore or Online Retailer

ABOUT THE AUTHOR

Dallas Gorham's books combine murder, mystery, and general mayhem with a touch of humor—all done with a PG-13 rating. His Carlos McCrary, Private Investigator, Mystery Thriller Series can be read and enjoyed in any order.

Dallas writes in the mystery, thriller, and suspense genres. (Take your pick: His novels have all three elements) His stories will get your heart pounding and leave you wanting more. He writes to hit hard, have a good time, and leave as few grammar errors as possible (or is it "grammatical errors"? Hmm.)

In his previous life, Dallas worked as a shoe salesman, grocery store sacker, florist deliverer, auditor, management consultant, association executive, accountant, radio announcer, and a paid assassin for the Florida Board of Cosmetology. (He is lying about one of those jobs.) If you ask him about it, he will deny ever having worked as an auditor.

Dallas is a sixth-generation Texan and a proud Texas Longhorn, having earned a Bachelor of Business Administration at the University of Texas at Austin. He graduated in the top three-quarters of his class, maybe. He has also been known to lie about his class ranking.

Dallas, the writer, and his wife moved to Florida years ago to escape Dallas, the city, winters (Brrrr. Way too cold) and summers (Whew. Way too hot). Like his fictional hero, Chuck McCrary, he lives in Florida in a waterfront home where he and his wife watch the sunset over the lake most days. He is a member of Mystery Writers of America and the Florida Writers Association.

Dallas is frequent (but bad) golfer. He plays about once a week because that is all the abuse he can stand. One of his goals in life is to find more golf balls than he loses. He also is an accomplished liar (is this true?) and defender of down-trodden palm trees.

Dallas is married to his one-and-only wife who treats him far better than he deserves. They have two grown sons, of whom they are inordinately proud. They also have seven grandchildren who are the smartest, most handsome, and most beautiful grandchildren in the known universe. He and his wife spend waaaay too much money on their love of travel. They have visited all 50 states and over 90 foreign countries, the most recent of which was Indonesia, where their cruise ship stopped at Kuala Lumpur.

Dallas writes an occasional blog post at http://dallasgorham.com/blog that is sometimes funny, but not nearly as funny as he thinks.

If you have too much time on your hands, you can follow him at the following social media links:

www.DallasGorham.com

 facebook.com/DallasGorham

twitter.com/DallasGorham